Chasing the Banyan Wind

Bernadette Gabay Dyer

LMH PUBLISHING LIMITED

Editor: K. Sean Harris
Cover Artwork: Bernadette Gabay Dyer
Cover Design: Roshane Anglin
Book Design, Layout & Typesetting: Roshane Anglin

Published by LMH Publishing Limited
Suite 10-11, Sagicor Industrial Park
7 Norman Road
Kingston C.S.O., Jamaica
Tel.: 876-938-0005; 876-938-0712
Fax: 876-759-8752
Email: lmhbookpublishing@cwjamaica.com
Website: www.lmhpublishing.com

Printed in the U.S.A.   ISBN: 978-976-8245-71-7

NATIONAL LIBRARY OF JAMAICA CATALOGUING IN PUBLICATION
DATA

Dyer, Bernadette Gabay
    Chasing the banyan wind / Bernadette Gabay Dyer.

    p. ; cm
ISBN 978-976-8245-71-7 (pbk)

1   Biographical fiction
I. Title

808.8382   dc 23

Dedicated to the late Anne Carey, who
read my manuscript and
genuinely loved the story.

And also dedicated to K. Sean Harris
and Siegfried Betterman
who both helped to make this a better
tale.

Acknowledgements

Thanks to my brother David A. Gabay who managed to recover my manuscript, when I thought it was lost forever.

Thanks to the late Maud Fuller who remembered being told how 'sweet' Jamaican soldiers looked in their uniforms.

Thanks to Jamaican percussion musician Dick Smith, who regaled me with stories about the training camp up at Newcastle.

And thanks to Toronto Public libraries for its tremendous wealth of research materials.

Chapter 1:
Toronto

I came to Toronto from Kingston, Jamaica, to escape a relationship that seemed to be going nowhere. Arriving in early November, I was astonished to see stark winter-white skies and feel the lash of brute-force winds. I huddled inside my padded coat, a gift from my father, and followed a group of passengers bound for the city.

We left the arrivals terminal to wait outside for a bus, and were exposed to walls of blowing snow that came down in great sheets. Icy pellets stung exposed skin like needles and I heard talk that if things worsened, public transportation would be crippled.

Huge snowdrifts piled up along the highway as the sleek bus bravely whisked us to the city. I kept craning my neck to peer out to observe strange white scenes of wonder. Pedestrians bustled under mountains of clothing; cars with thick pads of snow on their roofs travelled in long slow lines. The outstretched branches of trees looked bare though laden down with snow, as icy, picture-perfect patterns formed on windowpanes.

I don't know how long I sat frozen at Bathurst subway station wondering what could have possessed me to come into this bleak and beautiful weather. Were it not that my father lived here and arrangements had been made for an old family friend to meet me, I might seriously have considered turning back and taking the next plane home.

"It looks like they will have to send the ploughs out soon," said an old European woman, swaddled in a thick black shawl, sitting across from me massaging her stubby frozen fingers and dragging her mittens on.

"Do they send ploughs out when it's like this?" I asked innocently.

"You must be from the States?" she hissed, turning her small bird-like eyes to peer at me.

"No, I'm Jamaican. I just arrived."

"You don't look Jamaican. You must be pulling my leg. How come you're not black?"

I don't know how many times I, Charmaine Gunn, have met with disbelief when asked about my origins, and even after several years in Toronto, I am still obliged to explain.

Long or short explanations regarding my heritage has allowed me to disassociate from the mundane in order for me to emphasize and empathize circumstances, emotions, weather inclinations, world affairs, history and even diversity in tropical islands, to ultimately give credence to my existence.

Ever since childhood, I had been inundated with vivid stories. There were tales and memories that family held dear and imparted to me, and there were tales passed on by friends and acquaintances. All these stories stuck like an adhesive that bound me to the past as it tempered me and made me strong.

2

By my early twenties I was driven by the knowledge I carried. My goal was to preserve all that I had learned about our family. Like a prospector on a quest for fulfilment, I was determined to research and collect all the information I already had, with the intention of combining it with findings in family records, old sepia-coloured photographs and faded journals. I pored over ratty newspaper clippings in the island's record office, and with permission, family diaries, and church archival records. I even approached long standing shopkeepers, and political affiliates for fresh information which I pieced together like a jigsaw in conjunction with historical information kept on file in Kingston's poor house. I wrote pages and pages as a result of whatever I was fortunate enough to extract, only to find that ultimately my words read like a textbook.

I soon realized that our family history needed authentic sounding voices. And having no record of the words that were actually spoken by my ancestors, I therefore was compelled to use my imagination to allow them to speak.

These voices have empowered my research, it was as though my ancestors had given me permission to tell their story. Their story, which is also my story, began on the island of Jamaica, an island that has not ceased to awe and humble me.

Chapter 2:
Hedley

I grew up on the mountainous northwest coast of the island of Jamaica, where hot winds blow fiercely through sugarcane fields and straddle the coconut-laden cliffs that overlook the ferocious sea. The islanders say that that salty stretch of water near the village of Hedley is mesmerizing. They have heard its seductive songs and its moaning and roaring, and their tongues have been sharpened with the enticing taste of salt from its restless belly. Tales have been told through the ages, of persons foolhardy enough to risk their lives and plummet from the treacherous cliffs into the boiling sea below, in search of immortality. Legends say that some survived the free fall, but they do not speak of those who did not.

My grandmother, Wilemina Gunn, the widow of one Jonathan Gunn, a former English bookkeeper, lived at one time in self-imposed solitary existence on an isolated property not far from those very cliffs.

After grandfather's passing, her daily existence and rituals were marked as though in memorial to him.

They had come from England in the early 1920's and decided to settle near Hedley, a small village in the parish of St. James. They planted mango, avocado, cocoa and banana trees in the once-barren landscape immediately in the vicinity of their cottage. However, despite their efforts, nothing would grow near an old banyan tree that stood further upland, not far from the jutting cliff face.

The massive tree stood sentinel, and was visible from a large window at the side of the cottage. Its trunks spanned a good three yards and its thick branches, more than two feet wide at the widest point, seemed to shoot out like great fists grappling with its canopy of shady leaves. The tree's trunks were so curiously formed, that their bulges and indentations resembled crevices and cave-like hollows fashioned by human hands. From its monstrous upper branches cascaded long, sturdy aerial roots, locally called wisps, though they were thicker and stronger than ropes.

The three-bedroom cottage was built brick by brick, each one mortared with grandmother's joyful tears. Back then, the cottage had stood proud and new, easing, as it were, the gash of loneliness that would eventually rip against her widowed heart. My grandparents' industry in building the cottage had been assisted by strong-shouldered black men who brought bricks by wheelbarrow over the arid, bumpy terrain beneath the spreading banyan. The broad-hipped women from Hedley also came, wearing colourful head scarves and loose-fitting cotton frocks that revealed their muscled arms.

It was not unheard of to find them mixing and stirring mortar alongside the men. The hum of their rich, girlish laughter cascading jewel-like into the parched air.

Gangly, long-legged boys wearing outgrown short pants scurried about carrying splashing water jars and fetching the planks, boards and long nails necessary for floors and roofing.

In the midst of all the industry was Ezekiel Samuels, a young Jew who resided just outside of Hedley. The son of a retired builder, Ezekiel knew a thing or two about construction, having been taught at his father's knee. While he supervised the bustling activity on one hand, he wove tales of wonder with the other. Enchantment lived in him and seeped out in his delicious tales of mermaids, rolling calves and other strange beings.

Curious village children followed his every step, ears cocked, even as he shouted instructions to the workers, reminding them of the threat of ferocious storms, and ominous spirits with lightning bolts, and how to place a beam, just so.

Twenty-five-year old Ezekiel was as fair-skinned as my grandmother, though he was a year younger than she and was single. His hair was as black as the thick soot-encased coal stove used by the villagers down on the beach they frequented.

He had very much ingratiated himself with the people of Hedley. Unlike some of the other men, he even gave a hand with lifting and carrying cooking utensils down the steep incline to the open beach. Often the pots would have been laden with goat head soup, tripe, eels and crab and, on Sundays, curried goat.

Ezekiel's storytelling prowess and generosity earned him acceptance in Hedley, though it did not shield him from local gossip. Time and time again, his name was mentioned as a prospective suitor, despite the fact that the village women thought they were perhaps too dark-skinned and uneducated for his taste. It was common knowledge that he had graduated from Munro College and had studied abroad in England.

"Him handsome but is a waste a time, cause him not going go marry us," young women grumbled.

"Him baby would be so pretty, with good hair and clear skin," they whispered regretfully and hissed their teeth.

At thirty years old, my grandfather was not a handsome man; perhaps it was because of his red, tufted hair and sallow complexion, but there was no eclipsing the cheerfulness that peeped out from behind his pale blue eyes.

Although he was not a drinking man, it was said that there was a time when he had appeared inebriated. People in Hedley had it to say that when negotiations for his property were successfully completed, my grandfather was wild with joy. He grabbed a coconut bough and, with trousers rolled up to his knees, ran whooping and screaming into the arms of the sea.

As waves swirled around him, tongues wagged, and it was said that the cliffs, the sea, the straining palms, and even the narrow dirt road flanked with wild hibiscus and flowering alamander bushes had cast a spell on him.

The property had since came to be known as Gunn's Run.

Before Grandfather immigrated to Jamaica, his physician in Bristol had recommended a drastic change of climate for the sake of his health.

"Find a warm climate to live in, somewhere in the colonies perhaps. England will be the death of you. Your lungs are bad," Doctor Solmes had said gravely. "Clearly it is a difficult decision, but you ought to pull up roots, or you won't survive to see your children grow up. No doubt, sunshine and salt air will do you a world of good. There are countries like Jamaica, for instance, where you can live year-round at a fraction of what it would cost to live here. I'm sure you have sizeable savings, being a bookkeeper. It is time to consider using some of it, for you won't last too many more winters here. You just won't have the stamina."

For my grandfather, there was no question of facing another bleak British winter. As it was, he could barely breathe and he had developed a hacking cough.

Therefore, less than six months after that conversation with his physician, he and Grandmother departed from Southampton on a steamer bound for the West Indies. It was almost two months later that their two children followed.

The children—a boy, Dunstan, who would be my father, and his younger sister Eliza—arrived in Jamaica feeling spent, after having made the long, eventful sea journey across the Atlantic. My grandparents had eagerly anticipated their arrival, especially now that their home was habitable and the construction was near completion.

Hot, sticky winds barrelled down from the towering mountain ranges to greet the children, and their legs were wobbly from too many days at sea. Being curious, they had not confined themselves to the cabins. A great deal of their time aboard was spent up on deck under the supervision of a steward. From that vantage, they saw the sky's ever-changing palette between the hemispheres and experienced each extreme turn in the weather. When a storm blew up and the ship was incessantly lashed by gale-force winds and rain, they were afraid, as was everyone else aboard.

When Dunstan and Eliza were to descend the gangplank, they were instructed to place one careful foot at a
time on the narrow rungs. They noticed a long rope
running alongside for support, but they were fearful. The
rope looked flimsy and there were wide spaces between
the rungs, revealing the swirling sea immediately below. It
was no consolation that thick, strong ropes bound the
heavy vessel to the dock.

"Look there's mother and father!" ten-year old Dunstan
shouted, midway down. He fixed his eyes on the two
white people on the wharf amidst the locals, and found
courage to quicken his pace.

Eliza, too, wanted to bolt down the last few rungs, but
Dunstan held tightly to her small hand. He felt protective
and responsible, and stepped with confidence from rung to
rung. Feeling more courageous, he looked westward and
glimpsed a line of coconut palms that dotted the terrain.
He could almost hear their mournful rustle, as they flailed
giant, leafy arms in the blazing sunshine.

"Eliza, look, palm trees," he said hoarsely. "They look
like giant warriors, don't they?"

But Eliza did not look at the coconut palms; she tugged
at his sleeve, instead, and pointed at the dark-skinned
crowd below.

"Those are the Jamaicans," Dunstan whispered. "What
do you suppose they'll think of us?" He laughed softly,
already feeling warm in his English-made suit.

Before they reached the ground, my grandmother ran
towards them and stood, arms outstretched at the bottom
of the gangplank. Dunstan saw that she had pulled on a
bright scarf and was bravely wrestling with the wind that
lashed against her skirt. "Children!" she shouted through
tears, "your father and I have waited so long for this!"

Up close, Dunstan felt her warm breath, saw the palest of lines beside her blue eyes, and anticipated the scent of lilacs in her soft, blonde curls, which crushed against his damp, tear-stained cheek.

"Did you have a good voyage? Did you eat your meals? Are you too warm? We should have warned you about this heat, shouldn't we, darlings?"

Striding, then almost running, my grandfather joined them and pressed them to his heart.

The strong, emotional reunion loosened six-year old Eliza's tongue, for she had not spoken a word since her parents' departure from England.

"Papa," she croaked, and words flowed out from her like water from a deep gushing wellspring.

Though the lilting voices of the Jamaicans sounded melodic to the ears of the new arrivals, they were not sure of what was being said. "What do you suppose they are saying, father?" Dunstan inquired over and over as they walked along the long wooden wharf, their sea trunk and a grip carried with gusto by a large brown man named Laddie, who strode with such pride one would have thought he was on a mission for the king.

Along the beachfront adjoining the wharf, graceful-looking black-skinned market women called higglers, carried precariously balanced baskets of provisions on their heads. They called out urgently to the children. But neither Grandfather nor Grandmother took much notice. "Come youngsters," the women shouted. "Buy this pretty grapefruit, it sweet can't done, and me apple them is the best on the island."

The comings and goings engaged the children, even as they whispered behind their pale hands. They couldn't help but notice the inch-thick calluses on the women's bare feet and the men's muscles that rippled like shiny black snakes.

Their eyes were wide with wonder when thin, grey donkeys and dark-brown oxen laboriously pulled extremely heavy coconut carts to the foot of the dock, bright ribbons tied at the animal's throats. The atmosphere was carnival-like, and even more so when a thin-faced Indian man began to play a welcoming song on a home-made banjo. At his feet was a battered, empty tin cup, testament to his desperation to receive a few spare copper pennies from the disembarking passengers' bounty.

The children's high English voices brought curiosity seekers, who strained their ears, eager to catch their every word. Beggars earlier that day had seen the British ship approach the harbor, and congregated at the far end of the dock, their hands outstretched in anticipation.

"Beg you a sixpence, Sar!" and "Beg you a sixpence, Ma'am!" they chanted, before being hushed into silence and dispersed by the departure of the last of the disembarking crew.

"Sar, you and the missus mus' come a mi daughter wedding," one old woman shouted out as she handed grandfather a stick of sugar cane, a toothy grin on her face. Her name was Martha Rose and Grandfather would not forget her audacity.

Chapter 3:

Camaraderie

Sam Chung, the Chinese shopkeeper in Hedley, dreamed of travelling ever since he learned to read and write. He devoured anything with writing on it that came his way. Even the old newspapers that he used to wrap salt fish tempted him. His eyes would dart hungrily over the words, and he would read the same sentences again and again. It was because of his voracious appetite for reading that he developed a close friendship with my grandfather.

Sam Chung had no books, and he longed to someday own a small collection to keep on one of the narrow wooden shelves behind his shop counter.

Fortunately for him, a friend of my grandmother's named Mabel Davidson, who resided in London, decided to send grandmother an occasional bundle of British magazines in lieu of letters, to keep the family informed about events at home. The magazines were aimed at a female audience and informed its readers with news items, the latest in fashion, makeup, household etiquette and cooking, as well as short stories.

Grandmother cultivated the habit of passing on her magazines to Sam Chung as soon as the next bundle arrived. He was one of the few locals who knew how to read.

Sam Chung enjoyed the short stories most. He felt that they took him into the orderly and envious world of the British. In his mind's eye, he could almost hear the cadence of their clipped speech, and he perceived their lives as ideal.

Strangely enough, he knew little or nothing about China, where his parents had come from, and neither he nor his wife Chunty spoke Hakka, the language of their ancestors.

Chunty, who was darker-skinned than Sam, was a Spanish Town–born Chinese. Their two children Peter and Maggie, attended the village school, and lived and spoke in the same manner as did the other locals. If one had heard their voices without the benefit of seeing them, one would have been hard-pressed to realize that they were Oriental.

"Mi wife going make whole heap of mackerel and banana tonight, Mr. Gunn," Sam Chung said, gratefully accepting another bundle of magazines. "Mi going bring some over for your children, for them like it."

Sam Chung's gesture, bringing cooked meals to my grandparents' house became synonymous with the arrival of the magazines. As a result, the two men, my grandfather and Sam Chung, developed a close friendship. There were occasions when Grandfather would saunter down the dirt road to visit the grocery shop, and would find there East Indians and Negro labourers from the sugarcane fields, congregated for a smoke or a drink of rum. Sam Chung was usually behind the counter, replenishing his meager stocks of sugar, rice and flour, as he relayed information he found in the English magazines.

"The man them over there always have to dress in suit, cause it so cold. And all of them have umbrella. Rain come all the time there."

Hearing Sam Chung expound on a life that he had never experienced must have made Grandfather smile wryly, allowing the old shopkeeper to hold centre stage.

How far away Europe seemed to the threadbare locals who had never travelled, and how amazing the technology — radios in British homes.

Occasionally in the evenings, Ezekiel Samuels shared in the camaraderie at Hedley's only grocery shop. On those occasions, the men would entreat him to tell them stories for, as far as they were concerned, stories were as powerful and as real as the written word.

Whenever Ezekiel came, the women would stealthily begin to drift in, each one on the pretense of an errand. Children, too, would squeeze themselves between the women, staying well away from the drinking men's tables, ears cocked. Often, they would be rewarded with a tale.

Ezekiel never touched more than half a shot of rum; it was as if that amount was enough to unravel the enchantment in him.

"I'm going to tell you the story of the Bog Walk Gorge in St. Catherine," he said, wiping his lips on his cloth handkerchief, and accepting the wooden stool that Sam Chung quickly brought over to him.

"Once upon a time, long time gone," Ezekiel began — his eyes half closed as the words poured out from him — "there was a young man looking for a wife, but no matter where he went, he couldn't find the right woman. Then one night when he was coming home from a dance, and had too much to drink, he managed to get lost in the mountainous countryside in St. Catherine. All of a sudden, he heard a woman's voice singing. He had never heard anything as sweet, and he decided to follow the sound.

"Before he knew it, he found himself right inside the Bog Walk Gorge. But back in those days there was no bridge there, so it was impossible to cross over the river. The gorge was such a secret place that, for the longest time, not even the Spanish, who lived in Jamaica before the British, knew about it.

"The young man gazed longingly across the wide river. The shining, rippling waters looked strangely inviting. But as the moon sailed high in the sky, he saw that there were dark shadows looming and darting amongst the rocks, looking like the faces of hideous monsters.

"'Is anybody here?' he called out.

"'Nobody here but me,' a voice answered from across the river. It was a young woman with long, waist-length golden hair, sitting on a large rock, on the distant riverbank. She looked beautiful in the moonlight, though her face was partially hidden.

"'Come sit beside me,' she said sweetly, hiding more of her face behind her flowing hair. 'Come let me tell you something.'

"'I can't come to you,' the young man stammered. 'The river is too wide. I would drown ... I can't swim.'"

Ezekiel Samuels heard the collective catch of breath around him, and felt an "otherness" creep over him. He had felt it before when telling stories. It was as if an electrical current had shot through him, leaving him as strangely awed and as transfixed as his listeners.

"She goin' kill him!" a small boy hissed fearfully, but his mother boxed his ears and he too became perfectly still.

"Quiet!" she commanded, eyes bulging. "You must learn to listen when big man them talk."

The men were the first to draw closer then the older children and lastly, the women. Mothers balanced babies in one hand and covered their mouths with the other, while younger children who could walk gripped at their clothing.

"So what happen then, Mr. Samuels? The man drown or what?" A light-brown man known as Busha inquired, eager for the story to continue.

Ezekiel closed his eyes, and his countenance went slack and luminous as though he was in a trance. So rapt was the audience's attention that the only sound that could be heard was the sound of mosquitoes and other insects, and the occasional shuffle of animals tethered outside the shop. But when Ezekiel's mouth finally opened, the story flowed out.

"The woman on the rock smiled," Ezekiel said, and his captivated audience hung on to his every word.

"'You won't drown,' she said and as the water splashed all around her, the young man saw that she had no feet, for the lower half of her body was a huge fish tail! The young man was shocked to realize that she was a mermaid. He was so frightened he wanted to run, but his feet were rooted to the spot as she swam slowly towards him.

"'Don't be afraid,' she said sweetly. 'I could be a good wife to you.'

"As she drew closer, the young man became enchanted by her beauty.

"I am falling in love with her, he thought. But if she is a fish and I am a man, how can we marry?

"But no sooner than he thought those thoughts than the mermaid smiled knowingly.

"'Of course we can marry,' she said and laughed. 'I will take you to my river kingdom.'

"I wouldn't be able to breathe down there. I would drown, the young man thought.

"'Listen well, my handsome, mortal friend,' she said. 'In the future, many bridges will be built over this river gorge, but I will wash them away with floods and storms. Many mortals who venture into this gorge will meet their fate.'

"'And though I thrive on human souls, I will spare the soul of my lifelong mate. Promise me that as of this very night you will come to live with me forever so that none of the disasters I predicted will ever come to pass.'

"The young man's legs were unglued and he walked slowly towards her, full of regret at having to leave his home and his family behind. The mermaid rushed towards him, and the young man was so terrified he couldn't breathe — his heart and lungs gave out, and he fell dead with a great crash into the shallows.

"From that day until this, it is said that the gorge is haunted, and that is why there are tragic accidents there and bridges are always washed away. It is all because the mermaid is still angry about losing that handsome young man."

Ezekiel Samuels stretched his long legs, rose from the stool, and took a few short steps to the counter, where he had placed his shot glass. He drained the drop or two that were left in it and without another word or looking back, he walked out of the shop door into the night.

"That Mista Samuels can sure tell story," a young woman named Isilda said, eying the doorway. "I wonder if him not fraid when him tell story like that. I for one is not going walk out a here alone."

Isilda came from the parish of St. Elizabeth and like

many others from that district, was light-skinned though Negroid in appearance. She had come to Hedley to live with her grandmother and hoped to find some kind of work on the north coast.

"Good evening Sir," she said, nodding at Grandfather, who entered the shop at that precise moment, intending to buy cigarettes. So intent was he on his mission that he barely looked up as he mumbled evening's greetings to all within earshot and laid his coins on the counter.

"I was wondering, Sir," Isilda said, approaching him more boldly, "do you have any days' work over at the house, Sir? I can wash, cook, clean and even look after children, Sir. I know that plenty of your workmen gone, so nobody is there to give a hand." She spoke in practised English rather than patois, and her attempts at a genteel manner made an impression.

Pocketing his cigarettes, Grandfather stopped momentarily and looked at her, and he seemed to carefully weigh her suggestion.

Sam Chung, who was hunched over at the shop counter, was working diligently at separating husks and weevils from the rice barrel by lamp light. He looked up sharply to meet Isilda's eyes. No doubt her pretentious tone dismayed him.

"Leave the gentleman alone," he hissed. "You is not to bother the people them who come in here. Why you don't go down a Mobay or Kingston?"

But Isilda Greaves was not to be cowed. She bent her head and approached my grandfather, desperation in her downcast eyes. "I beg you, Sir. I need to help out my poor granny."

"It's all right Sam Chung, not to worry," Grandfather said. "My wife could use some help. She spends far too much time doing housework and we can't have that, can we? Why, I think this young lady would do us all a world of good. Perhaps she could pop over soon and speak with my wife."

"Well, Sir," Isilda replied, excitement mounting in her throat, "if it convenient, I can walk over there with you tonight. It is in my way."

Chapter 4:
The Dream Place

A nd so it was that Isilda Greaves, an uneducated Jamaican peasant woman, became part of the "English people's" household. Every morning at six-thirty she cooked breakfast on the wood stove, and afterwards made beds and cleaned shoes. By midday, she would have tidied the house and taken the family's dirty laundry to be scrubbed and beaten out on the rocky shore of a nearby stream.

Other women from Hedley frequented the stream to do washing but, being envious of Isilda, they gathered in groups further along the waterway to gossip. They laughed about Isilda's coarse, kinky, reddish hair, saying that it looked untamable.

"Comb can't pass through that," they whispered mockingly.

Some of them cackled aloud and said that Isilda's sensuously swollen-looking lips were caused by insect bites. They giggled about what was, to them, her unnaturally pallid complexion. "She look even whiter than the white people. She's a 'red nayga' that is what she is," a stout black woman said with a smirk. "She lucky she get work with English people. Cause them pay good, and them clothes not too hard to wash either."

Isilda would return to the house in time to set the lunch table with bright, white linens and Grandmother's "everyday" cutlery. Dependent on the weather, the table was placed outdoors under the shade of the huge banyan. The family enjoyed Isilda's tasty lunches of roasted sweet potatoes, boiled green bananas, fried fish with onions, peppers and pimento, and even her spicy bully beef sandwiches. It was a far cry from the bland fare they had been accustomed to in England.

When the gentle sea breezes came inland as far as the slope where the banyan tree stood, the family could glimpse the distant, emerald sea between the swaying branches. It would invariably remind them of their voyage across the Atlantic, and thanks would be given to God for food, health, family and this dream place they now called home.

After lunch, when the children would take to exploring the nooks and crannies of the banyan, oblivious to their parents' discussion of schooling, world affairs, the fall of the British pound and opportunities, if any, to make a living on the island.

"Since we have a car, I could perhaps get a position as a bookkeeper in a Montego Bay hotel, though the roads are awfully bad," Grandfather said. "And you, Wilemina, might like to do something from the house. Would you consider taking in sewing or baking? There's a need for such skills here, I dare say."

"I beg your pardon, darling; you don't know me at all, do you? I'd rather sell pickles and preserves. If I have my way, that's what I'll do; and there will be lots of provisions coming from our garden once it gets more productive. Don't you agree?"

The sun would be high in the sky before my grandparents would excuse themselves from the table. At that time of day, it was my grandfather's habit to settle in a swayback chair nearer to the beach to enjoy a smoke and, perhaps, to think his own thoughts. As for my grandmother, after the spread at the lunch table, she would reward herself with a long walk along the lonely shore. Even then, it was as though she was constantly searching for solitude. However, she was unaware that her lean frame, her thick, blonde curls and her beauty attracted envious, as well as discreet, admiring glances.

Left to her own devices, Isilda planned meals for the evening. She peeled Irish potatoes, washed rice, chopped onions and Scotch bonnet peppers, and marinated fish, pork or the occasional chicken. Her broad hands would caress the English-made pots and saucepans with fondness. She had never used utensils like those and felt that her meals were successful because of them.

Produce was scarce on the island, though my grandparents, being foreigners, were privy to the freshest supplies from the market and the grocery shop. Isilda's meals stood as testament, and her pots constantly steamed and spluttered as she daydreamed about Grandfather.

She wasn't sure when it was that she had first started to fantasize about him, but her body felt strangely excited and aroused the more he consumed her thoughts.

Grandfather, oblivious to her state of mind, complimented her housework, and this small attention flamed her desire. He sometimes left the house for a day, to pursue job opportunities. Jobs were becoming scarce, though some American tourists continued to visit the island's hotels, and there was talk that conditions over in Europe might deteriorate. It was no wonder that Grandfather felt an urgent need to protect his savings. On those days, Isilda would miss his presence in the household.

Ezekiel Samuels had heard gossip in the village shop. There was no escaping the talk around him, from sullen-faced women who came to listen to his stories.

"That Isilda Greaves, she think she white, and is just cause she work for white people," one woman said, spitting out the words in disgust.

"Them people must be fool though, cause them can't see that all she want is man," hissed a bony-faced woman.

The woman standing next to her commented, "What wrong with Mr. Gunn? Him don't see that she a make moon eye at him?"

At first Ezekiel put it all down to jealous talk, but it wasn't long before he had his own suspicions.

After three months of free rein, it was decided that the children should be sent off to boarding school in Montego Bay. Their long, carefree days of wading, swimming, shell gathering, and lunches under the banyan tree were swiftly drawing to a close.

"Mother, I'm not going to like the school, am I? There will be all sorts of rules and nothing but schoolwork. I can't see me liking it one bit."

"Come, come, Dunstan darling, there will be lots to learn, but you'll enjoy it; and you'll make new friends too. After all, as it is, all you have here are Peter and Maggie Chung, and you hardly ever see them; they spend so much time in the shop."

"But I like Peter and Maggie. They get on splendidly with Eliza and me. And just this morning, Peter and I found a jellyfish and we dissected it, and Peter says he wants to study marine life when he grows up, and I think I might like that too."

"My word, darling, there will be lots of time to decide about your future, but right now it's school for you and Eliza. You both have been away from classes for an awfully long time."

There was great excitement in the household as plans were made and the children's suitcases packed and repacked. Isilda was kept busy, not only with housework, but occasionally with drying tears. Though she kept her eye on the children, her thoughts were crowded with Grandfather's needs. Were his clothes clean and starched, were his meals sufficient, and was he contented?

Neither Grandmother nor Grandfather noticed her extra diligence. Neither did they notice the little droplets of thick, clotty oils she stealthily added to Grandfather's portion of meals. She took to carrying a small bottle of "Oil of Stay with Me" in her apron pocket and whispering incantations, familiar to those from St. Elizabeth who practised obeah.

It would seem that there was no way to prevent events from coming to a head.

Not even late one August evening, when Ezekiel Samuels decided to enjoy the evening breeze, as was his habit, and set out for his usual walk. It occurred to him that he might visit the Gunn children before their departure for school. Also, if the opportunity presented itself, he thought he might voice his suspicions to Grandfather regarding Isilda.

Stopping briefly at the grocery shop, he bought the children a brown paper bag of red-and-white mint balls and Paradise Plum candies, as well as a few pencils. The cool evening air exhilarated him and, since he was familiar with the terrain, he confidently made his way along the pitch-black path near the cliffs. There was never any danger that he might lose his footing, though he stopped near the edge to admire the rich silver hues of the sea and the sky from the safety of the black foreboding landscape. Waves crashed ominously against rocks far below him, and brought to mind tragic tales he had heard in the village. It was no wonder that the lonely cry of sea birds nesting in the rock face startled him.

Ezekiel hurried through the hibiscus and alamander, and noticed that my grandparents' house was in darkness, for no one was home. He turned on his heel to return home, when he was surprised by a low whistle.

"Who's there?" he asked, staring into the darkness.

"Is me, Isilda," a female voice replied as Isilda slowly separated herself from the shadows and approached. Her legs seemed unsteady, and there was a faint whiff of alcohol on her breath. "I watching the house," she slurred. "The family gone go Mobay, cause Mr. Gunn get a job there. Them going move, and them won't need me no more. But I watching the house."

"Are they coming back tonight?"

"Yes, them coming back tonight."

"I brought a little something for the children. Maybe I'll come back another time."

"Leave it with me, Mr. Samuels. I will give them."

It was quite late in the evening when my grandparents returned home. They parked the car a short distance from the house, as was their custom. The children had fallen asleep on the journey, and were gently roused when the car engine stopped and they heard their parents whispering in excited voices.

"A job at last, Wilemina darling. Isn't that splendid! Now, we won't have to depend entirely on our savings. We can supplement it with my wages."

"Darling, that's the best news I've heard today, Jonathan."

"Yes, we'll move to a house closer to the children's school. You'd like that, wouldn't you? I'm pretty certain it will have a proper kitchen, and bathroom too."

"I am rather happy, darling, though I'm sure we will miss this house. It has a certain charm, wouldn't you say?"

They were in mid-stride when a slight rustle in the bush attracted their attention.

"Who's it? Show yourself!" Grandfather demanded, pulling Grandmother closer, as she gripped the children's hands. Dunstan and Eliza, being half asleep, were unaware of the urgency.

"Is me," Isilda replied sheepishly, pushing the bush aside.

"Isilda, you gave us rather a start. What on earth are you doing out here at this hour?" Grandmother asked, relaxing her hold on the children.

"I was watching the house till you get back."

"But it's rather late, Isilda," Grandfather added. "There's no need for you to watch the house. You shouldn't be out here at this hour. Anything could happen. Mrs.

Gunn will take the children in to bed, and I'll walk you over to the village. I shouldn't be long, darling."

That was the last time Grandmother was to see my grandfather alive. Four days later, his body and that of Isilda's washed up on the shore beneath the cliffs.

Their bodies, bloated and swollen from sea water, gave no indication of foul play or signs of a struggle. Village gossip had it to say that Isilda had been distraught over the English family's impending departure. No doubt it was she, in her deranged state of mind, who pushed Grandfather over the cliff then jumped over to join him in his watery grave.

Not even the two sleeping, fair-haired children, Dunstan and Eliza, could stay the sadness that filled my grandmother up like a vessel. For when Grandfather did not return that night she was fearful, and the house felt like an island in a well of darkness, more remote than ever. Grandmother lit a kerosene lamp, and her heart raced as she took up post by the window. For hours, she fidgeted restlessly with a string of fake pearls she wore, trying in that small way to hold back a flood of tears. Through it all, the children slept soundly, unaware of their mother's anguish.

In the morning, when a grey dawn approached the mountains, Grandfather had still not returned. Grandmother rose from her weary vigil and pulled on a pair of hard-soled shoes. Then, without waking the children, she locked the front door and made her solitary way down the bushy path to the village.

Sam Chung was just opening up his shop when he glimpsed her on the dusty road out front. It was rare indeed to see her in the village, not to mention at that hour. Flustered by her unexpected appearance, he did not notice how disheveled she was. She was still wearing clothes from the night before, and her hair was unusually unruly.

"Mrs. Gunn." Sam Chung smiled shyly. "How can I help you, Ma'am?"

"Sam," Grandmother said, holding herself erect and barely hiding tears, "if it's not too much of a bother, I wonder if you've seen Mr. Gunn? After he walked Isilda home last night he didn't come home. Do you know where she lives?"

Sam Chung creased his forehead and his eyes became lively as he glanced up and down the road, shaking his head. "No good will come from that girl," he muttered. "Let me call my son Peter. He will show you where her house is. Come Mrs. Gunn, rest you feet, you been walking long."

Isilda was not to be found. Her grandmother was alone. The old woman tottered around her shack, trembling from the news she had just heard, a tin can of bush tea bubbling on her coal stove.

"That girl don't listen to nobody," she grumbled, wagging her head. "She don't come home last night. Who know what she go get mix up in. Me did tell her that she going get in serious trouble long time now. See all them powder and oil all over the place … is her thing them."

Before long, it was not only Peter Chung who was helping with the search; volunteers and willing hands appeared as quickly as word spread.

School was closed that day and many school children combed the beach, while adults, lead by Ezekiel Samuels and others, searched caves as well as the hollows in the banyan and even in the overhangs along the cliff face. But nothing was found.

That afternoon, Chunty Chung brought freshly made beef soup to Gunn's Run. It was her first visit to the house, and she insisted that Grandmother and the children should eat. Over the next few days, it was her coaxing and generosity that kept the family going.

"Chunty, you've been awfully kind to the lot of us." Grandmother sighed. "How can we ever return the favour?"

"Some things don't need payment, Mrs. Gunn. We Jamaican people help out when someone needs it. Your husband and my husband is good friends, and Peter and Maggie get on so well with your children."

How prophetic her words were.

As fate would have it, Martha Rose, the old woman who had given Grandfather a stick of sugarcane at the wharf, was the person who discovered the bodies on the beach. Her piercing wail sent others running, and there was a great uproar as the startling news spread unbridled.

The one church in Hedley rang its bell ominously, and the entire village fell into silent grieving.

It didn't take long before there was talk that the house at Gunn's Run would surely be haunted. Hundreds of suggestions came forward as to how to cleanse the house of spirits or duppies, as they were called locally. For two days the property was overrun with sympathizers and curiosity seekers, the Chung family, Ezekiel Samuels and the school teacher George Ellis, amongst them.

It was a bright morning with birds wheeling in the sky, when Grandfather's body was solemnly taken by a boat overflowing with floral wreaths and tributes, to be laid to rest far out at sea. A church minister came from Falmouth to officiate, and the entire village came out to the beachfront to pay their respects. Grandmother and the children, buoyed by the support, stood firm in the midst of the mourning.

"Look how she hold up strong," the women whispered. "If it was me, me would bruk down. But stop, them must be give her something strong to drink."

On the other hand, that morning before daybreak, Isilda's body was swaddled in crocus bags and packed in melting ice before being taken by donkey cart to be buried in an unmarked grave far from the village. No one was in attendance except for her grandmother and the cart man, who had to be paid five shillings for his trouble. Isilda's last journey involved taking deliberately roundabout routes, to prevent her spirit from finding its way back to the village.

Unable to afford the car Grandfather had rented and boarding school fees, my grandmother and the children continued to reside at Gunn's Run. They lived frugally from the last of Grandfather's savings and depended on fresh produce from the garden. Once in a while, a woman would come from the village to help out. But Grandmother's dwindling savings were cause for concern, and she was desperate to find another source of income.

Dunstan and Eliza were enrolled at the government-run village school in Hedley, along with Peter and Maggie and thirty other children.

The students sat three abreast in rustic wooden desks, with hardly any room to stretch their growing legs. A narrow shelf ran the length of the underside of the desk, though it was almost too narrow for their slim exercise books.

The students were dirt poor, though the boys sported cheap homemade khaki uniforms with short pants, and the girls a blue tunic with a white inner blouse. Footwear did not matter, since students often came barefooted.

Mr. George Ellis, who ran the school, was vigilant and a strict disciplinarian who strived to see his students successful at scholarship. He was grateful for assistance from Ezekiel Samuels, who lent a hand not only with marking papers but also with reading to the children, and teaching geography and literature. One other teacher completed the staff, a Mrs. Joy Rodney from Kingston. Mrs. Rodney carried a thin, black switch, and many disorderly students had felt its sting. She was divorced, and gossip said that she would often take her anger out on the children.

"If she get friendly with Mr. Samuels, that might soften her up," one young boy commented hopefully after being the recipient of her wrath.

It was said that Ezekiel Samuels had found his niche because, since the passing of his elderly father, he appeared to be released from restrictions and constraints that might have been placed on him. He even "walked out" with a handful of village women, though it was clear that he seemed to be still searching for something intangible.

"Him not going settle," one feisty woman complained. "All him want is to tell story, and all me want is to get him to give me him baby. And that man not even so much as touch me!"

"Wonder if him funny?" a young woman with thick braids chimed in.

"No, I know that him not funny. I see how he look at woman, him eye light up, but something a hold him back."

Chapter 5:
The Changing Landscape

Grandmother hardly noticed how over the years, her children had grown. They were not unlike the wild hibiscus bushes that grew profusely without the guidance of her hand. Her self-imposed isolation prevented her having a part in it, and the English-born children embraced without restraint the tropical land and the sea. Grandmother would hear their voices echoing along the windy shore and, occupied indoors with one insignificant task or another, it became impossible for her to distinguish their voices from that of the village children.

She walked through sun-drenched rooms and felt the warmth settle like a mantle around her slim shoulders and imagined her husband still there, holding her. Smiling softly, she would gently close the bedroom door and go into the kitchen to remove his blue bowl from the top shelf and press it against her heart. Then in the living-room, she would set the bowl on the small side table beside his rocking chair. In her mind's eye, she could almost see him sitting beside the wide window that overlooked the band of aquamarine sea. Tears would come as she headed out to the wooden veranda.

Everything she touched reminded her of him: he had built the three-bedroom house to last them forever. She remembered their shared excitement when furnishings were brought over from England, never imagining that so soon he would no longer be there.

How is it, she wondered, that she had not noticed the children growing tall, and that fourteen-year old Dunstan was already handsome and soon approaching manhood. How is it, she wondered, she had not noticed that his cheeks were as ruddy as his father's, though his hair and complexion were golden from long exposure to the Caribbean sun. As for curly-haired Eliza, she was already ten years old and showing signs of the beauty she could become.

My children have become Jamaicans, my grandmother thought dreamily, hearing their excited shouts from the beach.

Chunty Chung's was the voice of reason that gently stirred Grandmother from her dreaming. Once in a while, Chunty would take it up on herself to bring a piece of salt fish, mackerel or pig's tail to Gunn's Run, knowing that the family lived on the edge of poverty. Grandmother would return the favour by giving her bananas, avocados and mangoes from the property.

"It not that safe out here anymore," Chunty said one day, bustling about, putting her bundles away in the kitchen. "Things change, Mrs. Gunn. You going need somebody to stay out here with you."

"Whatever for, Chunty? There's no problem."

"Things not like when you and Mr. Gunn did just

come. Lots of changes happening in Jamaica that you don't know about. Labourers getting laid off and some are even fired."

"So how on earth does that affect me, Chunty?"

"Mrs. Gunn, people discontent. If they don't get money, they steal and loot. I hear there's talk of an uprising. You could even get held up out here, and nobody would know. For God sakes, think about the children's safety."

"But Chunty, even if you are right, where could anyone stay here? We have only three bedrooms."

"Then build a small shack on the property. You still have lots of leftover board and zinc. Lots of people would help."

"But... what about bathrooms, Chunty?"

"Don't worry about that now, Mrs. Gunn. My husband Sam read in the paper that Kingston full up of people looking for work. But there's no jobs there. Is the same thing happening here too, so even a small job like this would be welcome."

"But Chunty, I have hardly any money."

"Don't worry 'bout money. All they will ask for is some bananas, cocoa or mangoes. As long as you have the building supplies, which you do, I can look about getting you a carpenter."

A small shack and an outdoor covered pit toilet were built at the back of the house. Chunty was right: there was no cost to Grandmother, except in fruit and vegetables. Then things were left up to Sam Chung who knew the community well, to find someone suitable to live on the

Gunn property. Many of Hedley's residents were afraid of the proximity to the cliffs nearby, with its legacy of death and suicides. Others feared that Isilda's ghost might return to drive them away. It was only a strapping black woman named Constance, who had just come from St. Ann, who agreed to the offer as long as she could bring her teenaged son Lucas. An agreement was made that the Gunn's food and cooking would be shared as payment enough for the presence of the newcomers on the property.

"Lucas don't want to go to school," Constance said, wringing her large hands in frustration. "I wants to keep him occupied, so I going get him to do the washing, the Gunn's and mine."

But when tall, strapping Lucas went to the river with the bundles of clothes, his lean, muscular black frame and his handsomeness attracted the washer women.

Day after day, they clustered around him, going so far as to take on his washing duties, in return for kisses.

For the next two years or so, disgruntled labourers roamed Jamaica's countryside, seeking out young men to join their ranks in labour unions. Sugar cane crops were failing as a result of the fierce competition from European beet sugar. There was even an outcry for the diversification of crops, and small farmers were encouraged to cultivate more bananas and coconuts instead.

It was also around that time that a countermovement began amongst young men who turned to Rastafarianism. This religious movement originated in the parish of St. Thomas, to promote an Afrocentric way of thinking. It preached a philosophy of blacks overcoming past and present persecution, and finding salvation in an Ethiopian god in the person of Emperor Haile Selassie.

Rastas, as they were called, grew their hair unconventionally long in dreadlocks and smoked ganja, a hallucinogenic drug, as sacrament. The lower classes viewed the movement as the answer to an oppressed society in search of cultural identity. But it was perceived as a threat by the Jamaican upper class as well as British nationals.

When Lucas disappeared from the property, it was assumed that he had left to follow either the labour unionists or the Rastafarians. His departure at that time was unfortunate, since only the two vulnerable women and the children were left to protect the property.

No one missed him more than Eliza, for there was a gentleness about the large, black young man that appealed to the child. She found to her delight that he was not beyond helping to construct banana leaf clothing for her stick dolls. And whenever she brought canisters of cooked food from the house for him and his mother, it was Lucas who was especially thankful. Two years after his departure, she still had not forgotten him.

"Do you think Lucas might come back one day?" Eliza asked one morning while walking on the beach with her mother. "I think it would be nice if Constance could read and write, because she probably would have heard from him. Don't you agree Mother?"

"Constance doesn't want to learn to read and write, darling. She feels she is too old. But no doubt I know she recognizes words like sugar and flour when she sees them on a shopping list."

"Have you asked her about Lucas? She must be fretting about him. What if it was Dunstan, wouldn't you fret, Mother?"

"Naturally I would fret, darling, but don't ever forget that some of these people are quite different than we are."

"I think you're wrong Mother. They are like us. It's just that we are white, isn't it?"

"Eliza, as you get older, you'll realize that a lot is expected from us just for being white, and we mustn't disappoint, must we?"

"That doesn't make a bit of sense to me, Mother."

The next time Chunty Chung came to Gunn's Run, Grandmother intended to speak to her about the conversation she had with Eliza. However, she thought better of it, seeing how Chunty seemed more inclined to be one of the blacks, though she looked quite Chinese.

"What's it like for you living here?" Grandmother asked tentatively. "Does it ever concern you at all that your children never get to mix with their own kind?"

"Why should that concern me?" Chunty laughed. "You mean you don't know that I am half Chinese. My mother is a black Jamaican. It's my father who is Chinese. Sam says that's why our children so pretty."

"Oh, now that I think of it, Chunty, Maggie is sixteen isn't she? She's rather pretty, with all that wavy hair and all, and your Peter is already seventeen. What a beanpole he has become. Where did the time go?"

"Mrs. Gunn," Chunty said, sounding conspiratorial, "our children been growing while we wasn't looking. Oh, that remind me — I almost forgot to give you this."

Chunty thrust an especially nice-looking piece of salt fish into Grandmother's hands. She had carefully wrapped it in newspaper to remind herself to discuss the latest news.

"Sam tell me that sugar not making much money in Jamaica anymore, and the country could bankrupt. Him getting old, but last night he come up with an idea. He say that if we had some land, we could plant ginger, cause ginger doing well. I think him right, and it make me think that you and me going need money to help our children. Now, if you allow us to grow ginger on your property, we could all share the profits. We could use the fallow land on the other side of the banyan tree. I can even get people to help with the planting, and in the end all of we will benefit. What you think Mrs. Gunn?"

"Chunty, please call me Wilemina. We've been friends for rather a long time, and I'm sure you know that I don't know the first thing about ginger."

"You won't need to know a thing. We will do all the work."

"Rubbish, Chunty, of course I'd want to help too, but what's so good about ginger anyway?"

"Well, you can use it in tea, bake with it and make beer. Some people even use it for stomach medicine. We Chinese use it in cooking and my father used to make nice dried ginger candies. And we mustn't forget that Indian people use it in curry."

"I must admit it all sounds rather interesting Chunty, and if you are right, I dare say it might just be the ticket.

Dunstan wants to study further once he is finished here — he's already sixteen — and Eliza's not far behind."

"It's the same thing with Peter and Maggie, and since Peter older he going finish school before them."

The two acres of land near the banyan tree was ideal for cultivating ginger. Not only was there an abundance of organic waste material in the soil, but there was ample exposure to sun and rain.

Chunty and Sam Chung brought several ginger seed rhizomes to the property and treated them in warm water to cure them for the required seven days before the actual planting.

"We going have to weed regularly," Sam Chung warned. "And another thing, we going have to mound the rows. I can get two or three young boys from the village to help us with that. Is a good ten months before it going mature."

"Sam, I hope it don't get no disease and waste our time."

"Chunty, how many times I must tell you that it not going get any disease. But we going have to keep down the insects."

It was one afternoon some months after the ginger was harvested and the first sales had come in that Ezekiel Samuels sought out Eliza Gunn in the school yard. The school had relocated to a larger building, since enrollment had gone up and there was now a staff of six teachers, each in charge of one of the forms. Ezekiel had no trouble finding Eliza. Not only was her blonde hair noticeable from a distance, but she was still the school's only white female student. As such, she was usually surrounded by interested and curious dark-skinned playmates.

"Eliza," Ezekiel Samuels said, calling her over, as all heads turned to listen to the conversation. "It's important that I speak with your mother. Could you please ask her if she is free on Sunday?"

A group of young girls with plaits giggled amongst themselves and nudged each other knowingly.

"If you come on Sunday, Mr. Samuels," Eliza said grinning, "she's going to want you to stay for dinner. But if you're coming to talk about schoolwork ..." Eliza paused, as though sizing up the situation, then laughed out loud before assuming a mock haughty posture. "If school is what it's about, perhaps you shouldn't come at all."

"No, Eliza, it's not about schoolwork," Ezekiel Samuels said, somewhat exasperated by the lack of privacy and Eliza's tendency to be disrespectful. "Just give your mother my message, and tell her I'm going to bring a nice snapper fish to cook."

No sooner than Ezekiel Samuels was out of sight, the schoolgirls who had been standing nearby during the conversation giggled some more. They hid their smiling mouths behind their hands, and whispered and joked amongst themselves as if in response to their own budding sexuality.

"Our Mrs. Rodney don't stand a chance with him now," they chanted songlike, then scampered off to a safe distance away from Eliza, who got more annoyed as they continued their chant. "She go wait too long to rope him, and now him a look at prettier prospects." Their words were clearly suggestive, and Eliza was no longer amused. She rushed after them angrily and swore never to speak with them again.

That Sunday, Ezekiel Samuels brought the promised snapper fish to Gunn's Run. It was generously spiced and marinated in vinegar, pimento, onion, garlic and Scotch bonnet peppers. Its delicious aromas filled the household as it slowly baked in the woodstove oven. What a welcome addition it was to the Gunn's meagre fare.

"That was a brilliant meal," Dunstan said, wiping his plate clean with a slice of hardo bread. "You should come over more often, Mr. Samuels."

Everyone laughed, though a visit from Ezekiel always meant there would be a good meal on the table, and perhaps a story afterwards.

"So what brought you out here, Ezekiel?" Grandmother asked. "I know it couldn't be about helping with the ginger cultivation, because it hasn't been much of a bother finding hands to help."

"How are the crops doing, Wilemina?"

"Rather well, thanks. Chunty and Constance and a few others, including myself, have really been putting our backs into the work. We have actually been making some money. Anyway, your visit is most probably about the children, isn't it? Are they misbehaving in classes?" She tossed her hair teasingly and folded her crisp white napkin, which usually indicated that everyone was excused from the table.

"Mother," Dunstan said hastily, closing his knife and fork, and pushing his empty chair back into place, "me and Eliza are going to the caves. Maggie and Peter are meeting us there. We're going to examine rocks, algae and stuff."

"Do be careful, darling. Don't forget it can be rather dangerous there."

A thin worry line etched itself on her forehead, and when Dunstan turned to meet her eyes, he couldn't help but notice how beautiful she was. Blonde ringlets framed her smooth face. She looked younger than he had thought she was. I must have been born when she was a teenager, Dunstan thought to himself, and it surprised him, for he had always thought of her as being so much older than he was.

"Not to worry, Mother." He grinned and he almost dragged Eliza from her chair. "We won't be going up on the cliffs, will we, Eliza?"

But Eliza didn't reply; she was never sure what Dunstan was up to, but whatever it was, she was glad to be included.

"Wilemina, the children have left the house," Ezekiel said, keeping his voice low, "so now I'll tell you why I've come over to see you, and I won't beat around the bush either."

"Whatever is the matter, Ezekiel? You look positively distraught."

"Who can blame me? There's political unrest everywhere Wilemina, not to mention gang warfare, the depression in America, and the fact that the British pound is taking quite a beating. All of this impacts on Jamaica's economy. Heaven forbid, but there might even be a war on the horizon! From what I hear, things don't look too good for the Jews either. Not only are we discriminated against widely, but in Europe it is said that Jews are being deprived of properties. All these concerns are quite troubling, Wilemina, and that is why I've decided to leave Hedley. I have become too complacent here. I need to go to Kingston, where I can find out if there is any way I can help to stop what might be inevitable. To put it bluntly, I want to help to prevent what could well be a massive and destructive war."

"My God!" Grandmother gasped, steadying herself

against the doorframe. "You are frightening me, Ezekiel!" She was suddenly aware that living isolated at Gunn's Run had cut her off from world affairs and politics, and had narrowed her view. She had not even stopped to imagine the possibility that a steadfast friend such as Ezekiel would no longer be in her world. She felt both exposed and vulnerable and, with thoughts racing, found that she could barely stand.

"I rather didn't expect this at all," she said. "I never considered that you would leave Hedley. You've rather thrown me for a loop, haven't you?"

She went to sit by the window; the skies were cloudy and gray, but she did not notice. She did not even see the sails of the small fishing boats heading towards the horizon, or the slow flight of gulls coming in for a landing.

Ezekiel came to stand behind her. There was no mistaking the tears on her cheeks when she turned her head towards him, and he was moved.

He hesitated at first, then softly placed his trembling hands on her shoulders. She moved her head to one side, her ringlets cascading, as she sighed deeply and brought her lips to his fingers.

"Ezekiel," she murmured, feeling his warm kiss in her hair and in the hollow of her shoulder.

"I'd better go now," he said hoarsely, "or else I might never leave."

Down near the caves, Peter and Eliza roamed the beach, pouring over conch shells, bright algae, starfish and a variety of corals. For more than an hour, they stuffed a cloth bag with their findings.

"These are really good finds," Eliza said. "Are you

going to dissect some of them in your room, Peter?"

"Yes, I plan to. I'm going to find out all I can about them. Maybe someday I'll use the information in my work."

"So, Peter, it sounds like you want to be some sort of scientist?"

"I want to be a doctor. The money from the ginger cultivation might send me to Kingston and then England. But look, Eliza, a squashed sea urchin! Too bad most of the parts are broken off."

"Where's Dunstan anyway? He could help us find a better one."

"Last time I saw him, he was going to the caves with Maggie. She used to say that she was afraid of places like that. But maybe she isn't anymore."

"Let's go find them, Peter. The tide might come in."

"It won't reach as far as the caves, Eliza. Anyway, let's go see what they found."

Dunstan and Maggie had entered one of the larger caves. Side by side, they bent low and followed a narrow tunnel for some distance until it widened. They found themselves standing inside a phosphorus-lit hollow.

They did not say a word to each other, so taken aback were they by the beauty around them. Maggie ran her hands along the walls, entranced by the glowing rocks.

"Who would think this was here," she said breathlessly.

"What a find," Dunstan said. "It's beautiful. Let's take back a rock or two for Peter."

He squatted in the sand and tried to loosen a piece of the phosphorus, and noticed only then that there was a huge pile of driftwood, over to one side. He went and pulled out a piece, hoping to use it as a tool for leverage. But the wood pile shifted, and a large portion of it scattered and fell with a clatter. Beneath the pile was an assortment of hundreds of human bones!

"Did you find anything?" Peter asked suspiciously, after seeing his sister quickly emerge from the cave with Dunstan in tow.

"Yes!" Maggie replied excitedly. "We found a huge pile of old bones and phosphorus rocks! It was frightening Peter — the bones looked like human bones. I for one will never go in that cave again!"

"Dunstan, what made you take my sister in there?" Peter shouted accusingly. No doubt dismayed by what he thought were incriminating streaks of dirt and moss on Maggie's clothing.

"We going home now, Maggie," he snapped sternly and grabbed her by the wrist.

"What's the matter with you, Peter?" Dunstan responded angrily. "Didn't you just hear that we found a cache of human bones? Get a lid on it, Peter. What do you think your sister and I were doing in there? Do you really think that I'm like that? Whatsoever you're thinking, you are wrong about me."

The sea lapped lazily along the stretch of debris-strewn beach, as the four young people, each caught up in their own thoughts, trudged through the sand. However, Peter kept to himself and made a solemn vow to himself as he walked.

If Dunstan hurts my sister, I swear I'll kill him.

Small birds flitted along the sandy ribbon. The wind rose, the sky darkened, and clouds moved in. The sea spat and hissed and roared, sounding as angry as Peter's thoughts. Eliza, with ringlets flying, raced ahead of the others with childlike exuberance.

"There will be bread pudding waiting!" she shouted into the wind, trying her best to ease the tension. "Last one is a rotten egg," she added with a laugh.

"We can't stay!" Peter said emphatically. He bent his head into the wind, his black hair flying, and Maggie followed nervously behind him.

"Not a word to mother about the bones, Eliza," Dunstan warned as they drew closer to the house.

"Mother, we've been gathering seaweed and shells!" Eliza shouted, bursting into the house. She approached the kitchen. Her mother was humming softly; the song sounded particularly melancholy.

"Where's Mr. Samuels?" Eliza inquired, clearly disappointed by his absence.

"We won't be seeing him anymore, darling," Grandmother said forlornly. "He's leaving Hedley."

"Are you sure, Mother?"

"I wish I were wrong, darling, but sadly it's true."

"But why would he leave? Is it because the school children teased him?"

"No, darling, not at all. It's all to do with grown-up things like politics and world affairs."

Eliza didn't want to believe her ears. She pounded the wall fiercely with her fists as tears came. And she couldn't help but remember Lucas, and how he too had gone, and how secretly she had loved him.

"Why couldn't you love him, Mother?" she screamed. "He might have stayed, Mother. People need to know they are loved."

"Darling, calm down please. This has nothing to do with love. Mr. Samuels wants to help people. He thinks there might be a war coming."

When the school term ended, Peter left for Kingston. He was to study at the Institute of Jamaica, located on East Street. The Institute was a known pioneer in science studies and, fortunately for Peter, Chunty's sister Phyllis lived in Kingston's downtown core, which meant there was a place for him to stay rent-free.

Peter didn't say goodbye to the Gunns. Unwilling to admit that he was wrong about Dunstan, he avoided them entirely.

Chunty had proudly packed two suitcases for him. Her son was going for higher education in Kingston. He would leave on a steam engine train from Falmouth. It was the biggest adventure of his life. How old and tired Sam Chung looked as he held his young son at arms length, tears at the corners of his eyes.

"My boy," he said, "you going out into the world. I am so proud of you. Imagine somebody like me, a humble shopkeeper, with an educated son."

Sam Chung turned his face away quickly and gave in to tears.

"Don't cry, Papa," Peter said gruffly, already embarrassed by his family and their country ways.

"Safe journey," Chunty called as the train pulled out,

leaving dark puffs of steam behind. And she couldn't help noticing that they were the only Chinese at the station.

Chapter 6:
Letters

Three weeks after Peter left, Chunty was at the shop counter when a market woman came to tell her that there was a letter waiting for her at the postmistress's. She quickly untied her apron and, almost running, went to find Sam Chung in the living quarters at the back of the shop.

"Sam, Sam!" she shouted. "I going have to run down to the post office. We get a letter. It might be Peter, so take over here. I'll run fast."

The letter was indeed from Peter. Chunty recognized his writing. She held the letter tightly in her fist and made haste to get back to Sam. She never admitted it, but Sam was still the only one of them who could read well. She always used the fact that she was Chinese as an excuse for not reading English properly, never mentioning that she was born and bred in English-speaking Jamaica.

She burst into the shop and quickly handed over the letter. She liked to hear Sam read aloud and since there was no one else to listen in, she enjoyed it more. "Read it Sam," she urged. "I wonder how him is."

Sam Chung ripped the letter open carefully with his fingernail and went to sit on the stool. Chunty, with her head over his shoulders, listened blissfully.

Dear Papa and Mama,
I hope you are well.
The train ride was exciting. Higglers were going to the market in Kingston. A woman gave me two oranges, she remember Papa from when he was young.
I did not know that Jamaica was so big. The scenery was like a painting.
I saw cows, horses, pigs and goats on the way.
Uncle Aston met me at the station. He lives near King Street. It is very busy here with many big shops and Chinese people.
Love to the both of you and Maggie,
Peter

"So him don't say one word about him studies?" Chunty inquired, surprised by the sparseness of the letter. "He don't even mention him Aunt Phyllis. I going have to write that sister of mine, for Peter not telling us nothing. Is what me going say, when people ask? He think me going tell people him get two orange on the train! Is what him think this is?"

"Come now, Chunty, that was only him first letter. He going tell us more next time."

Ever since Ezekiel Samuels had spoken out, Grandmother busied herself with reading The Gleaner, as well as newspapers from England.

She was more than surprised to learn that Ezekiel's findings were correct. There was worldwide turmoil. Jamaica's problems had increased, with rampant joblessness. However, she learned that trade unions were being championed by a young, charismatic leader named Alexander Bustamante. She admired him for courageously firing off letters to the Crown, disclosing the true state of affairs in the colony. There were several riots on Jamaica's estates and plantations that would not have garnered attention in Britain, were it not for Mr. Bustamante's letters.

As a result of these revelations, Grandmother visited the post office more than once a week. She said that she was awaiting magazines and newspapers from Britain. Never once did she mention Ezekiel, though he was never far from her thoughts. The memory of the touch of his hands on her shoulders and his brief kisses haunted her still.

One rainy afternoon, when locals traditionally remained indoors, Wilemina Gunn took an umbrella and made her way to Hedley in the driving rain.

Mrs. Cynthia Ward, the postmistress, was surprised to see her, since she had been wondering how to send word that a letter had arrived for Wilemina. Mrs. Ward had taken the time to examine the envelope carefully, as was her custom. There was no return address, and the stamp was local. Wonder who that from? Mrs. Ward wondered, eager for gossip and hoping that Grandmother would comply.

But Grandmother did not dally. She quickly retrieved the letter and hurried away. She only managed to wave to Chunty as she passed by the old shop before beginning the long trek home. Looking neither left nor right, so intent was she on her destination, she was taken by complete surprise when, in the middle of the bushy path, a tall black man stepped out of the rain and barred her way.

"Mrs. Gunn," he said, his voice deep and resonant. "It's me."

"Who are you?" she inquired, searching his face with her frightened eyes.

"It's me, Lucas. You don't recognize me?"

Grandmother was extremely relieved. There were any number of things that could happen to her while walking alone.

"Thank God it's you, Lucas," she said, finally breathing.

"Is everybody okay?" Lucas inquired, eyes bright with anticipation.

"Yes, we're all well, thank you. And you?"

"I'm well, Mrs. Gunn. I've been bettering myself, and I have also been making sure that you are all okay. It's because of me that you've all been safe on your property."

"Whatever do you mean, Lucas?"

"Is a long story, Mrs. Gunn. I'm in politics now. I belong to Mr. Manley's People's National Party. I'm well respected. You might wonder why no troublemakers have come to Gunn's Run, even though it's so far away from the village. The reason they are staying away is because human bones from slavery days are in the caves on your property. Mr. Gunn got the land cheap because of those bones. People here are afraid of the bones — they think they will rise up to haunt them. I myself tell hooligans to leave Gunn's Run alone because my mother and the girl I'm going to marry live there."

"Lucas, what nonsense. I must beg your pardon, but I'm not about to marry you."

"Not you, Mrs. Gunn. I'm going to marry Miss Eliza."

"Miss Eliza! How absurd to think you could marry her, Lucas!" Grandmother chuckled, then, seeing the seriousness in Luca's eyes, she regained her composure. "I suppose I should thank you for all that you've been doing to help us, Lucas. I'll tell the others that I saw you."

"No, Mrs. Gunn, don't you say one word. I'm not ready yet."

"Ready for what, Lucas?"

But Lucas didn't answer; he stepped aside and disappeared into the rain.

After her unexpected encounter with Lucas, Grandmother could hardly wait to get home. She practically bounded up the steps and was careful to secure the lock behind her. The nerve of him, she thought. How could he even entertain the idea of marrying our Eliza? And what rubbish about the caves. If there were bones there, I would have heard about it.

Taking a deep breath, she went to sit at the dining table, her thoughts in turmoil. Then remembering the letter, she took it from her pocket and opened it, a smile on her lips as she read.

Dear Wilemina,

I wanted to address you as My Dear Wilemina, but in the end I felt that I would be out of line. I have written a thousand letters to you in my mind, but each time I attempted to write them down on paper, cold feet prevented my doing so.

Ever since I came to Kingston, I have thought of nothing else but you. Please bear with me, Wilemina; I can be rather foolish and full of imaginings.

Nevertheless, I am hoping that you felt something that day when last I was at Gunn's Run. You might not have realized how difficult it was for me to part from you.

But I mustn't bore you with what might be, to you, my inconsequential feelings.

I am presently staying with a family in Kingston. The husband, Raymond Charles, is a customs broker, and his wife Blossom works as his secretary. They have contacts with businesses and agents around the world, so I am kept well informed, and I am able to send financial support to Jewish causes.

I have also been helping out at a Catholic school, tutoring boys, and have ingratiated myself upon Kingston Jews who also require extra lessons for their offspring. My dream of helping Jews abroad has become a reality in light of my contributions. However, I am going to stay here in the city to find out more about myself and my ancestry.

Did you know that there is a synagogue here, and also a Jewish cemetery? Some of the oldest marked graves in this country are Jewish. I feel very connected to my past. My father often hinted at being descended from Sephardic Jews from Portugal, but to see our name listed here among Jewish memorabilia confirms it.

Hoping you are all well, I look forward to hearing from you, and, with my heart in my hand, I hope that one day you might decide to come to see me.

Sincerely,
Ezekiel

Grandmother folded and unfolded the letter, kissed it, then read it again. All thought of Lucas vanished by the time the young people came home. Her cheeks glowed with passion from the sincerity of the letter as she opened the door.

"Why'd you bolt the door mother?" Dunstan asked. "You don't usually do that, do you?"

"Are you alright, Mother?" Eliza inquired, her blue eyes full of concern, for her mother looked quite flushed.

"Yes, darling, I'm quite alright; everything is as it should be."

"Mother, there was so much rain today, Dunstan and I stayed inside the school at lunchtime. But Maggie went home, and she says the postmistress told her mother Chunty that there was a letter for you."

"Oh dear, people do talk, don't they? Yes, there was a letter from Mr. Samuels."

"What did he say? Is he coming back?"

"Dunstan darling, he's in Kingston; he seems to be enjoying it. He didn't say a word about coming back here."

"I'm never going to leave here!" Eliza said. "Because people who leave never come back."

"That's not entirely true darling, why only ..." Grandmother was about to blurt out the fact that she had seen Lucas, but managed to stop herself in time.

"Why only what, Mother?"

"Oh it's nothing, Eliza darling. I was just thinking only this morning that it would be nice to hear from Mr. Samuels, and here it is, his letter came today."

Later that afternoon, while Dunstan was occupied with studies, Eliza slipped out of the cottage and went to visit Constance in her shack. Constance was peeling ginger, a tedious task that very few people would put their hand to. She looked up, surprised to see young Eliza watching her.

"Hello Miss Eliza," she said, setting aside her task. "Need something, Ma'am?"

"Not really, Constance, but I've been wondering if you've heard from Lucas at all?"

"No, my girl, not a word from him, I don't know if him alive or dead."

"Tell me about him, Constance. What's his last name? Things like that."

"Well, young lady, I don't know why you would want to know those things. But anyway, Lucas' name is Lucas Paynado. He was born on Frome Estate, him daddy was a Busha there. He was a brown-skin man, and though him was married him was good to us. Nothing but the best for me and Lucas, we used to get condense milk and bun and cheese, and even herring and bammy bread. But when Busha wife find out bout us, we had was to go."

"So, what happened to Lucas' father, Constance?"

"The wife shoot him dead when Lucas was three, but she make up story that somebody break in and shoot him. Them believe her, cause she white. But as God is my witness, I know is she do it. We been living from hand to mouth ever since."

"Constance, that is so sad. Was Lucas' father good-looking? I think Lucas is so handsome."

"Yes Miss Eliza, him sure was good-looking, and I was lucky that him love me."

"Do you miss him, Constance?"

"Yes, Miss Eliza, I miss the both of them so much."

"And I miss Lucas," Eliza said, feeling far more grown up than her fourteen years.

Buoyed by the new information, Eliza whistled jauntily and went to watch some young boys who had come to help weed the ginger. She took particular notice of their boney legs, large round knees, and stick-like arms. That must have been what Lucas was like, she thought with fondness.

A second letter came from Peter a few weeks later. Sam Chung himself went to collect it, since Chunty was unwell. When he returned with the letter, Maggie was by Chunty's bedside, dabbing her mother's forehead with a cloth soaked in white rum. "Mama fever getting worse, Papa. We going have to call the doctor."

"I going send go get him, Maggie, but I know Mama want to hear what Peter have to say first. So let me just ease myself down and read it to her."

It was a weary Sam Chung who tore open the envelope and bent his head to read the letter into Chunty's ear.

Dear Papa and Mama,

I hope you are well. We are all well.

Uncle Aston says things getting more scarce. Stores don't have much goods. Dock workers keep striking. It is confusing, since I don't know much about politics and things like that. Anyway, tell Mama Aunt Phyllis send love.

This might surprise you, but there is a Chinese girl name Patsy Lee, going to England with her family. I am going to go with them to study over there. Don't worry, Patsy's family know that me and Patsy love each other.

Please tell Dunstan that I will see England at last.

Your son,

Peter

Chunty pulled herself up and waved Maggie's swab aside.

"Rawtid!" she exclaimed. "You mean to say that we work so hard to send our big son to school, and now him talking rubbish bout him in love? Where him getting money from to go England? Not from me! Who is this Patsy Lee anyway?"

"Chunty, calm down," Sam Chung said. "Him can't be

serious. He don't have no money. Me better tell him to come home."

When a doctor from outside of Hedley came to see Chunty, he recommended complete bedrest and lots of fluids. He prescribed medication and entrusted Maggie with administering the proper dosage every four hours.

"You could lose her," Dr. Evan Isaacs said. "She must have picked up an infection. I'm hoping it's not Malaria. So I'm taking some tests."

With the advent of Chunty's illness, a worried Sam Chung put all thoughts about Peter aside. Every spare moment away from the shop counter would find him in the back quarters by Chunty's side. At times, he could barely manage to get Chunty to sip a small amount of chicken noodle soup, but most times she seemed to crave the sharp taste of lemonade.

In Kingston, Peter knew nothing about his mother's illness. When no letter or telegram came protesting his actions, he felt that his parents were as excited as he was about his impending voyage. In the interim, he and Patsy Lee grew closer.

Patsy Lee was the eldest of the four daughters of the well-known, wealthy Lee family, who owned and operated a large Kingston bakery called 'Lee's Patty Kingdom'.

Peter had met Patsy's older brother, Alvin Lee, who was a student at the Institute of Jamaica. They became fast friends, and when Alvin took Peter home to meet his family, Peter immediately fell in love with Patsy. Patsy was neither employed nor making plans for her future, confident in the knowledge that the family business would fall into her hands, as a result of Alvin's growing interest in lab work.

When the family had decided to migrate to England, Patsy convinced her parents to support her proposition to have Peter accompany them as a potential son-in-law. The senior Mr. Lee no doubt saw something in Peter's simple country manner that reminded him of himself when he had first come to Kingston from Savanna-La-Mar some thirty years before.

There was nothing Mr. Lee would not do for his children for, having come from a poverty-stricken childhood, his sworn intention was to make things better for his family. And his present wealth allowed him to do just that.

There was nothing demure about nineteen-year old Patsy Lee. Not only was she as aggressive as her father, but she also enjoyed dominance over the opposite sex. Since childhood, all her whims and wiles were always met and attended to by her doting father. Despite clever use of powder, rouge and lipstick, Patsy was not very attractive. Her face was broad and flat, and her eyes were small slits. It was her voluptuous mouth, large breasts and thick black hair that attracted.

It was not long before she and Peter Chung became lovers and, less than a month after his letter home, Peter boarded a steamer with the Lee family, bound for Liverpool, England.

My dear sister Chunty,

By the time you get this, Peter will be gone to England. I don't know bout these young people, but your son go get mix up with some rich Chinese people name Lee. The daughter name Patsy set her cap for Peter, and the poor soul didn't stand a chance.

The truth is, I think them is more than friend.

As you know, me and Aston don't have no children, but we

did look out for Peter like him was we own. But after a while, we get the feeling that we not good enough no more. I am so sorry my dear. We did our best, but now is only God can help.

Give my love to Sam and Maggie. How Maggie doing in school?

Your loving sister,
Phyllis

By the time Chunty Chung was well enough for Sam Chung to read the letter to her, war had broken out in Europe, and Britain was involved; and the years passed slowly.

The Jamaican army, called The Jamaican Infantry Volunteers, was in reserve. However, hundreds of young men from poor families, eager to make something of themselves, signed up for service in British forces. Some, who were as young as seventeen, saw it as an opportunity to learn a trade, while for others it was entirely the glamour of the uniform.

"The boy them look so sweet in them uniform," young women crooned. "Him shirt starch stiff caa done, and look how him boots so shine. Oh my!"

Young men relished the taste of freedom the army offered, and the once-in-a-lifetime opportunity to travel.

Electricity was conserved island-wide, and there were frequent warnings of "blackouts", which were impromptu power cuts to the electricity. Islanders were given the impression that, if there were no visible lights during the evening hours, enemy planes would have difficulty finding the island.

"I should be joining the army, Mother," Dunstan said. "It's only right. It's our war."

"Dunstan darling, we are safe here. Why would you compromise that?"

61

"What am I supposed to do, Mother? Many youngsters, even young men from Hedley, are going into danger for us."

"Dunstan, I'm not heartless, really I'm not. Far from it, but I'm rather afraid of losing another man I love. I don't think I could stand that — no, not at all."

Chapter 7:
War Time

"Mother, come quick look! Lucas is mentioned in The Gleaner!"

"What on earth are you talking about, darling? Lucas couldn't be in the newspaper, unless of course there's been a crime, or in the death announcements."

"No, Mother, he's no criminal. He's alive, and he's in Kingston! See for yourself."

"Where's it?" Grandmother asked nervously, knowing full well that Lucas was alive.

"Right down here, Mother!"

"Charismatic twenty-two-year old Mr. Lucas Paynado, an assistant to one of Kingston's PNP candidates, has successfully squashed a potential riot at Kingston's waterfront after nine hours of negotiations."

"That couldn't be Lucas, darling. What would he know about negotiating and politics?"

"Mother, I know it's him. How many people could be called Lucas Paynado? I want to go to Kingston to find him."

"Darling, there's a war on, gasoline is scarce, and we are barely surviving as it is."

"Listen, Mother, nothing's going to stop me!"

"Eliza darling, I'm not going to allow you to travel to Kingston alone!"

"So does that mean you'll come with me, Mother?"

"Please, Eliza! I want you to get over this childish foolishness. Lucas is not at all suitable for you."

"Is that because he's a Negro, Mother? I know it is! I'm not a child; I'm seventeen! I even know why you wouldn't consider Mr. Samuels as someone to love. It's because he's a Jew, isn't it! I'm warning you, Mother — I'm going to find a way to get to Kingston!"

"Darling, darling Eliza, you need to rest. You're all upset, and I'm sure you'll feel entirely differently tomorrow."

But the next day, Eliza did not feel any differently. She avoided her mother and instead confided in Dunstan about wanting to go to Kingston, though stopping short of mentioning Lucas.

Dunstan's plans to study abroad were put on hold as a result of the war. He had reluctantly taken a position at the school teaching the younger children. To his surprise, he found satisfaction in his work. He hoped eventually to receive proper qualifications, though thoughts of joining the forces weighed down all his plans for the future.

Maggie had wanted to study nursing but ended up helping out in the shop. At first, it was only for short periods but with Sam Chung growing frail, she had pretty much taken over running things. However, she arranged schedules with Chunty so that everyday she could spend the lunch hour with Dunstan. Together, they would enjoy memories and a good laugh. After lunch, they would occasionally stroll along the bushy pathway away from the eyes of the villagers. Friendship was all either of them dared hope for, having been scarred by Peter's outburst that day at the caves.

"Eliza wants to go to Kingston, Maggie," Dunstan confided one afternoon after school, the moment they were out of earshot. "Mother wants to stop her, but Eliza is headstrong. I'm worried, Maggie. I know she will go, regardless of whatever Mother says."

"Does she know anyone there, Dunstan?"

"I'm not sure, but I got the impression that she is actually looking for someone; she seemed rather reluctant to discuss it."

"Well, I could go with her if you'd like me to, Dunstan. At least there'd be the two of us to look out for each other, and I know you wouldn't be able to go, because of your work."

"Would you do that for me, Maggie? You're a real treasure but then again, what about your work in the shop?"

"I'd do anything for you, Dunstan." Maggie grinned. "Mama would gladly run the shop for a week."

"Are you sure now?"

"Yes, I'm sure. Me and Eliza could even stay with my Aunt Phyllis."

"Come here, Maggie. You're brilliant, aren't you; let me give you a hug."

Maggie came into his arms and Dunstan's heart raced. Can she hear the pounding? he wondered inwardly.

Maggie tipped up and kissed his cheek lightly. There was such a rushing in his ears that Dunstan didn't recognize it as his own heavy breathing. Trembling, he let his hands fall to his sides and began the walk back to Hedley.

"Maggie," he said, after some thought, "we shouldn't get mushy, should we? It could ruin our friendship. Besides, I have been thinking about joining the services."

A few days later during lunch hour, a letter arrived unexpectedly from Peter.

Chunty, who had grown quite broad, waddled into the back quarters of the shop and woke Sam Chung. Maggie said that there was a letter with an English postage stamp, and the return addressee was Peter. Chunty was so excited she could barely catch her breath.

"You better read the letter Maggie, but first you go tell Mista Dunstan to come in here with us," Chunty urged.

Maggie was already sitting next to her father's pillow when Dunstan, overhearing what Chunty had said, ducked under the hanging beads that separated the rooms, and joined them.

"Make yourself comfortable, Mista Dunstan," Chunty said with a smile, unconcerned about untidiness in the sparse room, and that sunbeams coming in at the window revealed dust floating in the air.

"But Mama, what about the other people out in the shop?"

"Them not going steal from us, Maggie, them know us since long time gone."

"I don't mean that, Mama. I mean, who going serve them."

"Them know we need a moment to ourselves Maggie, them will wait."

Bending into Sam Chung's ear, Maggie read the letter in a clear voice.

Dear Papa, Mama and Maggie,

I am hanging my head in shame. I have not written in years. It is not because I have forgotten you; it is because I love you and did not want to let you know the true state of affairs here.

England is not what I thought it would be. I wish I could say that things were happier. The cold and damp is easier to bear than the life that I have been living.

Patsy Lee was not the good person I thought she was. As soon as she came to England, things changed. She got tired of me. She said that if she got pregnant by me, she would flush the baby down the toilet. She spent all her time with new white friends, especially soldiers, and tormented me about my poverty. She called me "a poor thing country boy". I looked for work because I felt I was a burden to her, but couldn't find anything.

Alvin Lee, Patsy's brother, was very fond of me. He persuaded me to join the army; he believed that if I became a soldier, his sister would love and respect me again. I joined up and was surprised when Alvin joined too.

Me and Alvin were shaved and given kits, after a ridiculous medical exam. But we were put in separate squads and paraded and taught discipline. Being Chinese and Jamaican, I was often humiliated by drill sergeants.

I was told that many of us, especially me, would even end up committing suicide because we would not be able to stand up to pressure.

So even though I was not feeling well, I didn't say anything. All I could think was that I wanted to see all of you again. But when my battalion was shipped over to Europe, I became severely ill and was sent back to London. Doctors say that I have a mysterious tropical ailment, and I was discharged from the service. Though I cannot prove it, I have a feeling that some sort of germ was put into my food while I lived with the Lees. But my dear friend Alvin Lee has died; he was killed in a fierce battle over in France.

While I was in hospital, a black-skinned Jamaican man working there named Vincent Reid managed to get me a job cleaning the bathrooms. It is a low wage, but I manage by sharing a cheap London flat with Vincent. He knows other Jamaicans here. He says he is going to introduce me to a Chinese family from Linstead named Wong. There are days when I am so sick that I can't go to work, but Vincent, in his kindness, covers for me.

Please give my regards to the Gunns, and tell Dunstan that I was wrong about him — he will know what I mean — and let them know that I love them as though they were family.

I hope this finds all of you in good health, and may God bless you,

Peter

"My poor son." Sam Chung sighed, tears welling in his eyes. "I pray to God that I'll live to see my son again. Every day, I ask the Lord for just one more day."

"Don't cry, Papa. At least Peter has met somebody kind. We should be so grateful to Vincent Reid. The Wongs might be good people too. Try to rest Papa, and let's not think about the terrible things happening over there. May God have mercy on poor Alvin Lee's soul."

"Well, if I ever meet that Patsy Lee, I would wring her neck!" Chunty said, straightening her apron and heading back out to the counter.

"So how's you son?" someone shouted from inside the shop.

Chunty put a on a brave smile. "He's fine, thanks," she said, feeling close to tears.

Sam Chung, weary from the traumatic news, had drifted off into a deep sleep as soon as Chunty left his side. Dunstan, overcome with compassion, gazed at the old man curled up fetus-like under the thin covers. He noticed the deep hollows in the old man's cheeks, the dark, spreading lines under the eyes, and Sam Chung's grey, receding hairline, which reminded him of a dried coconut.

He was moved to touch Sam Chung's shoulder gently.

"You'll see Peter again," he whispered. "But it is I who'll go to fight the war in his place."

Maggie's eyes spilled over with unexpected tears. "No, Dunstan, I couldn't bear it if you left."

That afternoon, when school was over, Dunstan found Maggie waiting for him at the school gate. "Is everything all right?" he asked, certain that there was more bad news.

"Nothing's happened," Maggie said. "I just thought I'd walk over to Gunn's Run with you. It's as good a time as any to talk with Eliza about going to Kingston."

"Oh, and here it is I was thinking you were going to try to stop me from joining up for service, Maggie."

"No, Dunstan, I have decided that you should make up your own mind about that."

As the two young people strolled through the open bushland, they couldn't help but remember times past when Peter was healthy and would have raced ahead of them, stopping only to look at tree lizards, strange spiders, beetles and toads.

"It's very sad about Peter, isn't it, Maggie?" Dunstan said. "I could barely keep myself together when you read his letter, and it just goes to show that one never knows what lies ahead."

"Yes, Dunstan, you are right. Peter had such hope for his future."

For a few moments, neither of them said anything, though Dunstan found himself occasionally glancing at Maggie's profile; it was as though he could see something of Peter there. He couldn't help noticing how lovely she had become. Her wavy black hair framed her luminous oval face and, once in a while as she moved, stray strands of hair brushed seductively against her lips and her soft lashes. Dunstan let his eyes stray to her slim shoulders, but he turned his head away quickly, embarrassed by the rush of pleasure he felt.

"Peter was very serious about studying," Dunstan said, deliberately focusing attention away from his feelings. "He actually thought that both of us would become scientists."

"So have you given up that idea, Dunstan?"

"Yes, I suppose I have, Maggie. I rather enjoy teaching, and I still want to get qualified; I think I would enjoy teaching high school. I would really like to give youngsters a fighting chance."

"Dunstan, do you think Peter will come back? What I really mean is, do you really think Papa will see him again?"

"Peter is a very determined person, Maggie, and so is your father as a matter of fact. I remember how Peter used to set his mind to things, and then he would get it done. So I feel that if he wants to see the family again, he will."

"Do you remember how he yelled at us that day at the caves, Dunstan?"

"How could I ever forget that, Maggie?"

"Well, Dunstan, Peter was sure that you would have taken advantage of me, being alone in the cave. He said that all white people are like that. I'm glad that now he has at least admitted that he misjudged you. Underneath it all, Dunstan, I can't help but feel that Peter would prefer if I ended up with someone Chinese."

"Do you really think so, Maggie? I would never have guessed that Peter cared about race. I never have, but I guess Peter has come to his senses. Just look what's happened with him and Patsy Lee."

As they drew closer to Gunn's Run, the sea came into view and Dunstan fixed his eyes on the stark aquamarine line on the horizon, shimmering in the sunshine. The view never failed to mesmerize him and bring back a rush of memories, and he chuckled softly.

"What's funny, Dunstan? Is it what I said about Peter?"

"No, Maggie, far from it. I was just thinking about how I used to dream of sailing back to England in a fisherman's boat with Peter, when I was a child."

"Dunstan, you just gave me an idea."

"Have I?"

"Yes, you have, but that can wait."

They came upon a clearing and saw a shabby, old barefoot man eating a mango and watching his small herd of skinny, brown goats and squealing, black pigs; and the old man nodded as they went by.

"Good evening, James." Maggie smiled and, aside, said to Dunstan, "He comes to the shop. It must be so hard looking after animals. But who am I to say. I've never owned anything, not even a plant."

"Well, Maggie, there's something you've got to see

then," Dunstan whispered as they came over a steep rise. "Hope you won't mind stopping a moment."

"I don't mind, but what's it?"

"It's an old tree, Maggie. It's where I used to play when I was a boy. It's quite special to me."

Grabbing hold of Maggie's hand, Dunstan led her over the rough terrain, past the cliffs and wide grass-like ginger cultivation fields, and into the very arms of the giant banyan.

"What a big tree!" Maggie exclaimed. "What kind of tree is it?"

She stood stock still, struck by the massive size of the tree, for its great trunk and wide bulging branches were testament to her own insignificance.

"I can see why you loved playing here," she murmured, keeping her voice low, as though in the presence of something holy.

"It's a banyan tree, Maggie. They are rather splendid, aren't they? Come, I'll show you something else. I'm sure you noticed that it has many trunks. Would you believe there are wide openings in some of the trunks, almost like caves? Duck down and I'll show you."

"It's wonderful here," Maggie said, stooping low and following Dunstan's lead.

They found themselves inside an unusual deep, natural opening that seemed to be a curious formation of the main trunk and secondary trunks. Being inside its interior felt almost like being within the very womb of the tree.

"Does anyone ever come here, Dunstan?"

"No one does, Maggie. The locals are afraid of the ghosts of slaves who probably hid in places like this years and years ago. Remember the cache of bones we found in the caves? They might have been slaves' bones."

If those were probably slaves' bones, no wonder the

locals are afraid, Maggie thought, her palms growing clammy. She couldn't help but be shaken by Dunstan's revelation for, though time had passed, the trauma of the discovered bones was still fresh. Her throat felt constricted, and her heart pounded so hard she thought it would burst out of her chest. She had an uncontrollable impulse to run away but thought better of it. It wouldn't do any good, she thought, if Dunstan perceived her as being as backward as the other locals.

She took a deep breath, steadied herself, and forced herself to act as normal as possible.

It was dim inside the opening, but she fixed her attention on how Dunstan's hands moved with surety in his examination of the bumpy walls. She saw how his shock of blonde hair would often fall over his forehead, and how blue his eyes were even in the poor light. I mustn't stare, she told herself, and reluctantly turned her eyes away from him. She feigned interest in patches of stark white mushrooms that grew on the interior bark, and thought they reminded her of strange, spongy shelves. Just below them, at her feet, was a thick carpet of mosses. How soft it would be to lie there, she thought.

There in the tranquility of the hollow, in Dunstan's companionable silence, she felt far removed from conflicts. If only the world could be as peaceful as this place, she thought, revelling in brief imaginings.

Then, Dunstan surprised her. He twirled himself around exuberantly, the way he used to when he was a child. "It's a very special place, isn't it?" he said excitedly. "I always believed that there's magic at work here. Don't you agree, Maggie?"

"Yes, I agree," Maggie said, finding her voice as she laughed softly; and when Dunstan joined in, their laughter echoed through the tree's branches, its leaves and its hollows, and it sounded as though the tree itself shared in their laughter.

Less than an hour would go by before a wild wind gusted from the sea below, to moan and sigh in every crevice of the banyan, to resonate haunting and flute-like as the banyan reverberated with the mighty wind's exquisite song. Its unparalleled sound was destined to live in their memories forever.

"I feel so privileged to have heard the banyan wind's song, Dunstan," Maggie whispered in awe. "I'll never forget it, and you know what else, Dunstan? There's no doubt that this must be the most beautiful place in the world."

"Maggie ..."

"Yes, Dunstan?"

"Can I kiss you?"

"You don't have to ask, Dunstan."

Dunstan took a few short steps and gathered her in his arms, and Maggie clung to him fiercely. The ground beneath them was soft and pliable as in desperate eagerness, they caressed each other and there on the mossy ground, gave in entirely to years of suppressed passion.

"And your brother thought he was wrong about me." Dunstan laughed. "If only he knew how I feel about you, Maggie."

"Dunstan, I have wanted to hear you say that for so long."

"But do you have feelings for me, Maggie?" He grinned.

"Yes, more than you ever knew."

"Maggie, I'd like to help to bring Peter home, if you'll let me."

Eliza had been sitting on the verandah, looking out to sea, and her blonde curls blew like flags. She was still cross with her mother and refused to concede, though aware that travelling to Kingston by herself was not feasible. She knew that several violent disturbances had recently broken out in the capital and was in a quandary, for being a white female could easily target her for harassment and, at the same time, being white had its privileges. She momentarily wondered if her fixation on Lucas might indeed be childish but couldn't explain why the thought of him charged her with such mature passion. She had never felt this way about anyone. There was no forgetting Lucas' long, lean, black frame, his curly, wool-like hair that invited touching, and his thickly lashed eyes, filled with gentleness.

She was on the verge of calling a truce with her mother, for perhaps only then would her mother agree to accompany her. But then again, she didn't want her mother there when she finally found Lucas.

She was thinking about packing a few things in readiness, when she saw Dunstan and Maggie approaching. They were a long way off, on the strip of beach, and they appeared to be holding hands. Eliza couldn't be sure, but when they drew closer, she saw that they did not pull apart, even when she rose from her seat and went down the steps to meet them.

"Eliza." Maggie smiled. "I was hoping we could have a little chat."

Maggie looked radiant. Her shiny hair tumbled around her shoulders, and there was a sensuous looseness to her gait. Eliza couldn't quite put her finger on it, but she sensed there was something different about Maggie. Given the opportunity, she would have scrutinized her more carefully but, just then, Dunstan pressed forward and gently took her hand.

"Eliza," he said softly, his voice hoarse with emotion, "you didn't come into Hedley today, so you probably don't know that there's been word from Peter."

"Is he all right, Dunstan?" Eliza inquired, her blue eyes filled with concern.

The brother and sister stood side by side in the wind, blonde hair streaming. Eliza sensed that whatever was going to be said would be ominous and unavoidable. But she knew that Dunstan was protective of her, and she would trust his judgement.

"Peter's had a rough time of it in England, Eliza," he said. "In fact, he's rather ill, and the girl he went over there with ended up causing him quite a lot of pain. To add to it all, he was in the services and his only friend was killed. He wants to come home, Eliza. He's been reduced to cleaning toilets! Can you imagine, someone like Peter doing that?"

Dunstan barely held back tears, and when Maggie put her arm around him comfortingly, Eliza saw something in their eyes. She sensed a change between her brother and Maggie. No doubt they were more publicly affectionate, but there was something else too, and Dunstan's swift kiss on Maggie's cheek confirmed it.

"How's he managing to live day to day?" Eliza asked, never once taking her eyes off the couple. "And how is he going to afford the money to come home?"

"He's sharing a flat with a Jamaican man he met while he was in hospital," Maggie said through tears. "But I know that he can't afford to come home. Mama and Papa barely manage to make ends meet with their little savings. On my way over here, I remembered that Mama had set aside some ginger money for me to be able to study, but I'd gladly give that up for Peter."

"Oh, Maggie, I'd have liked to help too, but the little I have will only take me to Kingston and back. And I want to go there so badly."

"You are very kind, Eliza. Thanks. But Dunstan has offered to help; we've only just discussed it. But that reminds me, you and I need to talk about Kingston," said Maggie, winking discreetly at Dunstan and, as if on cue, he pressed Eliza's hand softly and brushed his lips against Maggie's forehead.

"If it's alright with both of you," he said, "I'm going inside to tell Mother about Peter. She will be rather shocked, I think. And meanwhile, both of you might like to take a stroll down on the beach, out of earshot."

Chapter 8:
Making Plans

"Eliza, the reason I want to talk with you is because I told your brother I'd go to Kingston with you. But I'm wondering why you want to go so badly," Maggie said, trying to sound as nonchalant as possible yet knowing that, in the turbulent political climate, going to the capital together was rather an important decision.

Eliza, with no further thought of personal safety was so thrilled she jumped high in the air excitedly and scattered sand in all directions. In exuberance, she grabbed Maggie and hugged her as fiercely as the wind that whipped against them.

"Maggie, you are wonderful!" she said, teary-eyed. "I'm so happy I could die."

"So, Eliza, will you tell me why you want to go to Kingston?"

"I'm trying to find somebody, Maggie."

"Is it somebody I know?"

Eliza didn't answer immediately. Head down, she dragged her heels, undecided as to whether to tell Maggie everything. No one takes you seriously when you are as young as I am, she thought. But perhaps I'll have to trust in the strength of Maggie's long-standing friendship with the family.

"We have been friends for so long." Eliza sighed, looking towards the sea, where waves rushed in relentlessly, and it occurred to her that she herself was not unlike the waves, for she too was irresistibly drawn towards something far beyond her control.

She met Maggie's gaze, and there, in Maggie's almond eyes, she saw honesty and a yearning that spoke volumes.

"I might be wrong, Maggie," Eliza began testily, though she barely flinched, despite the deeply personal nature of what she intended to find out. "I've been wondering," she began again, noticing faint worry lines and nervous anticipation in Maggie's expression. Eliza's thoughts rushed to the surface like a swiftly boiling pot that threatened to spill over and unable to suppress things a moment longer, she blurted out, "Are you are in love with my brother?"

Maggie was taken by surprise, not having anticipated such a question and furthermore, quite unsure of how Eliza might react to her answer. It was not lost on her that there was a bond between Dunstan and Eliza. At times, it had almost seemed that their thoughts were one and the same. She knew that when their parents had migrated, the two children in the care of English relatives had grown closer and dependent on each other. Eliza might well regard her as an usurper to that splendid attachment between them.

The sand that seeped into Maggie's sandals were sharp and biting against her skin, and it reminded her that pain was never far off, despite the happiest of circumstances. She chastised herself for being momentarily complacent by allowing herself to be buoyed by the memory of Dunstan's sweet kisses. How could she have forgotten Peter's pain, and that of her aging parents? In the midst of her joy from having just loved Dunstan, there was the shame. She gritted her teeth against the realizations and stared intently at the horizon, as stark white clouds sailed across the broad sky.

I mustn't allow life's misfortunes to drag me down so low that I cannot recognize that I am loved and capable of reciprocating love.

She felt as transparent and as exposed as the dry skeletal leaves and fern that dotted the beach at that time of year. Has Eliza somehow guessed, she wondered, that Dunstan and I have been intimate? Does it show on my face, or even in the way I move? I hope to God it doesn't, for nobody must ever know what transpired between me and Dunstan. It would kill Papa, and everyone else would be disappointed in me. Thank goodness Eliza wasn't anywhere near the banyan tree.

With that sobering thought, Maggie braced herself, took a deep breath, and heard herself speaking: "Yes, Eliza, no use my denying it. I am more than just fond of Dunstan."

The words tumbled out like a wall between the two women, dividing the very air they breathed. For, though each of them had strong feelings for Dunstan, they were acutely aware that only one of them was privy to his deepest desires and could satisfy him fully.

Eliza turned her head away, not having anticipated that the honesty in Maggie's words would throw her off kilter. She felt left out, for she and Dunstan had always shared everything. Things had changed and no doubt would continue to change. Tears stung at her eyes, though she knew she was being foolish.

I am such a child, she thought, feeling more rational. Why shouldn't Maggie love him? Nothing can take away what Dunstan and I share and besides, Maggie's so close to our family she's almost like a sister. I only wish Lucas was here and that my feelings for him will not tear everyone apart.

"Maggie." Eliza sighed in resignation. "Perhaps now that you have deep feelings for someone, you'll understand what I'm going to tell you."

Eliza felt assured that only a woman in love like herself could make any sense of what she was feeling for Lucas.

"What is it, Eliza?"

"Maggie, I'm in love." Eliza smiled, and she made no attempt to hide the excitement she felt inside.

"Are you serious, Eliza? I wouldn't have guessed. I know you had lots of school friends, but I hardly think it would be one of them."

Eliza shook her head. Here we go again, she thought, a smile playing at the corners of her lips, for she had come to realize that it was almost delicious to be able to have one up on another person.

"So why couldn't it be one of them, Maggie?" she said, barely concealing the satisfaction she felt in baiting her. "Would it be because they were all black-skinned and I'm white?"

A flushed faced Maggie, embarrassed by her assumption, could do nothing but stare aimlessly into the sand. "I didn't mean that the way it came out Eliza."

"Well, Maggie, you might be glad to know that it's not one of them, but he is black-skinned nevertheless."

Maggie was astonished. Her first thoughts were how

could blonde, blue-eyed Eliza fall in love with someone black-skinned? What would people think? But then again, what would people think about her and Dunstan? But at least I'm not black-skinned, she rationalized. Then she remembered that one of her grandparents was part Negro, and she couldn't help but laugh softly at her own foolishness and in apology, she hugged Eliza as they continued along the shoreline.

"Consider me nosey, Eliza, but who you are in love with?"

"Well, Maggie, even saying his name excites me." Eliza giggled. "I'm sure you, of all people, would understand. Mother doesn't understand a thing about love. His name is Lucas Paynado, and I think he is just wonderful."

"Where did you meet him, Eliza? Have you known him long?"

"Oh, Maggie, I met him here at Gunn's Run. I was just a child then, but he's a year or two older than Dunstan."

"I never heard mention of him, Eliza."

"He wasn't really in my social class, Maggie. Lucas used to live on our property in a shack with his mother Constance. He disappeared after a few months. But I recently found out that he is working as an assistant to one of the political candidates in Kingston, so I'd say he's made something of himself. Don't you think so?"

"Sounds like it, but does he know that you are in love with him, Eliza?"

"No, Maggie, he doesn't. How could he? But I plan to tell him; that's why I'm going to Kingston. And now you know everything."

"What a romantic you are, Eliza. It took me absolutely years before I had guts to tell Dunstan how I feel about him. As a matter of fact, it wasn't until this afternoon."

Eliza exploded into peals of laughter. "You're quite the one, aren't you? No wonder I noticed something a little different about you, Maggie. What did Dunstan say when you told him? Does he love you? Oh my God, I can't even imagine the two of you together. You don't have to look so surprised, Maggie. It's just that he is my brother and all."

"Yes, Dunstan cares for me Eliza; he told me so."

"But Maggie, has he told you he is considering going into the services?"

"Yes, but whether he goes or not won't stop me from having feelings for him."

"I know just how you feel, Maggie."

"Eliza, there's a fisherman from Montego Bay who comes to the shop a few times a week. His name is Kenton Johnson, but we call him 'Kenny'. He sells fish up and down the coast. He will do anything for us. Papa likes him. I'm sure I could ask him if he could take us to Kingston in his boat. Because, as you know, with island-wide gas shortages, buses only travel here once in a while, and trains are so expensive nowadays. I'm sure Kenny would only charge us a few shillings, since his boat would be going to Kingston anyway."

"Maggie, you are brilliant. I could pack a few things – not much though, because I wouldn't want Mother to know that I'm going. She'd certainly try to stop me. Would you believe it, Maggie, Mother was already married when she was my age!"

"She was? Well, Eliza, that's proof positive that you are no longer a child, though sometimes it's hard for all of us to believe that. Anyway, going back to Kenny, he usually picks up supplies in Kingston for Papa and other grocers, basic things that they can't get from Montego Bay anymore. I don't think he would say no to a couple of paying passengers."

"Is it a small boat, Maggie, like the wooden ones that land near Gunn's Run?"

"Oh no. Kenny's boat is roomy; it can seat six, and it looks very sturdy. Did I mention that it has a motor? We'll be seeing a lot of the island's ports before we get to St. Andrew, where Kingston is. And another thing, I'm sure Aunt Phyllis in Kingston will put us up for the few days."

Chunty was never happy about keeping secrets from anyone, least of all from my grandmother. She was not one to practise any sort of deception. Perhaps that was why she always made it known that she was not full-blooded Chinese, though she resembled one. "My Jamaican family is the Watsons," she used to say proudly. "You should see how dark them is. But just look at my children them. They come out 'Chiney', just like Sam and me."

When Maggie told her that she and Eliza would be going to Kingston, and that Mrs. Gunn was not to be told, Chunty was not pleased. However, she kept her feelings to herself, deciding not to visit Gunn's Run over the next few days, to entirely avoid the issue. Furthermore, she thought that there would be no sense in ruffling Maggie's feathers, since Maggie had agreed to help to bring Peter home; and to Chunty's surprise, Dunstan Gunn was also willing to make a sizeable contribution to that end.

Arrangements were made. Kenny's boat would pick up

the two passengers along the beach near Gunn's Run at 5:30 in the morning the next Friday. It was decided that Dunstan would accompany Maggie from Hedley, then meet up with Eliza on the beach near the house.

Dunstan woke up early that morning. All week, he had wanted to discuss plans for the future with Maggie, but there wasn't an opportunity. Now that she was going away for a few days, it became more urgent. He slipped out of the house discreetly, but not before letting Eliza know that she had only two hours of sleep left before he would meet her on the beach. Eliza had giggled, and pulled the covers up over her shoulders.

The moon was high in the sky, and a cool breeze blew through Hedley. Dunstan was unusually eager to see Maggie, though he rapped gently at the shop door. She answered his knock almost immediately, but Chunty was by her side. Chunty seemed particularly nervous as she held Maggie's small suitcase.

"Good evening, Mr. Dunstan. Is so good of you to come," she said, sounding relieved. "Please carry this grip for Maggie. It going be too heavy for her."

But before Dunstan could take the suitcase, Chunty leaned in and swiftly kissed Maggie's cheek. "Bye, Maggie. Be good," she said huskily. "Take care of her, Mr. Dunstan. I didn't like the idea of her walking through the bush alone, and I know that nothing would stop her. Please tell Mr. Kenny to look out for the two of them, you hear. And Maggie, don't you forget to tell Aunt Phyllis to call Hedley post office. The postmistress will give me the message, and me and Papa will know you get there safe."

Though half asleep, Maggie could hardly contain her excitement. The thought of having Dunstan by her side in the early morning hours was thrilling. When he took her by the hand and walked through the sleeping village, she almost wished everyone was awake to see them. So taken was she with the impressive figure that Dunstan cut, she hardly noticed the blanket he carried rolled up under his arm.

As they headed into the bushy path, Dunstan put his arm around her, and she rested her head on his shoulder. So contented was she that she named it the most beautiful night of her life.

Leaves rustled in the cool breeze and sounded like a thousand whispering voices. In the distance, a lone donkey brayed pitifully and tethered animals in the open pasture shuddered and wheezed in the darkness.

"Maggie," Dunstan whispered, pulling her closer, "I didn't have a chance to tell you, but I've signed up for service. It's only a matter of time before I'll be called."

Maggie felt the bottom fall out of her world. It was as though she was given a swift kick in the shins, and her stomach turned a summersault.

"Oh no, Dunstan!" she cried, sounding as pained as if she had been shot with an assassin's bullet. She dug her fingers into his side and held him more tightly than ever. "Don't you know you are going into danger? I am so afraid for you."

"Maggie darling, you shouldn't worry so much. It mightn't be that bad. Why don't we talk about it when you come back from Kingston? I was thinking that perhaps we could get married before I have to go overseas. But the question is, would you have me?"

Maggie held him even more tightly, tears already at the corners of her eyes.

"Of course I'd marry you, Dunstan... please hold me ... I'm shivering."

"Maggie darling, I brought you a blanket. You'll probably need it on the boat to ward off the cold."

Maggie gazed at the blanket in surprise, suddenly realizing it was meant for the weather, though at that precise moment she herself could have thought of a better use for it. "You are so thoughtful, Dunstan," she heard herself saying. But it wasn't at all what she would have wanted to say, for she had hoped that he would have laid the blanket down and loved her then and there. It occurred to her that whenever she was with Dunstan, she was never quite honest with herself, for she had always felt as if she were playing an assigned role, and that person wasn't always who she felt she was. "Thank you, I never thought to bring a sweater," she said.

The beach was deserted when Eliza left the house, discreetly carrying a small suitcase and one of the lanterns that used to be in the cottage's front room. She hoped Dunstan and Maggie would be there on the beach, but instead she was alone. She had the forethought to pull on a sweater, for the temperature had dropped, as she kept sentry under the darkened sky.

How lonely the beach was, and how cool the wind that blew in from the sea. The driftwood, the rocks and the raised sand bars, in the absence of daylight, loomed threatening and foreboding on the dark beach. And the ink-black sea muscled its way into shore with waves capped in the moon's silver glow.

My God, where's Maggie and Dunstan? Eliza thought fearfully, the stars low in the sky seeming to watch her every move.

With a trembling hand she lit the hurricane lantern and went to stand at a higher elevation. Once there, she felt exposed in the lamp's glow and feared discovery by anyone other than Dunstan and Maggie. It was with great relief that she saw a silver-white boat approaching the landing not far from where she stood. The boat had to be Kenny's, for Maggie had told her that it was called Star of the Sea, and the name was clearly visible. The moment Kenny saw her, he cut the engine and waved. "Good morning, Ma'am!" he shouted. "Is you Miss Eliza?"

"Good morning to you too and yes, I'm Eliza," she replied, climbing down from her perch, suitcase and lantern in hand.

"It cold out here tonight," Kenny said. "Is good you wear a sweater. Where's Miss Maggie?"

With a broad hand to shield his eyes in the moonlight, Kenny scanned the lonely beach as Eliza juggled with her suitcase, the lantern, and the hem of her skirt to climb into the boat. "My brother went to fetch Maggie," Eliza said, catching her breath. "They should be along soon." There was something likeable about Kenny, she thought, and his dark brown skin reminded her of Lucas.

Up close, Eliza saw that Kenny was middle-aged and hazel-eyed, with a face that was heavily lined and furrowed. To her, it seemed that Kenny's eyes were the saddest eyes she had ever seen, though his smile seemed always at a ready.

"Well, them better hurry up," Kenny said. "The day soon start, and we want to avoid the hot sun later on. Come, Ma'am, mek me help you. We going have to leave."

Then Kenny saw a small frown on Eliza's pale face and, though she didn't say a word, her blue eyes pleaded. He knew her disappointment and softened. "Okay, Ma'am, we'll maybe wait another twenty minutes," he said with a grin.

"They'll be here," Eliza said confidently, though she was quite unsure if Dunstan and Maggie might not have taken the opportunity to spend more time together and were delayed.

"Sit back so, Ma'am," Kenny said, taking her suitcase and waving his hand at a long wooden seat behind him. "Mek me just signal with you lamp."

"This is a rather nice boat," Eliza said, feeling the boat heave and toss under her like a stallion, as eager to be on its way as she was. Kenny smiled broadly; there was no mistaking how much he loved the boat. It even showed in his swagger, as he went to stand near the railings and he ran his long black fingers along its smooth surface.

"I lease this here boat from an American man," he said proudly. "It have a single cylinder engine, so it really up-to-date. And see those big wicker baskets hanging at the side in the water? That is where I carry some of the catch. That door there lead down to storage below. I can carry all kind a thing in there. And this railing is real strong, Miss Eliza, so you mustn't fraid of falling overboard. Four or five fisherman usually comes to sea with me, but this morning is just going be the three of us. Yes, Ma'am, this is a good boat alright, and the fishnet them strong can't done."

The glow from the lantern cut through the darkness, and from a distance it almost appeared to be a star twinkling on the water.

"What's that?" Maggie said, coming through the trees with Dunstan and noticing the swaying light in the direction of the beach.

"It's the boat signalling, Maggie. We'd better hurry!" Dunstan urged, grabbing hold of her hand and running.

Maggie ran as quickly as she could and trailed the blanket behind them in the wind like a sail, and Kenny saw them.

Chapter 9:
On the High Seas

"Please take care of my girl," Dunstan said as Kenny started the engine, "and watch out for my sister too; they are precious cargo."

Kenny grinned broadly. "Yes, boss, you can be sure I'll watch over the two of them good."

The sky was streaked with purples and black, though a faint orange glow threatened to permeate the clouds, as the boat pulled out from the landing.

At first, the boat bobbed like a cork on the slippery water then settled into a smooth rhythm to part the waves with each thrust of its engine. Once it was out on open sea, Maggie and Eliza lost sight of boundaries; they could not distinguish where the land or the sea and the sky began or ended. All around, faint orange light slowly emerged from the darkness to streak the sky and dapple the waves, like the brush of an impressionist painter. The wind blew cool and fierce, as though angry at their presence on the restless water.

Maggie pulled the blanket around her shoulders, too exhausted and too cold to appreciate the beauty around her. The heaving boat unsettled her, and her scattered thoughts were filled with Dunstan's impending departure. She longed for shared sympathy and comforting but couldn't bring herself to discuss Dunstan's plans in Kenny's presence. She curled herself up on the rough bench like a child, and surrendered herself to much needed sleep.

"Let Miss Maggie sleep," Kenny said softly. "She did look real tired to me."

No doubt Kenny must have appreciated the fact that Eliza was alert and awake. After many years of fishing, he was well aware of the effects that sea air can have on the body's rhythms. He knew how easily fishermen could fall asleep in their boats, only to drift endlessly and become lost at sea. He also knew that the rhythmic waves lapping against the vessel were as comforting and sleep-inducing as a mother's hand rocking an infant's cradle.

Kenny kept his ropy hand on the steering wheel and his bright eyes on the sea, occasionally glancing round to check on the two passengers. "Miss Eliza," he said ominously, "when we get to Port Maria, I going stop to get more gas."

One hour passed, and then another as the boat chugged on, and the sunlit sea sparkled with bands of pale blues, deep indigo and aquamarine. There was no land in sight. Far above, gulls and John crows dotted the sky like ravenous watchdogs waiting to be fed.

"Is a good thing we getting close to Port Maria, cause

we a' start to drift," Kenny said.

"Is that normal, Kenny? Can we make it in to port?"

"No, Ma'am, it don't look too good, but I think I see something in the distance. Look Miss Eliza, look over dey. You see it? It look like a ship."

"Yes, I can see it, Kenny. You are right. It is a ship," Eliza said, pointing at the ship's dark shape on the horizon.

Maggie awoke to their conversation and rubbed her eyes in disbelief as she followed the direction of Eliza's pointing finger. "It's a warship," she said matter-of-factly. An alert Kenny turned to glance at her. "You sure bout that, Miss Maggie?" he said. "That not good at all."

"Yes, Kenny, I'm sure. Look, there's mounted artillery. It's probably a destroyer. I've seen pictures of destroyers."

"I hope it's not a German U-boat," Eliza said gravely, "because if it is, we are done for. And Kenny says we are starting to drift."

"Ma'am," Kenny said hastily, "a U-boat is a submarine. That don't look like no submarine to me. It got to be a warship."

"Let's hope they don't notice us then," Maggie said. "We are as small as an ant in comparison. That ship is as large as a dozen elephants standing on top of each other."

"I think them must a notice us, Miss Maggie," Kenny hissed, his anxiety mounting. "The ship look like it a come this way."

The phantom-like ship sailed smoothly on the diamond water as it careened silently against wind and waves, only to loom large a short distance from the small boat.

It was the largest and most impressive vessel either Eliza or Maggie had ever seen. It was metallic and monstrous, with huge rigging and rotating weaponry, and its decks swarmed with uniformed men.

Clearly there was brisk activity aboard, and some of the sailors scurried to lean over the vessel's expansive railings to observe the drifting boat. The small boat seemed to be pulled magnetically, for it appeared to settle on its own near the manned portholes along the enormous vessel's side.

Instinctively, Eliza searched for evidence that might identify the ship, but neither she nor Maggie nor Kenny could see anything. They were acutely aware of an eerie silence as their boat drifted against the length of the ship, going past one armed porthole after another, reminiscent of one animal inspecting another. I mustn't be afraid, Maggie repeated silently and hardly dared to breathe.

"I didn't know warship was in our waters," Kenny whispered, "but anyways, me never did go out this far."

"What a mess I've got you both in." Eliza sighed. "If anyone is to blame, it's me, isn't it?"

The wind changed suddenly, and uncommonly rough waves nudged and banged the boat about against the ship's steel sides. The three shaken passengers held on for dear life, barely noticing the faces of the sympathetic and bemused sailors above them.

"Having a spot of trouble, are you?" someone with a British accent shouted from up on deck, and Eliza realized that it might be a Royal Navy vessel. She stood bravely at the railing, the boat heaving and bucking like a mule under her. Her blonde hair flew in the wind, almost blinding her as she attempted to hold on to her skirt, which in turn pasted against her slim frame, and exposed her shapely legs.

She was immediately inundated with hundreds of catcalls and wolf whistles. But the ruckus was silenced on the command of a senior officer who addressed her directly.

"Good morning, Madam!" he shouted. "Is everything all right?"

"No Sir," Eliza replied. "Our boat is adrift. We had hoped to make it to Port Maria to refuel, but we haven't had any luck."

The men aboard who had been leaning over the railings huddled together in heated discussion, and it was some time before the senior officer spoke to Eliza again.

"Is Port Maria your destination then, Madam?" he asked.

"Not really, Sir," Eliza replied. "We had hoped to make it to Kingston."

Further discussion amongst the sailors resulted in two or more senior officers joining the ranks of men at the railing. To Eliza, it seemed as though a year went by before one of the new officers addressed her.

"This is a Royal Navy ship, Ma'am," he said smartly. "It's not our usual practice to allow civilians aboard during wartime. But it looks as though your situation warrants a rescue mission. We are actually bound for Kingston Harbour. If it's all right with the lot of you, we could easily bring you aboard."

All three passengers were transferred safely aboard ship clinging to thick, knotted ropes dangled over the ship's side. Eliza couldn't help but remember how, as frightened children, she and Dunstan had disembarked from the steamship, and how she had counted on his steady hand. Yet here she was, years later, horrendously clinging to a rope to board a ship, and considering it an adventure. Perhaps in desperate times, she thought, one finds strength to undertake previously impossible tasks.

There was Maggie balancing steadily on the ropes without complaint, and Kenny was already heaving himself aboard.

Kenny's boat was hauled out of the blue waters and hoisted up with thick ropes attached to heavy metal hooks and a series of pulleys. It didn't take long before it finally rested safely on the battleship's deck.

Once aboard ship, Eliza, who was conscious of the salacious attention of the sailors, kept her eyes down and hoped to find somewhere that was out of their way. But that proved entirely impossible, for the deck was a beehive of activity. The vessel was so large it reminded her of the length of a cane field, and there was no disguising the ever-present evidence of weaponry. This must have been what it was like for Peter, she thought. He must have felt entirely out of place in the army. When she looked up, Eliza noticed huge, manned tower-like structures that reminded her that she was under constant surveillance.

"I'm Admiral James Elder," a young dark-haired officer said, interrupting her thoughts as he came forward. "You probably haven't had a bite to eat, have you? Please follow me. Don't be put off by the men, ladies. There are no women aboard ship, so it's only natural that they will stare."

Over hot barley soup and crackers, a group of officers made the three passengers comfortable in a small, poorly lit room below deck. Its furnishings were spare and the amenities were at a minimum, but the aroma from the thick, hot soup was welcoming.

"So you are all Jamaican, are you?" one of the officers asked, casually passing a plate of soda crackers.

"I born and raised here," Kenny said, suddenly more inclined to be talkative with the soup spoon halfway to his lips.

"Me too," Maggie said, and the officers eyed her unusual and exotic beauty quizzically, as though expecting further information. But Maggie, unaware of their interest, ate in silence and was not forthcoming.

"How about you, then?" Admiral Elder asked, nodding at Eliza.

"Oh, I'm English," she said. "I came here when I was quite small. My parents bought a property near Hedley in St. James some years ago."

Admiral Elder smiled at his companions knowingly. "I did say she sounded a bit English, didn't I?" he said, and the other officers nodded and returned his smile, though it was clear they had just lost a bet.

No longer smiling, Admiral Elder shoved his bowl aside and assumed a more serious demeanour. He leaned forward conspiratorially, as though the very walls might be privy to the information he was about to impart. "We are in very dangerous waters here in the Caribbean," he said in hushed tones. "The lot of you could have been in rather serious trouble, had we not been a British vessel. The truth of the matter is, these waters are under direct threat from German submarines."

Eliza's eyes opened wide. "Are they?" she said, suddenly acutely aware of danger. "I didn't know the war had reached here."

"So them submarine could a kill us?" Kenny said nervously, and his spoon slipped out of his hand and fell with a clatter. He hastily bent down to retrieve it. At ground level, he saw the men's hard, sturdy army boots and military stance, and it occurred to him that despite their present hospitality, these were men at war; and he fell silent.

Admiral Elder, with his eyes on Eliza, continued the conversation without pause. "German subs are in the Caribbean territory hunting for oil tankers and bauxite carriers en route to Britain and America. Oil and bauxite cargo are essential to our war effort, and to that of our allies. Even small boats such as yours could be at grave risk if caught in the wrong place at the wrong time. There are huge nets set at many of the ports to help to prevent subs from landing. We have personally and successfully captured and dealt with a few."

Maggie's heart pounded. She could well imagine what the 'dealt with' implied but couldn't help but stare at the admiral in admiration. "So that's why you're here," she said. "You're protecting Caribbean cargo."

"Yes, you might say that Ma'am, but rather we are mainly here to guard ports and POW camps, some of which are right here in Jamaica."

"Sir, you mean to say that we does have POW camps here on we island?" Kenny blurted out in disbelief.

"Yes, there are camps up at New Castle near Kingston, as well as at Up Park Camp in the city, and many others out in the countryside."

Chapter 10:
A New Day

The sun was beating down on Gunn's Run when Dunstan awoke. It was almost midday and the house seemed unnaturally still. He looked out his window to see waves lapping against the shoreline, and his thoughts flew to Maggie and Eliza out at sea.

I hope they'll arrive safely, he thought, as he swung out of bed and went in search of a cup of hot cocoa. Where's mother? he wondered. Shouldn't she be up already? He went past her room and saw that her bed clothes were already neatly folded, as was her custom. So he went to the back of the house and looked longingly towards the banyan, remembering the splendid afternoon there with Maggie, and the majestic tree seemed somehow diminished and lonely without her. Then he saw his mother not too far off from the tree. She was dressed in a loose white cotton dress that gleamed in the sunlight, and she was engaged in conversation with three young village boys who, for a few pennies, had come to weed the ginger. Her back was straight and her hair pinned up out of the way, and the slant of sun and shadow that fell across the plains of her face made Dunstan acutely aware that she was still beautiful. He stood his ground by the door, unable to take his eyes off her. His decision to go into service would surely break her heart, and he was quite uncertain as to how she would react regarding his feelings for Maggie.

She must have felt his eyes on her, for she looked towards him, smiled and waved, and Dunstan watched as she crossed the field with great strides to come to him.

Up close, he saw that her blue eyes were watery, and that there were stray strands of grey in her blonde hair. He felt as though his insides might burst from the secrets he carried, and he longed for the days when, as a boy, his mother's strong, pale arms would have comforted him.

"Dunstan darling," she said, coming over to embrace him. "Don't say a word. I know."

He was quite unaware of what she might be referring to, and he held his breath until his chest ached. "What do you know, Mother?" he finally said, holding her at arm's length and noticing the tear stains on her cheeks.

"Eliza's left us, darling." She sighed. "She's off to find that horrid young man."

"What young man, Mother?"

"His name is Lucas, darling. Don't you remember him, Constance's son?"

"Are you sure about that, Mother?"

"Of course, I'm sure, darling. He wants to marry her."

"How do you know that, Mother?"

"He told me himself, darling, and as for Eliza, she's had a silly crush on him since she was a child."

"She's hardly a child now, Mother, wouldn't you say?"

"I know, I know, darling, but he's so wrong for her."

"Well, she obviously doesn't think so, Mother. And by the way, weren't you married at her age?"

"Yes, darling, but what's that to do with anything?"

"Think about it, Mother. Eliza's in love, just like you were. What's so horrid about Lucas anyway? Is it that you're jealous, Mother, or have you forgotten what it's like to be in love? Don't look away, Mother. I think you have prevented yourself from loving anyone since Father died. Do you realize how beautiful you are? You are like the rarest of orchids that's been kept hidden away in this godforsaken place. Have you been hoping that love wouldn't find you? Well, Mother, love has indeed found Eliza, and me too, for that matter."

"No, Dunstan darling, not you too!"

"Yes, Mother, I'm rather fond of Maggie Chung, and I plan to marry her before I am shipped overseas."

"You've joined the services? How could you, darling! Look what's happened to Peter! Dunstan darling, you shouldn't even be talking about marriage, should you? You've hardly known anyone else besides Maggie. Shouldn't you be meeting other girls before making such a rash decision?"

"Nonsense, Mother, I love Maggie, and that's all there is to that. I'd wager anything that you are beginning to sound a lot like your own mother. I remember Father once told me that your mother wasn't too thrilled about him either."

"That was different, darling."

"No, Mother, it wasn't, and you might as well accept it."

When the Royal Navy vessel sailed into Kingston Harbour, it was early afternoon. The seas were calm, the sky was clear, and the weather announcement on the local radio station called for "fair to fine weather". Eliza could hardly wait to disembark and, just as she and Maggie were getting ready to do so, they were surprised when Admiral Elder requested privacy from his men and took the two women aside. There wasn't anything disquieting about his nature, Eliza thought, for his eyes were soft and his words were kind. If anything, he seemed daringly rakish yet likeable. It showed in the line of his firm jaw and the ghost of a smile that played on his thin lips. Unfortunately for him, though, both Eliza and Maggie, who had earned his admiration, were both missing other men. Eliza had expected that perhaps in the end the Admiral would require payment in one form or another. But she was more than surprised when his only request was for permission to visit with them at an early opportunity. The women were in no position to refuse his request, considering the kindnesses they had recently received from all aboard ship.

When finally they disembarked, they found Kenny and his boat already on the pier, patiently waiting for servicing and fuel.

"Kenny," Maggie said delighted to see that, in spite of their delay, he had not abandoned them. "I just want you to know that since Miss Eliza and I are going back to Hedley before you, we will take the train home. Thank you for everything. Here's a little something for you." She discreetly handed him a crisp white envelope with two five-shilling notes enclosed. Kenny grinned broadly and shook his head in disbelief. "I didn't earn this. Is the captain on the battleship that get you here safe, and it look like him like you. I don't deserve to get this much pay."

"Yes you do, Kenny," Eliza said. "You were there with us from the beginning of the journey till now."

"Thanks then, Ma'am. You been very kind. But it look

like I won't see you until next week in Hedley. Walk good."

The two young women couldn't help but be amused when hordes of street vendors and higglers mistaking them for tourists, eagerly approached them to peddle trinkets, fruit and souvenirs. Eliza couldn't resist speaking to them in the broadest patois she could muster, and the vendors could barely hide their disappointment in discovering that she was a local.

"Me did think you come from foreign," one market woman said, hoisting her fruit basket back on her head.

"Well, me grow right yah so." Eliza grinned. "But since you have nuff star apple, me could buy some next time."

The higglers and vendors hearing her speak broke into raucous laughter and cleared a path allowing her and Maggie free passage through them.

At the foot of the busy pier, Maggie noticed a stand with cars and drivers for hire and, with their few belongings in hand, the two young women managed, after much haranguing, to procure one to take them to Barry Street, where Aunt Phyllis' haberdashery was located.

In spite of the war, Eliza thought that Kingston's streets appeared vibrant and crowded, for there were hordes of people, bicycles with tinkling bells, rumbling pushcarts, trucks and cars with honking horns, and a rattling tram line. Business appeared brisk and the open markets were crowded, despite the fact that stock was in short supply.

The hired car raced through the bumpy streets, flew around narrow corners, and on several occasions mounted the pavement to avoid pedestrians as well as stray dogs and goats, and even a donkey that ventured out into the road. A breathless Eliza had to hold on fearfully to a strap on her side of the car as the driver cursed and swore at anyone or any vehicle that dared approach his vehicle.

When finally he screeched to a halt in front of the haberdashery, it was to the delight of many curious and envious onlookers.

"Is you that, Maggie? You should a let us know to come pick you up. Anyway, come give you aunt a kiss," Aunt Phyllis said, rushing out of the shop to greet them. "And who this? Don't tell me this is Eliza. She's real tall and pretty. And Maggie, last time me see you, you was just a little girl. You don't even look like Peter, for look how you pretty. Come, come inside. Uncle Aston cant wait to see the both of you."

Thin and talkative, Aunt Phyllis had a mouth that easily curved into smiles and, although older than her sister Chunty, she seemed more youthful. She wore her hair short in a fashionable bob, dressed in smart city clothes and, to Maggie's surprise, she even wore lipstick.

"Aston, come see you niece!" she shouted on entering the shop. "By the way, you speak Hakka?"

"No, Aunt Phyllis," Maggie replied, "we never learned."

"Your Uncle Aston can speak it good," Aunt Phyllis said with a grin. "Him use it in the shop all the time, and over the years I start catch on. Sometimes when we don't want nobody to know our personal business, we speak it together."

Trailing behind Maggie, Eliza entered the shop, her eyes wide and curious. She felt as though she was on the threshold of some sort of enchantment, for the narrow shop overflowed with intriguing items, both old and new. Some of the dust-covered stock had sat on the shelves for years. Yet there was something endearing, she thought, in the stuffiness that hung in the air for, to her, it spoke of dreams and waiting and wanting, and items handled and mulled over with longing, and she couldn't help but feel that the pursuit of something desired could surely result in the fulfillment of a promise.

Dreams, she thought, were there in this shop, from floor to ceiling, where pots, pans, clothes, cigarettes, exercise books, pencils and bedding jostled for space with drinking glasses, cutlery and bath towels. It was a place where dark, mounting dust did not seem to matter or to diminish the delight, and she longed with all her heart that she could share that sort of magic with Lucas.

"Baby Maggie!" Uncle Aston shouted the moment he caught sight of his niece, and he excused himself from his wide-eyed customers to come to greet her.

He was shorter than Maggie remembered, though his welcoming mustached smile had not changed. His hair had become streaked with gray, and there were visible lines around his eyes, which his thick round glasses could not disguise.

"Uncle Aston!" Maggie cried out as she fell into his arms.

"So you not going introduce Eliza?" Aunt Phyllis said with a laugh, tugging Eliza's wrist and pulling her forward. Even Maggie had to laugh when Uncle Aston dramatically extracted himself from her hold to throw his plump welcoming arms around a startled Eliza.

"Uncle Aston is a real joker," Aunt Phyllis said through laughter. "Anyway, call us Aunt Phyllis and Uncle Aston, cause you feel like family. But come upstairs. Let me show you your room. Is the same one that Peter did stay in."

There was a tiny rain-streaked window in the room that overlooked a dilapidated tenement yard, and Eliza could see an old, withered black woman washing clothes in a bucket near a standpipe where ragged, barefoot children rolled metal cart wheels and scurried to and fro in the resulting clouds of dust.

"This is your bed," Aunt Phyllis said, breaking into her thoughts as she pointed out a thin-looking iron bed on the far side of the dusky room. "And this one is Maggie's. You can put your things in this bureau. The bathroom is on the other side of that door. I wish you was staying longer. Me and Uncle Aston really miss having youngsters in the house. Is how long you staying anyway?"

"Only about two days, maybe three," Maggie said.

"You going do some buying for you daddy shop?"

"No, Aunt Phyllis, I just came because of Eliza. She's trying to locate somebody here."

"Somebody I know?"

Eliza reluctantly turned her eyes away from the animated tenement yard below and smiled weakly. "I don't think you'd know him," she said, "but I'm just wondering how to get in touch with Lucas Paynado."

"Lucas Paynado!" Aunt Phyllis said in surprise. "Isn't he the one in politics?"

"Yes."

"Everybody in Kingston know bout him, if of course him is the same person. Uncle Aston could take you in him car to Hope Road tomorrow morning. Because, if I'm not mistaken, Mr. Paynado's office is up there."

Eliza could hardly believe her ears. Imagine Aunt Phyllis

knowing where Lucas might be! The thought of him being even remotely near filled her with unexplained joy and her body ached with newfound longings.

"Thanks, Aunt Phyllis, I really appreciate it," she said, then, suddenly remembering Admiral Elder, reached out and took Maggie's warm hand. "By the way Aunt Phyllis, Maggie and I forgot to mention that we met an Admiral Elder, who was on a battleship in the harbour, and he might be coming over to visit us one of these days."

"Him coming to this house?! You serious, an admiral coming to this house? Is how you get to know him, anyways? Me going have to straighten up the place again." With a quick wink, Aunt Phyllis swept out of the room before either Eliza or Maggie had a chance to respond.

Chapter 11:
Kingstonians

Eliza did not sleep that night. Every sigh and sound in the creaking building kept her awake. Besides, her imagination was filled with dozens of scenarios about meeting Lucas again. What if he didn't remember her, she thought; and what if he did not reciprocate her feelings?

She pulled herself up on her elbows and listened in astonishment as an argument escalated between a man and a woman in the tenement below the window. A hungry baby cried pitifully and reminded Eliza that there were milk shortages. She would have given anything to be able to have gone out into the night to find out if she could offer assistance but, in the end, common sense prevailed.

The night was charged with the shouts of players slapping down dominoes and, once in a while, a low drumming like the heartbeat of the night permeated the air.

Towards dawn, Eliza kicked off her thin cover and

crossed the room to peer outside. The skies were empty except for stars; there were no passing planes nor any military presence at ground level, though after her experience on the battleship, she was more aware than ever that the country was at war.

Despite determination to be with Lucas, she felt estranged from Hedley and Gunn's Run. She longed for the ever-present roar of the sea, the wild wind in the banyan, the treacherous cliffs, and the uncultivated bushland. She couldn't help but wonder if those at home had come to understand why she had to leave. She hoped that Lucas would become a bridge rather than a barrier to her relationship with them. But it was Dunstan that she missed most. She glimpsed a horse-drawn cart out in the night, lit from underneath by a kerosene lamp, and the sight brought her amusement that she would have liked to share with him.

How long it seemed for that night to end! It dragged like a long, dark veil over the heavens, wound itself silently along streets and lanes, and attempted to silence and smother the entire city. But the city would not have it so, for it writhed and raged with its awakenings, pushcarts rumbling and low, murmuring voices escalating to shouts.

Dogs, mostly strays, awoke with a gnawing hunger as they bit furiously at fleas and barked and growled at friend and foe. Urban roosting chickens, startled awake, fussed and flapped their wings loudly while roosters crowed at the coming morning. A few brazen motor vehicles with dreadful honking horns sprang into life only to cough, splutter and backfire, and inadvertently awaken the city from its long dreaming.

The sky was painted in broad strokes of mauves and pinks and a blazing burst of orange that smoldered against the ebbing darkness; and Eliza, who had been standing at the window for hours, grew weary and heavy-eyed from watching. She was pent up with an excitement that burned in her loins. She returned to bed and dozed off just as the sun was rising.

She awoke well after nine o'clock, to the distinct aroma of fried fish and onions, only to be momentarily disoriented, for she thought that she was back at Gunn's Run. But the room seemed strange, and the sunlight that streamed in at the window was muted with flecks of dust. The floors beneath her feet were bare and devoid of mats, and there were no flowers on the bureau, as she was used to at home. On her side of the room, she noticed an unaccustomed blue pitcher and a basin for toiletries on a small table outside the bathroom door, and she remembered.

She looked for Maggie across the room, but saw that the bed was empty and the sheets crumpled. She washed hurriedly and took one careful step at a time down creaking stairs in the dimness. She ventured into a small, dark kitchen situated behind the partition where the shop counter was. On entering, she was surprised that neither Maggie nor Aunt Phyllis was there. It was only Uncle Aston who laboured at the stove, his brow creased and sweaty from the heat as the flame occasionally flared up from the blackened stove to caress his frying pan. Another shallow pan, black with soot, contained dumplings and stood on the counter next to him, evidence of his industry.

Behind him was a heavily bolted door that led outside. It was presently left ajar, perhaps because of the heat in the kitchen. The scent of the sea was faint in the air but, through the narrow opening, Eliza glimpsed a dirt lane with a tumbledown wood fence and scattered refuse. She was taken by surprise when she made out two shadowy figures crouched right there close to the doorway.

"Good morning, Eliza," Uncle Aston said, looking up

from his cooking to greet her, his face creased into a smile like a laughing Buddha. "You sleep good?"

"Yes thanks, Uncle Aston, but it took rather a long time."

"I thought as much," Uncle Aston said, flipping thin strips of fish as he spoke, "because that's how it usually is when you sleep in a strange house. But on the contrary, I hear that Maggie sleep good all night."

"Where's Maggie anyway, Uncle Aston?" Eliza asked, already missing Maggie and ready to make plans for their day.

"She gone with her Aunt Phyllis to the Syrian people shop next door. Mrs. Lazarus love a good gossip. But as for me, I have no time for that. I just come in from mass up at the big cathedral on North Street. Every morning at six, that's where you'll find me since my school days at St. George's up the road. My parents did even think I was going to be a priest. But oh no, when I met Phyllis, that was the end of that."

Uncle Aston's jaws shook as he laughed, and he turned the fish over once more and placed fried onions, thyme and Scotch bonnet peppers on top of the batch. "It ready," he said dramatically, "but two pickney outside the door, waiting for a little something." It was only then that Eliza realized that the two shadows outside the door were two dusky, barefoot children.

"Me usually give them a little something when me can," Uncle Aston said, turning aside to beckon to the two frightened children. "Come ya," he said in broad patois, and his familiar gesture appeased the children's fear.

"Fitzroy and Lena," he said with a flourish, "this is Miss Eliza. Don't frighten, she not going go lick you down with a big stick. Just take the food plates to you mother, and scram."

The two black-skinned children barely looked at Eliza, though their skeletal fingers trembled as they gripped the two plates of food tightly and nodded appreciation. Eliza was overcome with compassion, for it was impossible not to notice the rags that looked more like strings stretched across the children's boney backs as they bolted from the room. That could have been Lucas, she thought, fighting back tears.

"Them mother don't have nothing," Uncle Aston said. "Some of these Jamaican black people think that we Chinese don't have no heart. They think we have money because we have shops, but them wrong. They don't know how hard we have to work, and the long hours and the bookkeeping. They even forget that is because of us they can get things in grocery shops on trust. All us Chinese have long lists of people who owe us money, people who it would take a lifetime to pay us back, yet we allow them to carry on. Eliza, I can't help but be moved by the suffering around me, especially when it involve children."

"You're a good person Uncle Aston," Eliza said huskily. "And I want you to know that I am concerned about poor people too."

"Yes, young Eliza, there's still time for you to do a whole lot of good. And I hear that you want a drive uptown to see one of the politicians. Well, whatever you want to see him about can only be for a good. So right after we eat, I'll take you up there. Aunt Phyllis will watch the shop, so you don't have to pay it no mind."

After Uncle Aston said grace, Maggie and Aunt Phyllis bowed their heads into the meal, and Eliza ate in silence.

The fried fish brought back memories of home. She knew that Dunstan would have wanted a large portion of the fried dumplings, and that her mother would have enjoyed the stack of spicy onions.

"So you ready to go, Eliza?" Uncle Aston said, draining his last cup of hot cocoa. "I can drop you off and come pick you up later. Or if you want to find your way back by yourself, that alright with me too."

"Perhaps we could find our way back Uncle Aston," Maggie said. "I know you are busy, and Eliza might like to see something of Kingston."

"Did you remember we have to telephone your mother, Maggie?" Eliza said, thinking that perhaps she too could send a message to Gunn's Run.

"Yes, I called this morning, so Mama knows we've arrived safely. Mrs. Lazarus has a telephone in her shop. You wouldn't believe it, Eliza, but Mama was at the post office at eight o'clock this morning. She must have been waiting for the call. And by the way, I told her to let your family know that we are all right."

"Do you need any help to pay for the call, Maggie?"

"Oh no, Eliza," Aunt Phyllis said, waving her fingers. "That won't be necessary. I took care of that already."

"Well, let's get going before the day get too busy," Uncle Aston said. "The car have enough gas to get us there and back, and the spark plugs are in good shape."

Eliza was astonished at the contrasts that were Kingston. Even the downtown core was a grand mixture of opulence and poverty, with its luxurious hotels, elegant palm trees, stately buildings, ornate theatres, and well-built churches and hospitals. Yet there was the unforgiving evidence of poverty culminating in tumble-down shacks as the landscape deteriorated in close proximity. The impressive edifice that was the Institute of Jamaica brought Peter to mind, and Eliza imagined how proud he must have been to have studied there.

As the car nudged its way out of the downtown core, the landscape uncoiled to reveal the presence of the middle class. Stores, grocery shops, banks, hairdressing salons and petrol service stations lined the route from Crossroads and up as far as Half Way Tree, where churches, schools and government buildings stood near the shadow of the impressive clock tower. The modern homes in the vicinity evoked the financial status of their owners, for some were lavish and sprawling, while others showed architectural restraint. However, most of the homes boasted wide verandas, pristine lawns, hedges and cultivated gardens. It was clear to Eliza that these were the homes of the privileged.

"These people have maids," Uncle Aston said, confirming her thoughts as he nodded at the affluent homes. "Maids start working at six or seven in the morning, cooking, cleaning and washing until well in the evening. Some maids even have to look after the children. And see those houses with clothes lines in the backyard? Well, by mid-afternoon you should see the amount of clothes hanging out there. And see that man over there, cutting grass with the cutlass? He is a yardboy. Yardboys do the garden work, and they better make sure the property look good all the time, or else they could lose their job. People up in these parts can afford to hire and fire help, but not we. We in the shops have to struggle on we own."

Eliza couldn't believe how much there was to learn about the city from Uncle Aston. For at first, Kingston had deceptively appeared to be a well-oiled machine run by diversified peoples from various stations in life. But underneath it all, as she came to realize, there was an underbelly of rivalries, class discriminations, deceit and even danger, though on the surface rich, poor and middle class appeared to mingle amicably.

But despite Kingston's splendid reputation as a melting pot of society, Eliza missed the intimacy of Hedley and the sea in all its moods.

Theirs was not the only car that trundled through hordes of clanking bicycles and pushcarts with bells that jangled; once in a while, slow-moving cars would swerve dangerously close to their vehicle. Uncle Aston considered those drivers foolhardy and annoying, though he seldom retaliated with a toot of his foghorn.

Though his interpretation of the landscape was interesting and informative, Eliza, in her eagerness to see Lucas, felt that the journey was interminably long. Maggie, on the other hand, appeared disinterested in her uncle's anecdotes, for her face was expressionless as she stared unseeing out the car window. She must be missing Dunstan, Eliza thought, and it occurred to her that Maggie had become less than forthcoming ever since their arrival in Kingston. But she kept the concern to herself, nervously anticipating her own upcoming reunion with Lucas.

"This is the office," Uncle Aston said, interrupting her

thoughts and pointing to a new-looking white building with gabled roofs and dark green awnings.

"You will have to go in by yourself, Eliza. Me and Maggie will wait out here. We don't look high-class enough, like you. So you just go see if Mr. Paynado is there, then come tell us."

That's nonsense, Eliza thought; who would think that she looked more upper class than anyone else? But she didn't say a word. Her heart felt like bursting, for she was all wound up. She had no idea where she found strength to even open the car door. Her legs wobbled, her hands felt as useless as putty, and she was sure that she appeared unsteady as she made her way up the paved walkway.

A hedge of hardy red and yellow rose bushes were in bloom on either side of the walk, its bouquet scenting the air as she held her head high and entered the building.

The foyer's freshly scrubbed tiles were immaculate and leafy shade plants grew profusely in ornamental pots. From where she stood, Eliza saw that the room beyond was quite spacious. She glimpsed vases of fresh-cut flowers on mahogany tables and desks, and there were framed photographs and paintings along bookshelved walls. Comfortable wicker chairs stood in front of the desks, though Eliza's eyes were drawn to the ink blotters, pens and stacks of paper, imagining Lucas at work there. There was such a haunting stillness in the room, that it surprised her when suddenly she heard the steady tap of a typewriter's keys and the occasional bang of its carriage. She peered over the top of a low mahogany bookshelf and saw that a young, light-complexioned black woman was sitting there, engrossed in typing.

"Good morning," Eliza said cheerfully, though her palms were damp with nervous sweat. The young woman looked up reluctantly and smiled, and Eliza saw that her eyes were hazel and there were dimples in her cheeks.

"Good morning, Ma'am," the woman replied, with a practised English accent. "May I help you?"

"Yes, please," Eliza replied with a giggle, feeling all at once at ease and childish. "I'm here to see Mr. Paynado."

"Do you have an appointment, Ma'am?"

"No not really."

"Then you'll have to make one with me, Ma'am. Mr. Paynado is presently in St. Thomas, speaking with sugarcane workers."

"Do you know when he will be back?"

"I'm afraid he's scheduled to visit Bath as well, so the earliest he'd be back here is next Tuesday. Should I make you an appointment, Ma'am?"

"But that's almost a week away!" Eliza blurted out, coming to the realization that she and Maggie should be returning to Gunn's Run in less than two days.

"It's the best I can do, Ma'am," the young woman said. "But if it is an urgent matter, I could telephone or send him a telegram."

"No, please don't go to all that trouble. I'll make the appointment."

"What's your name, Ma'am?"

"Susan Jenkins," Eliza replied, saying the made-up name a little too quickly and hardly disguising the hint of mischief in her voice.

"Okay, Miss Jenkins, I've made you an appointment for 11:00 a.m. Is there anything else I can help you with?"

"No thanks, I'll be here next week."

"So them tell you that Mr. Paynado is in St. Thomas until next Tuesday. What you going do, Eliza?" Uncle

Aston said, starting up the car.

"I'd like to stay in Kingston, if I may, Uncle Aston," Eliza replied, looking longingly at the office building. "But I have a feeling that Maggie won't be able to stay, not with the shop to run and everything. Am I right, Maggie?"

"I suppose that's true, Eliza. I would have wanted to stay, really I would, but I can't, not with Papa's health the way it is and Mama's running things alone."

"Our poor dear Maggie," said Uncle Aston. "No wonder me and your Aunt Phyllis decide that we going pay your train fare home, so that you will have one less thing to worry about. Meanwhile, here's two five-shilling notes: go enjoy yourself with Eliza this evening. Aunt Phyllis and I will be happy to put Eliza up for the few extra days; that is, if she can put up with us."

It was a day after that conversation that Maggie left on the morning train for Falmouth. Chunty, who had been called regarding the departure, had assured Maggie that Dunstan would be asked to meet her and bring her home to Hedley.

Eliza had overslept and only awoke to glimpse Maggie with suitcase in hand, moments before her departure. Maggie's eyes were downcast and despondent, and though that past evening, she and Eliza had gone out for a meal at The Myrtle Bank, which was considered one of Kingston's finest hotels, the occasion had not served to lighten her solemn mood.

Maggie doesn't look like a woman going home to the man she loves, Eliza thought, and she wondered what on earth could be wrong with her. And, as if in answer to her concerns, Maggie turned aside from the sunlit doorway where she had stood, and where her yellow dress was rendered transparent, revealing her flat belly, her firm rounded breasts and her slim legs. No doubt she must have felt Eliza's eyes on her, for she self-consciously leaned away from the revealing light and came towards her.

"Oh, Eliza," she whispered hurriedly, urgently. "I can't seem to stop myself from thinking that I might never see Dunstan again if he goes off to war. These past few days, I've been hoping that he might change his mind. But I'm being selfish, aren't I? And I can't stand selfish people. I am so confused."

Eliza hurried from her bed, threw her arms around Maggie and held her tight, her own warm lips close as she whispered reassurances in Maggie's listening ear. "Don't imagine the worst, Maggie," she said bravely. "Dunstan is a man of his word. If he says he will come back to you, nothing will stop him. That's just the way he is, and I should know. When you get home, give him my best regards, and tell mother that I love her. Try to explain why I had to stay here, and tell her that I hope she will forgive me."

Chapter 12:
Reunion

When Maggie's train pulled into the sleepy station at Falmouth, she had already steeled herself, having decided not to let Dunstan know how she felt about his decision. She was sitting alone on a bench not far from where higglers displayed their painted calabashes alongside fresh papaws and newspaper-rolled packages of spiced shrimp. Her sight was so set on seeing Dunstan that it was no wonder she was unaware of it when a smartly dressed young woman in a broad hat approached her. Maggie hadn't even looked in the woman's direction as she scanned the few people who poured into the railway station, for she knew immediately that Dunstan was not there. She had looked for his fair hair, his tall frame and his laughing blue eyes and, not finding him, felt uneasy and quite isolated in the unfamiliar surroundings. If only there was some way of contacting Dunstan or her parents, she thought.

She was more than surprised when the young woman whom she had only briefly glimpsed at the corner of her eye walked right up to her. Her second surprise was that the woman was Chinese, for everyone else in the proximity was Negroid and dark-skinned.

"Hello there," the young woman continued, sounding to Maggie more English than Jamaican. "You must be Maggie Chung," she said, with an engaging smile tugging at the corners of her lips. "I hope I didn't alarm you. Did I? I'm Rita, your sister-in-law."

"I'm Maggie Chung," Maggie replied cautiously, eying the woman with suspicion. "But there must be some mistake. I don't have a sister-in-law."

Examining the woman's open face, Maggie noticed her arresting, softly lashed brown eyes, her pearl-like complexion, her firm jaw and her mouth, which seemed kind. She is probably not insane, Maggie thought, but why on earth, is she claiming to be my sister-in-law?

"I'm Peter's wife," the woman said convincingly. "There's been absolutely no mistake." Her manner was so matter-of-fact that, when she extended her pale hand, Maggie took it with her own firm hand.

"Please call me Rita," the woman said. "Your brother and I were married in England a few months ago. He recently received a telegram from a Wilemina Gunn, regarding an urgent matter here that Peter should attend to. But we were delayed and were able to arrive here only yesterday. If there is any doubt in your mind, you might want to speak to Peter himself. He is actually outside in the in the car; his legs can't take standing for too long."

"Peter's here?" Maggie said, trying to come to terms with the possibility, though it hardly seemed possible. She had not seen her brother in years, and the boy who had left home would surely have become a man. She could barely find her voice to speak, and the sound that came out of her throat was practically inaudible. "So you are serious? You are his wife?" she said. "I'm surprised that Peter didn't even tell us anything about being married."

Rita wrinkled her nose and laughed as she held the seated Maggie at arm's length. Her gentle touch on Maggie's shoulders was warm and reassuring, and her manner disarming. Maggie couldn't help but feel that Peter could not have done better than having someone as charming as Rita for a wife. She remembered how serious-minded her brother used to be and the many hours he used to spend squirreled away from the family, examining one scientific thing or another. Not to mention the endless plans he made for his future as a scientist, plans that did not include a wife and children.

"Yes, your wonderful brother wanted to surprise all of you," Rita said. "He has made me so very happy. I'm rather pleased to meet you, Maggie; and your parents are such dears."

"You've met my parents?" said Maggie, jumping to her feet, suitcase in hand, and all the while her eyes darting towards the few cars parked outside the station. And all of a sudden she remembered Dunstan. "So if Peter's here," she said hesitantly, "where's Dunstan then?"

"I'm afraid Peter says that his friend Dunstan has enlisted and was called away unexpectedly. It's quite likely Dunstan is either in Kingston being briefed or crossing the Atlantic just now."

Maggie's small suitcase fell from her limp hand with a thud as she collapsed like a folding tent into Rita's arms. Higglers idling close by rushed to offer assistance, but it was Rita who cradled Maggie on the hard bench and removed her own broad hat to fan her with.

"Must be the heat that make her faint," one of the higgler

women surmised. "Them say light-skin people can't take the sun like we."

"She's just had a bit of a shock," Rita said calmly. "She'll be all right."

"Give her this cup of water," one stout woman said. "Is what me give me own daughter when she did faint."

"Thanks so much," said Rita. "I appreciate your kindness."

When Maggie came to, she was sitting up in the back of Peter's car, where two strong higgler women had managed, with Rita's help, to take her. She opened her eyes to find Peter's face before her.

"Peter!" she gasped, for he had changed. Though his hair was still thick and dark, his face had become more angular, there were pale lines under his eyes, and his smile was slightly lopsided. His once-firm jaw seemed to have sunken. But despite it all, his eyes were as alert as ever. What pleasure danced in those eyes! thought Maggie as he leaned over the car seat, mouthing kisses.

"What's the matter, young lady?" he said softly, and his English accent surprised her. "Have you not eaten?" he inquired. "Should we be getting you something? We can't have you fainting like that again, can we?"

Maggie managed a weak grin and, as the brother and sister gripped hands, all the years of their separation fell away in an instant like a collapsing wall of bricks. "I can't believe how much you've changed." Peter laughed. "How could you be the wingy little sister I left at home. Just look at you, love, all full of curves. How pretty you've become. I told Rita you'd be rather skinny and plain, so I'm sure she wasn't expecting anything like this."

Maggie smiled, though tears welled in her eyes, for she had never seen Peter as animated. "It's wonderful to see you, Peter," she said, her tears flowing freely. "I've really missed you. How's your health anyway and, by the way, did you see Dunstan?"

"Questions, questions," Peter said with a laugh. "First of all, let me just say that my wife has been just splendid. Haven't you Rita? Without this woman beside me, I couldn't have gotten around and she's even helped you to get to this car, Maggie.

"So much has happened since I last wrote home. As you can see, I married this wonderful woman, Rita Wong. Rita's family are from Linstead. They went to settle in England, and Rita was born over there, weren't you, darling? The Wongs are close friends of the Jamaican man I mentioned in my letter, the one who has been so kind to me in London.

"But we have a lot of catching up to do, Maggie. I wasn't even going to mention it now, but I've had a stroke. My left leg is paralyzed, and I have to use a cane. I haven't been well since Europe, but dearest Rita makes sure I stick to the diet prescribed by my doctors, which means absolutely no spices, not even salt and black pepper for me."

"Oh Peter," Maggie said. "Why did all this have to happen to you?"

"Perhaps God didn't want me to take part in this war," Peter said. "He most likely has other plans for me, wouldn't you say so, Rita darling? We are going to stay here in Jamaica, and who knows, we might even have a family one day."

"But, Peter," Maggie said, her heart in her mouth, "tell me something, did you manage to see Dunstan before he left? Did he say anything?"

"No, Maggie, I didn't see him at all, and that really

bothers me, because it was Mrs. Gunn who sent me a telegram requesting me to return home urgently. At first, I thought it was bad news about Papa. Didn't I say so, darling? But when I went to see Mrs. Gunn directly after seeing Mama and Papa, she told me that she had wanted Dunstan to speak with me personally so that he would realize the horrors of war as a reality. She told me that she would go to any length to prevent him going over to Europe, and she even paid my fare here."

"Oh, Peter!" Maggie sobbed as she fought with her emotions, for even after all the years since the cave incident, she was still inclined not to want to reveal her true feelings to Peter concerning Dunstan. "I can't stand to think what might happen to him," she said, hoping Peter would not notice the slight quiver in her voice and the tremor in her hands. "And worst of all, Peter," she continued, biting her tongue against words she thought that he should not hear, "I never even had a chance to say goodbye to him."

Peter smiled wanly. "Please don't cry, Maggie," he said sympathetically. "Dunstan has been like a brother to us; I'm sure he knows how we both feel about him. All we can do now is wish him Godspeed and good health, and pray for his safety."

It had rained in Kingston continuously after Maggie left and, when Eliza tried to look out the bedroom window, she had found a thick layer of dust and condensation on the window pane. She patiently wiped away the buildup with her handkerchief and through the pelting rain, glimpsed figures in the tenement yard below, scurrying with only flimsy newspapers for covering.

She stared intently when she saw a small, ragged girl let free a paper boat into the streaming water that slowly filled the yard. The boat seemed almost merry, cascading in the rushing water and speeding over gravel and stones before it finally settled in a buildup of silt. The girl stood lonely and ankle-deep in the mud for the longest time, as though in deep contemplation, and Eliza thought, that girl could have been me, not really knowing what to do next. Then to Eliza's consternation, two rough, barefoot older boys came splashing through the water to run off with the girl's flimsy boat.

That's how life is, Eliza thought. There is always the danger of someone coming along to shatter your dreams. She turned away from the window, feeling strangely unsettled, and decided to go downstairs.

Aunt Phyllis was at the counter making bookkeeping entries in her large black ledger. She looked up with a smile as Eliza approached, though Eliza had the distinct feeling that Aunt Phyllis was not entirely contented. Her brow was wrinkled and even her laughing eyes were drooped, perhaps lamenting the fact that business was down, for the shop was absolutely deserted.

"It look like it going rain all day, Eliza," Aunt Phyllis grumbled, putting aside the ledger and her pen. "Business bound to be bad, cause most people don't go out in the rain. But anyway, Eliza, if you hungry, we have some patty in the patty pan in the back, or you can have bun and cheese if you'd rather that. I would have offered you tea, but I don't really know if you prefer cocoa tea, green tea or even aerated water. Just let me know whatever you feel like."

"Thanks, Aunt Phyllis, but I actually don't feel like having anything just now."

"Eliza, you should eat. Look how you thin! You going

need your strength. Anyway, I was looking at The Gleaner this morning, and it says that the warships in our harbour have been recalled to Europe, so I don't think your captain friend going come see us now."

"Oh, Aunt Phyllis," Eliza said with a sigh, "I haven't even thought about him and, besides, I think it was Maggie that interested him."

"Well, Eliza, if that is the case, then is just as well him don't come, since she not here. You must be so bored without her, you keep to yourself so much. Sometimes I wonder what you think about all the time. But Uncle Aston tell me that you didn't even get to see your friend the other day. Maybe when your friend comes back, he will have interesting things to occupy you with."

"I don't know about that, Aunt Phyllis. I haven't seen Lucas Paynado in a long time, years actually and, come to think of it, I am not even sure what his interests are."

"Sounds to me, Eliza, that you going have to get to know him all over again."

"Yes, I suppose so, Aunt Phyllis, and I intend to do that."

"Is he an old school friend then, Eliza? Maggie says he lived near Hedley at one time."

"Not really, Aunt Phyllis. In fact, he didn't want to go to school in Hedley when he was there."

"Oh, he must have worked on your property then?"

"No, Aunt Phyllis, he didn't work at Gunn's Run. My family just knows his mother well; she lives near us."

"Now I see," Aunt Phyllis said with a laugh. "I did start to think him was a boyfriend."

"No, he's not, Aunt Phyllis. He's just a family friend."

The conversation might well have continued had Uncle Aston not come bursting into the shop. "Phyllis!" he panted, mopping his brow, and looking wild-eyed. "Mrs.

Lazarus just call me in from the road, cause Chunty was on the telephone. Chunty call with the bad news that poor old Sam passed away last night!"

Aunt Phyllis rushed out from behind the counter and none too soon, for Uncle Aston was unsteady, though he managed to grip the counter to bolster himself and quickly made the sign of the cross.

"Good God!" Aunt Phyllis gasped. "What wretched news! Now don't you go faint, Aston!" she cried out, her voice as thin as a reed. "You all right, dear?"

Pressed up against the counter for support, Uncle Aston removed his glasses, wiped his eyes, and dabbed sweat from his forehead as he gently reassured Aunt Phyllis. "I'm okay," he said. "I did just feel a little dizzy."

"You better not get sick, Aston. I love you and can't afford to lose you, and I don't know what Chunty going do now. Sam was her life!"

"Phyllis, them say that everybody in Hedley is saying that old Sam was just holding on to see Peter again before him pass on, and is a good thing Maggie manage to be home when it happen. But guess what, Phyllis? Peter was there too! Peter come home from England with a wife, and Sam even did get to meet her!"

Aunt Phyllis wrinkled her brow and shook her head in disbelief. "Aston," she said through clenched teeth, "you sure she say Peter married? Cause I for one hope the wife is not that Lee girl him was so crazy bout when him was here."

"No, Phyllis, is somebody else him go marry. Somebody we don't know. But my goodness, you must excuse me, Eliza. Here you are all this time, and I almost forgot that Chunty say that your big brother Dunstan gone go fight in the war."

How alone I am, thought Wilemina Gunn, sitting on the veranda overlooking the bright sea where dried sea weed and bramble blew lazily along the shoreline. Birds swooped overhead in the clear sky, and she could hear the harsh cries of village children permeate the air as they taunted the hungry sea. There could be a drowning today,Wilemina thought as sail boats bobbed on the sunlit water, for the sea seemed particularly expectant and marked with wanting. And for the first time in many years, she imagined herself aboard one of those boats, sailing away from Gunn's Run. Jonathan Gunn's memory had clung to her like a ghost in all her dreams, and saddled her thoughts to him. Though now left alone to rattle about in the empty house that he had built her, Wilemina felt, for the first time in years, cut off from his bloodline and far removed from him. She could barely remember his haunting touch or what she had called his "fiery red kisses". And now that his children were gone from her like the pellets from a slingshot, perhaps never to return, what use was it all, she thought, in the long run? Bringing Peter home had served no purpose, she surmised, but to dry dear Chunty's tears as, together, they united in widowhood.

How I miss the company of an intelligent man, she mused, a man who can challenge me, and whose touch is so vivid it will awaken all my sensitivities, though as far as I'm concerned there is no such man in Hedley.

As the salt wind blew feverishly, it put her in mind of a jet of air from a warm mouth. And as her curls rose and fell in the breeze, an aroused Wilemina slowly caressed her own breasts, her strong thighs and her belly. She allowed her hands to be stilled only when, at the hollow of her shoulders, she remembered Ezekiel Samuels.

"Ezckicl," she said aloud pitifully, "why was I so foolish as to let you go?"

Sam Chung's funeral was scheduled for the very afternoon of Eliza's impending meeting with Lucas Paynado. Uncle Aston and Aunt Phyllis, who would be attending the service in Hedley, were reluctant to leave her in the city. However, she assured them that the shop could be closed since, after her appointment with Lucas, she would take the first train home, because with Dunstan gone, her mother would be feeling quite alone.

That morning, upon rising, she found the room bathed in sunlight. She washed and brushed her hair until it shone, then slipped into a pale pink off-the-shoulder frock and donned a floral straw hat, a gift from Aunt Phyllis.

I look like a tourist, she thought, her hair tumbling over her shoulders, beneath the hat's bright flowers.

Hearing movement downstairs, she quickly glanced into a hand mirror she found on top of the bureau and stopped momentarily to pinch colour into her pale cheeks.

"You ready, Eliza?" Uncle Aston shouted from the foot of the stairs. "We going have to be at the train station early, but we can drop you off at Mr. Paynado's office first."

"Yes, I'm ready, Uncle Aston," Eliza replied, grabbing her small suitcase and taking one last glimpse out the sun-drenched window.

The little girl she had seen with the paper boat was at the standpipe, assisting her mother with washing off a dirty younger sibling. But the little black-skinned girl never once looked in Eliza's direction, and neither did the mother, whose shabby clothing hung in shreds off her frame. I wonder what will become of them? Eliza thought.

"Mrs. Lazarus is downstairs here!" shouted Aunt Phyllis. "She was kind enough to bring us some ackee and salt fish for we breakfast before we go."

After all the goodbyes were said and Uncle Aston's car finally disappeared from view down Hope Road, Eliza felt strangely alone. She had long looked forward to the meeting with Lucas though now that it was to become reality, she was overcome with apprehension.

Uncle Aston had dropped her off at his office far earlier than her appointed time, but the receptionist on duty was courteous and friendly.

"Good morning, Miss Jenkins," she said. "Your appointment seems to be not until eleven, but you might like to make yourself comfortable in the waiting area. There are magazines and hot coffee there if you wish."

"What time is it now?" asked Eliza, gazing longingly at one of the office rooms she assumed was Lucas'.

"It's only nine thirty, Ma'am."

"Is Mr. Paynado back from Saint Thomas?"

"Yes, Miss Jenkins, he is. He should be here shortly. He's usually quite punctual."

Eliza was tempted to ask her more about Lucas but thought better about compromising herself, and it took her by complete surprise when the receptionist was more forthcoming.

"We have all been waiting to see him," the receptionist said with a smile. "He always has such interesting things to tell us when he comes back from trips. In fact, all the secretaries here have pooled together and bought him flowers. He is the nicest man."

Eliza felt strangely deflated walking back towards the waiting room, for never once had she imagined that Lucas might have admirers other than herself. *I am such a fool,* she thought. *These are all grown women here, and he's sure to think I'm just a silly little girl.*

She was soon bored with the magazines she found in the waiting room, and it seemed to her that minutes were stretched into hours. She watched as the well-dressed clientele were called into offices, and she couldn't help but feel ill at ease in her plain country clothing. She glimpsed her reflection in the glass of one of the framed photographs and was astonished by how childish she appeared, and she stuffed her thick hair under her hat. With the rim pulled down jauntily to conceal the upper half of her face, she was sure she had achieved some degree of sophistication.

Every sound and every footstep from the adjoining rooms quickened her heart, and every male voice outside the room startled her. As she grew more anxious, she imagined that every secretary in the building was watching her, and she was glad that she had decided to wear a pair of nice sensible shoes.

As she grew more agitated, she went to stand in the foyer to stretch her legs, and she gazed unseeingly out at the garden.

A large black hired car drew up in the driveway, with four male occupants. Overcome with anxiety, Eliza quickly returned to her seat in the waiting room, her face as flushed as a beet.

Four men dressed in dark business suits and ties spoke animatedly as they filed past the room without a second glance. But Eliza hid under her hat, feeling sure that Lucas was one of those men.

"Good morning, Mr. Paynado," she heard the receptionist say in a businesslike manner. "A Miss Jenkins has been waiting to see you since early this morning."

Lucas Paynado might have mumbled something in reply, though Eliza never heard a word. She imagined a dozen scenarios, and to her it seemed like a good nail-biting ten minutes before the receptionist came to get her.

"Please come this way, Miss Jenkins," she said, eyeing Eliza with new-found curiosity.

Lucas' office was down a narrow hall, and the door was slightly ajar. Eliza could see a mahogany desk with neatly stacked files, journals and ledgers. Over to one side of the desk was a crystal vase containing a stunning bouquet of dried wood roses and fresh wild orchids.

As she entered the room, Eliza couldn't help but notice the elegant welcome back card propped up against the flowers.

There was no mistaking Lucas Paynado's lean, muscled frame, though he was standing with his back to her as he rifled through a file.

Eliza took a deep breath to steady herself and when he turned around, she saw his eyes, those very same eyes that she remembered with so much love. He barely looked at her as he gestured to her to take a seat, and her heart drummed uncontrollably. She could hardly breathe, the thought occurring to her, as he took his seat, that only the broad dimensions of his desk separated them.

He had hardly changed, she thought, for he was as dark as ebony, his lips looked soft and inviting, and his close-cropped hair was the exact shade of a tamarind seed. And what a wonderful nose — it wasn't flared like his mother's; perhaps he inherited it from his father, who surely must have been part Portuguese. He was, as a matter of fact, more handsome than she even remembered.

"Good morning, Miss Jenkins. How can I help you?" Lucas said, and he reached across the desk and shook her hand. To Eliza, his grip was firm and sensual, and his touch sent a tremor of excitement through her, though he hardly took his eyes off the file before him.

"It's a complex family matter," Eliza said, her voice coming out controlled and stilted, "though of course it might be of interest to you, Mr. Paynado."

"And why would that be so, Miss Jenkins? Does it involve legalities and property settlements? If so, I must let you know right up front that I am not a lawyer. I have no real training in that field. I'm more inclined to be involved in mediations and negotiations of a different kind."

"I already know that, Mr. Paynado," Eliza replied, and she held her head low so that the brim of the hat covered her smiling blue eyes. "I just wanted your opinion on an urgent matter, that's all."

"Okay, Miss Jenkins, but I cannot promise anything. My colleague, Mr. Nesmith, is a lawyer, and he could be of more assistance."

"Oh no, Mr. Paynado, that wont be necessary. It's your opinion that I require."

"Well?"

"There is an old Jamaican woman," Eliza said with a grin, "who is living on a property owned by an English family. The English family's house is on the property, and so is the old woman's. Now, Mr. Paynado, if the English family deserts the property because their daughter has fallen in love with the old Jamaican woman's son, could the old woman claim the property?"

Eliza held her breath and studied Lucas' young face, and for one brief moment thought that surely he had seen through her charade.

"That sounds preposterous, Miss Jenkins," he said, a smile playing at the corner of his lips. "Are you representing the old woman or the English family? And where's this so-called property?"

"It's Gunn's Run," Eliza replied with a laugh as she removed her hat and allowed her blonde curls to tumble free.

"Eliza Gunn! Is that you?" Lucas gasped in genuine surprise. "I didn't recognize you! What the devil are you doing in Kingston? Just look at you — so grown up, and beautiful! I was beginning to think there was some truth to your concocted story."

"Oh, Lucas," Eliza said, laughing. "The part about the daughter in the story is true."

"Eliza Gunn, are you saying you're in love with me?"

"Yes, Lucas Paynado, I have always been."

"But you were just a little girl when I knew you! Little girls don't fall in love."

"Well, I fell in love with you back then, Lucas, and now that I'm grown, I couldn't wait to see you again."

Lucas stood up slowly and, to Eliza, he seemed to look as contemplative as the little girl she had seen in the tenement yard. "Does your mother know you are here?" he said finally.

"It's a long story, Lucas, but let's just say that she does know."

"Why do I have the feeling there is something you're not telling me, Eliza? Anyway, where are you staying?"

"I was actually staying downtown with the relatives of some family friends. But since they had to leave Kingston today, I was planning to go home by train after seeing you."

"Eliza, do you really have to leave today?"

"No, Lucas, not really, I don't. It's just that my brother has left home, and mother's alone now. Why?"

"Well, Eliza, your mother's not exactly alone if my

mother's still there on the property. So you know what I'm going to do? I'm going to have my secretary telephone and book you a room at the Bougainvillea Manor Hotel on Constant Spring Road. You could stay for a day or two if you'd like to. I know they will take good care of you there. We need to talk, Eliza, but there are a few things I need to catch up on here at the office first. Allow me to get a car to take you to the hotel, and I'll see you there at around three this afternoon."

Eliza could hardly believe the luxury to be found at the sprawling Bougainvillea Manor Hotel. Not only was the hotel set amidst manicured rolling lawns, but it boasted antique ceiling fans, marble-looking tiled floors, a spacious lobby, lavishly decorated rooms, patios, and even an outdoor pool.

Eliza was pampered from the moment of her arrival, for she was met with a chilled rum cocktail, and a hotel maid proffered a tray of finger food.

After having had a swim in the outdoor pool, she took time to enjoy a light shrimp salad for lunch. The patio where she sat was located under the shade of a fragrant poinciana tree that was cleverly incorporated into the elitist landscaping. She was exhausted after having had to wake up early that morning, and she went to rest on the smaller patio that adjoined her room. She sat for a while, feeling extremely lazy, with nothing to do except observe the other guests congregated in and around the pool area.

It occurred to her that there were no dark-skinned persons at the hotel, except for the servants. Judging from the accents she heard, the guests were mostly British and American Caucasians; and she wondered if Lucas would have been welcome there. She fell asleep in her deck chair and awoke a few hours later with a start, when there was a sharp knock at her room door.

She had been wearing a robe provided by the hotel but quickly slipped into her own clothes, realizing it might be Lucas.

"Who is it?" she called out, straightening her skirt and running her fingers through her unruly hair.

"It's me, Lucas," came the reply and Eliza, filled with excitement, could hardly even catch her breath as she unbolted the door, restraining herself from running into his arms.

"Is it three o'clock already?" She laughed, seeing him there before her, still dressed in his business suit, and she could hardly believe that the time had gone by so quickly.

"Yes, Eliza, it's a little after three," Lucas said, striding into the room, displaying unqualified familiarity with his surroundings, choosing a soft chair situated nearer to the picturesque window. "It's good to see you again," he said with a smile. "I hope you don't mind if we sit inside; it's much cooler in here than out on the hot patio."

"But of course, Lucas," Eliza said as she pulled up a chair across from him. "But before I say anything else, Lucas, I mustn't forget to thank you for putting me up here in this hotel, though it is a little highbrow for me. For I'm not really used to such luxury, as you might well know."

"Nothing is too good for you, Eliza Gunn, and I mean that," Lucas said, and his dusky lashed eyes met hers for the first time. "There's something I must say too, Eliza. Not only was I really surprised to see you here in Kingston this morning, but I was even more surprised when you said that you are in love with me. Hearing you say those words was like a dream come true.

"Eliza, I might not exactly be the innocent you might think I am. Many women have thrown themselves at me, and I must admit there were times when I almost gave in completely to their attentions. But believe you me, dear Eliza, you are the only woman I have ever wanted. I set very high standards for myself: I went back to school, studied hard, and improved my lot. Yes, Eliza, I am told I am quite articulate, but it is with humility and honesty that I am confessing that I am in love with you, foolish as it might seem, considering that we are from such different backgrounds."

Lucas got up from his chair and went to stand at the window, though it was clear that he was unconcerned with the bathers who splashed in the pool outside, or with the birdsong that permeated the air. A muscle worked at his jaw as he clenched and unclenched his fingers, and Eliza realized that he was every bit as nervous as she.

"Lucas, do you know how beautiful and fulfilling it is to hear you say that you love me?" she said, and she went to stand with him, taking his hands in hers. How comforting it felt, for his hands were warm and welcoming.

Tears flowed freely as she buried her damp cheek in his heaving chest, and when she searched out his smooth, dark face, she saw that hers were not the only tears, for Lucas' eyes too brimmed with joyful tears.

"My darling, darling Lucas," she murmured, as he cradled her in his strong arms, and she couldn't decide whether she was actually dreaming or awake.

"I hope you know I'm yours, Lucas, anytime you want me," she whispered, and her whole body trembled with the anticipation of him. But Lucas only smiled and held her even closer.

"Come, come, Eliza darling," he said softly. "If you mean what I think you do, I'll be up front with you: I don't want a casual relationship. Nothing good would come from that. And I would never want you to feel cheapened or used. To me, you are a princess, Eliza, and if I am lucky enough to ever know you sexually, I want us first to be man and wife."

"Are you serious, Lucas? Do you know how full of surprises you are? I've often heard it said that a Jamaican man would jump into bed with a woman given the flimsiest of excuses. But Lucas, what you said to me just now is contrary to that stereotype and, in fact, it was the nicest thing I could ever have heard."

Lucas leaned down to whisper in her ear, and his cheek briefly brushed against Eliza's soft cheek. "I don't suppose I am your typical Jamaican man, then," he said with a laugh, "because, not only am I a man in love, but I am a man of principle."

When his lips sought hers hungrily, she felt as though he might consume her, her fingers eagerly reaching up and burying themselves in the softness of his hair.

Chapter 13:
Army Life

"**M**aggie, I am writing you two letters. One is short and unemotional, and that is the one you will receive. In it, I can only say that I am well and that I arrived safely. I cannot tell you my location or about my rigorous training or about the friends I have met over here. There is so much I cannot say, not because I don't want to, dear Maggie, but because of regulations. One lives by rules here in the army. We are told when to get up, when to eat, and even when to rest and exercise. We are like one large body of well-oiled machinery.

"This letter, my real letter to you, is written in my heart; and someday, if God spares my life, I hope to reveal all of its contents to you in person. But now, all I am capable of is carving these words inside."

Dearest Maggie,

How I miss you. It is unfortunate that I was unable to see you before you came back from Kingston, because if I had, I would have married you before my departure. How wonderful it would have been to have addressed this letter to Maggie Gunn my darling wife.

Do you ever think about that afternoon we spent inside the banyan grove? I think about it often, because to me that was the exact moment when we stopped being two people, for we became one there. And whenever the wind blows furiously here, which is often, it brings back so many memories, and I chase that banyan wind in my mind, for it leads me back to you.

So much has happened since I came over to England, and though it is my homeland, I feel like such an outsider, a complete stranger, for at heart I have become Jamaican.

We are stationed in a base camp in the north of England, and the conditions are not that bad, but the weather can be appalling. It is rather damp and sometimes freezing cold, and many of the Jamaicans who are here have taken up smoking cigarettes, perhaps attempting to ward off the cold. I myself have an aversion to smoking, for I remember how my father was literally a slave to his cigarettes. Do you remember how he used to walk those miles into Hedley just to buy cigarettes at your shop?

Thus far, conditions here in England have been fairly stable, though there have been evacuations and war efforts on the part of civilians. At any moment, I expect my battalion to be crammed into army lorries and taken to the nearest port to be transported over to the continent, where there is action.

We, the contingent from the West Indies, were surprised when we first saw ourselves in uniform, for only then was it brought home to us that we are no longer civilians; we are now soldiers. I am known as Private 128429, and being an anonymous member of this beehive sometimes causes me to forget that I was once called Dunstan Gunn.

You'll be surprised to learn that some of us islanders have been sent off to be trained for the Royal Air Force and others for the Royal Navy, and some of us have even been sent as far north as Scotland, where I hear it is even colder. The rest of us lot will probably be designated as foot soldiers. We have been taught how to handle Bren guns, tie complex knots, drive lorries, and practise defense techniques in various forms of combat situations. Some of us, like me, have become familiar with the workings of weaponry and artillery. But there are others more skilled in the repair of combustion engines and vehicles, including tanks. Sad to say, there are contingents of ours that have gone over to the continent, and not a single man has returned. We have been advised not to dwell on those casualties, though I am sure that each of us, in his own mind, cannot help but wonder if we might be the next to go.

From the crack of dawn we are drilled. We participate in rigorous physical exercise, as well as long-distance marches. I wish you could see how lean I am, Maggie, and how they have scraped my hair off so that now it is mostly just blonde bristles. You'd laugh, Maggie; I'm sure you would.

I must also mention that there is no Jamaican food to be found at camp, not that I expected it, but it is pretty bland fare here.

However, I mustn't forget to mention that I have become friends with a chap from Kingston named Aynsford Collins. He is rather funny, and even at the worst of times, he manages to keep our spirits up. Needless to say, he is mixed race, a mulatto, sort of like tea with lots of milk. Last week, we were lucky enough to have two days' leave. Aynsford and I and a group of other Jamaican soldiers went down to London, where some relatives of his have resided since emigrating from Jamaica.

You would have been as surprised as I am by London. I'm not talking about the architecture and the crowds and the gasmasks, the shortages or the underground air raid shelters. What I am talking about is the prejudice! The black-skinned soldiers in our group were shunned everywhere we went. One man told me that it is because Americans have brought their own brand of prejudice and racial intolerance across the Atlantic. There are hundreds of Americans here, Maggie. They are verbally abusive to Negroes, and even go as far as not sharing tables in pubs with-black skinned soldiers, and a Negro soldier has next to no chance of being put up for the night in a hostel. I am not used to this kind of intolerance and I abhor it, even as a white man. How easy it is for civilians to forget that these Negro men are fighting and dying in the war in their stead.

We stayed two nights in London's East End with Aynsford's aunt, a portly woman with a heart as large as the entire universe, for all ten of us camped out in her three-bedroom home those two nights. Her name is Sheila Reynolds, and you should taste the stew peas and rice she made us! It was so good it took me right back to Gunn's Run, and ultimately to you.

I wasn't going to mention this, Maggie, but perhaps I might as well, for there is talk that my battalion is going to be sent to patrol the upper and lower Rhine, or else sent over to North Africa. It will be my first experience at the front, and I ask only for prayers as I head out. And may God protect you all at home.

Dear Maggie,
This is to let you know that I am well and have arrived safely. I hope all is well at home.
Yours truly,
Dunstan

When Maggie received this spare, unemotional letter that Dunstan had written from England, she cried. She knew absolutely nothing about the things he mentioned in the other letter, which was never to be sent. The letter had taken two months to arrive at its destination. She was excited to have received it but wept alone when she read it for, because of it, she felt entirely disconnected from Dunstan.

Hiding her tears, she avoided both Peter and Rita, who were running things at the shop and expanding the business to include an ice cream parlor. How strange it was that Peter, who was unable to stand without the use of a cane, found his niche, for his business sense was invaluable, though his interest in things scientific had not waned.

Chapter 14:
A Time of Joy, a Time of Sorrow

After Sam Chung's death, Chunty took to spending more time over at Gunn's Run. It was not only because she felt that the young married couple at home needed more time alone to get to know each other more fully, but also because she genuinely enjoyed Wilemina's company and that of Constance. All three women, though from different stations in life and racial backgrounds, were all women in grief.

Wilemina Gunn, the youngest of the three women, felt that she had grieved for far too many years, and was beginning to become more inclined to accept change and move on. She did not, however, mention a word about her feelings to the other women. Wilemina, instead, expressed her desire to visit Eliza in Kingston.

Eliza had not returned to Gunn's Run since leaving for Kingston with Maggie. It was clear, without her having to say so, that she had no desire to be separated from Lucas again. Wilemina was not pleased with the turn of events but told herself that she needed to see Eliza in person to convince her to come home. Deep inside, Wilemina knew that that would never happen, so perhaps it was the possibility of seeing Ezekiel Samuels again that enticed her.

It was a distraught Maggie who, alone in the banyan grove, shed tears in the very place where she missed Dunstan most. It was there under its shelter that she finally admitted that, after missing two menstrual cycles, there was a good possibility that she was pregnant. She had lied to Chunty concerning her bouts of morning sickness by pretending to have developed a weakness in her stomach in reaction to certain foods. Rita had recommended Peter's spare diet, but Maggie was unable to keep any of it down and was repulsed by everything that was offered. Even Peter, in his sorry state, empathized. She eventually resorted to eating plain soda crackers and drinking flat ginger ale, and she decided that no one in the household should know about her predicament.

So inordinately ashamed and disgraced was she, by what she considered her indiscretion with Dunstan, that there was no doubt in her mind that the entire Chung family would share in her disgrace. She imagined that all of Hedley's residents would consider her to be nothing more than a common stray dog that should be shunned.

Without Dunstan there to guide her, she was confused and undecided about the future. It occurred to her that, since she didn't yet show any outward signs of pregnancy, no one would know about it if she went to Kingston at the earliest convenience. Not only would she escape the inevitable country gossip, but she could have the baby and await Dunstan there where, unlike Hedley, the whole community did not know her.

After her decisive visit to the banyan grove, Maggie retired to the shop's small storage room, away from prying eyes, to put pen to paper.

Dear Aunt Phyllis,

I hope you and Uncle Aston are well. I have been wondering if it would be all right for me to visit you again. Perhaps I could even help you out in the shop. Peter and his wife Rita are running things nicely here. At times, I feel like a fifth wheel, if you know what I mean. I have been thinking of studying nursing, and I would take the opportunity to investigate the hospitals there, with that in mind.

Though my friend Eliza is in Kingston, I don't know if she has been in touch with you, for I have not heard from her recently.

Mama has often said that young married people like Peter and his wife are better off alone, and now that Mama no longer works, she spends most days over at Gunn's Run to get out of everyone's hair.

I hope to hear from you soon.

Your loving niece,

Maggie

"Eliza darling," Lucas said one morning as he drove her into the city, "I want us to be married as soon as we can. Because if we were married, we'd be living together and we would be able to express our love openly and freely every living moment of the day. It wouldn't be like it is now, darling, with you living elsewhere and me in my own home. It is such a frustration not being with you. I never knew how physically painful that could be Eliza; but believe you me, it is. It doesn't have to be an elaborate wedding, just something simple. What do you think?"

Two months had passed since Eliza had checked out of the posh Bougainvillea Manor Hotel. Lucas had found her a place to stay in a boarding house located on middle class Beechwood Avenue, outside of the downtown core. The well-kept property was owned by an East Indian couple, a Mr. and Mrs. Anthony Timol, who had been supportive of Lucas' political endeavours.

Lucas, being a man of principle, as he said he was, would not have stood for Eliza sharing his own three-bed-room home on Cargill Avenue without the benefit of marriage. No doubt he might even have given consideration to the implications that such an arrangement would have had on his budding political career.

"Lucas darling," Eliza said, reaching for his hand, as though to draw strength from him. "Of course I want to marry you as soon as possible; it's what I've always wanted. I remember how much I ached inside from being apart from you, and even now that we are in the same city, it is no better. But I'm going to be eighteen next month, on May 15. Maybe we could have our wedding then, on the beach at Gunn's Run, so that Constance can be there. It would be wonderful, wouldn't it, with the sea, the palms and the sand? Wouldn't you like that, Lucas?"

Lucas' heart beat faster. Everything had seemed unreal to him since Eliza had confessed her love for him. He had not drawn a single breath without giving thanks for that love. Every glimpse of her translucent face, her sky-blue eyes, and her hair that tumbled like a halo around her excited him. He had never felt that way about any woman, and his fear was that one day he might awake to find it had all been a fantasy. How could it be possible, he often thought, that a woman as irresistible as Eliza Gunn could actually be in love with him? What was it, he wondered, that she saw in him, and he would laugh silently to himself and praise God for such a blessing.

"But, Eliza, my dearest," he heard himself say, and his voice came out rich and resonant, "have you given any thought to your own mother coming to the wedding?"

But when Eliza didn't reply immediately, Lucas pulled the car over to stop beside a vacant lot, his forehead visibly creased with concern. "Darling Eliza," he said, "do you really think there's any chance that your mother is ready to accept your marrying a black-skinned man like me? We have to be realistic, Eliza. I really don't think she will. Colour might not matter to you, but I am sure it does to her. And another thing, darling, don't forget that she probably still thinks of me as the low-class barefoot boy who used to run around on her property."

"Lucas," Eliza said, and her eyes swam with tears, "please don't berate yourself; it really hurts. You have been such a gentleman, even my mother would have to respect you. I know she would. Granted, darling, neither of us can change the colour of our skin. But she might come round once she sees that you have made something of yourself. At your age, it is remarkable that you own a home and have been doing such good work. I wouldn't even have to mention how much we love each other. My only disappointment, Lucas, is that my dear brother Dunstan, who is away at war, can't be here at our wedding."

"Eliza," said Lucas, kissing her hand, "don't you think that perhaps it might be better if we got married right here in Kingston? We could have a small service, nothing fancy, and I could bring my mother here, for I know she would want that. She could stay in my home — there's room enough — and you could invite your mother too, so it would be entirely up to her if she wanted to come or not."

"Lucas," Eliza said, after much thought, "I have to agree with you, darling. You are more sensible than I am. Yes, let's get married here; I really don't need anything grand at all. All I need is to be your wife, regardless if Mother witnesses it or not."

Lucas moved closer to her in the car and nervously unbuttoned the top two buttons of her shirt. Feverishly, he kissed the top of her breasts, her shoulders and her warm neck, and when his hungry lips found hers, Eliza responded in kind, and it felt to her as though a jet of fire had run through her.

It was only a week or two later that Eliza was fortunate enough to have found rewarding work in downtown Kingston, volunteering her services in an alms house not far from Parade Gardens.

When first she went to the house, she had found the stench of carbolic soap, disinfectant, and the general rot associated with the poor overwhelming. However, as she had stood by the entrance, she had looked up and saw words carved into the door frame that were to have a profound effect on her: *"Come to me all you that are laboured and are burdened, and I will refresh you."*

She passed over the threshold, where several beggars had congregated, and was surprised when not even one of them accosted her. She thought perhaps it had to do with the fact that she was wearing white and they might have thought she was a nurse. She was moved by the sight of their sunken faces and the round frightened eyes of a group of three hungry children who silently followed her inside.

On entering the building, she found herself in a large, airy room. One of its two tall windows was open, and bright sunlight filtered in, and Eliza found herself missing the pungent scent of the sea. In the white haze of sunlight, she saw ragged men and women pressed up against each other on low wooden benches along the walls. She heard the low hum of their voices, hushed and murmuring, as once in a while a name was called out by someone whom Eliza imagined was employed there. The incessant waiting reminded her of when she herself had waited in Lucas' office; however, unlike those elegant surroundings, here she was confronted by the haunted faces of Kingston's poverty-stricken.

She had never encountered such a place, nor was she ever exposed to such curious odours. Moving slowly through the room, she hardly dared let a breath escape her, for surely her eyes would swim with tears that she feared might spill over. Towards the back of the room, she noticed a doorway that led to a small kitchen-like addition. She peered inside and noticed its sooty walls and grease splattering, and atop an old kerosene stove were huge soup pots bubbling. Flour, sugar and rice stored in wide mouth bottles stood on a rickety shelf, and on the floor in a wooden crate were bottles of iodine, strong disinfectants, rags, and brown soap. Outside the door where she had stood were carton boxes filled with filthy, discarded clothes and what Eliza assumed must be soiled bedding gone ragged and torn.

As she turned towards the large room she had first encountered, it seemed to Eliza that it was no better than a war zone, for all around her in that room was a field of broken souls.

One of the female employees, who had been occupied with darting about the room trying to attend to one case or another, encountered Eliza in her wandering, threw her a roll of bandages, and beckoned to her to follow. Before long, Eliza was to find herself ensconced in the unmatched odour of unwashed bodies and clothing, as she gave the woman whom she came to know as Vivian a helping hand. Everywhere Eliza rested her eyes was evidence of the good work done by the hard-working employees and a smattering of volunteers, and it inspired her.

At first, her duties were light ones and included distributing milk and a few morsels of food, but she had never felt as useful.

The old and the battered came daily, not only to request food, but often perhaps just for a cot to lie on. Eliza was moved to offer assistance, though it might be nothing more than a kind word. She encountered women there, no older than herself, burdened with three or more children in tow and with nothing to offer their starving offspring. She saw them day after day and wondered how they found strength in their ravished bodies to even have dragged themselves there.

The alms house was known among those masses as the "poor house", and a large percentage of Kingston's underbelly was entirely dependent on it for sustenance. The needy of indeterminable ages came as a result of the war's detrimental effect on Jamaica's economy. For not only did the war in Europe drain Jamaica's natural resources but, lately, it had also drained her manpower.

There were those Eliza saw in the poor house with open sores, missing limbs and various deformities, who were directly affected by circumstances and unable to find employment or afford medical assistance.

The small amount of funds that helped to keep the house operational came from the government, and an ever smaller amount of funds came from donations garnered from church parishioners. But even Eliza, the newcomer, was aware that the house operated on a shoestring, and that every new day threatened closure.

At first, even the hard-working staff might have been suspicious of Eliza's presence and her motives for being there. But most unusual, they thought, was to find a young white woman volunteering to work shoulder to shoulder with them. It did not go without their noticing that she would daily roll up her sleeves and, in true service, take on back-breaking tasks without complaint.

It took two months to garner their trust, and Eliza was made responsible for cooking the thin vegetable broths ladled out in such shelters. Her days were divided, working in the hot kitchen and assisting the other staff with their various duties, and finally, exhausted, she would be driven home to the boarding house by Lucas Paynado.

Everyone was aware of Lucas' political connections, but they were beside themselves with wondering what his connection to their Eliza was. It was no surprise that Eliza Gunn was beloved, and she came to be known amongst the needy and the poor as "Lady Eliza".

One afternoon, leaving early from work and feeling adventurous, Eliza decided to try to find her own way to Uncle Aston's haberdashery. She telephoned Lucas' office and left a message with his secretary to tell him to pick her up at Chin Yap's Haberdashery, an hour later than was usual. As she was leaving the compound of the alms house, a lame boy on crutches, whom she knew as Ivan came up to her at the gate and smiled at her.

"You going home, Lady Eliza?" he asked.

"No, Ivan, I was actually going to try to find Chin Yap's Haberdashery on Barry Street."

"Then I will walk with you, Ma'am. Is not safe for you to walk alone."

"Thank you, Ivan. Is it far?"

"No, Ma'am, it not far, but all kind a bad people bout here."

"Are you sure about that, Ivan?"

"Yes, Ma'am."

As Eliza walked alongside the young boy, she found herself involved in deep conversation with him. He pointed out dangerous lanes, rum shops to avoid, suspicious persons who might be pickpockets, and even those persons who Eliza thought appeared indifferent but who Ivan said were petty criminals, who posed as yardboys and could wield sharp machetes dangerously, with no intention of gardening. There were others, Ivan said, who had knives hidden on their persons, to use as prospective weapons. Ivan knew them all, but Eliza was never sure if his observations were astute or coming from his active imagination. Most surprising to Eliza though, was how many of Kingston's poor knew her. "Good afternoon, Lady Eliza. You out for a walk?" was what most of them said as she passed by and acknowledged them.

As soon as they approached Barry Street, Eliza recognized where she had stayed with Maggie, and she stopped on the pavement outside the shop.

"Thanks, Ivan, you were a wonderful escort," she said with a smile. "Here's a shilling for your trouble."

Ivan grinned broadly as he accepted the shilling and leaned heavily on his crutch.

"Is true that you going get married, Lady Eliza?" he said mischievously, his ears burning with curiosity.

"How did you know I'm getting married, Ivan?"

"Everybody knows, and them say is a black skin man you going marry, but me don't believe that, Ma'am."

"Well, Ivan, they are right. Mr. Paynado is black, and I love him very much."

"Lady Eliza, me going go tell everybody what you did say, and me glad to hear."

Chapter 15:
Friends among Foes

Mother, I cannot write you a letter with all the details that you might require, so I am passing this information on to a friend, Aynsford Collins. He and I have made a pact that, in the event that one of us does not survive this war, the other will inform both our families of the details of our existence over here. These are the things I have told him:

As a result of fierce battles and relentless enemy action on the European front, our training was intensified, leaving no real opportunity for most of us to write home. We were suddenly informed of our imminent departure from England over to the continent and were told to be ready at a moment's notice.

I will not forget how convoys of army lorries sped through the beautiful English countryside as they carried hundreds of us soldiers away from the relative safety of our camps and on to where we might be met with certain death in intense direct attacks. Neither will I forget how the skies seemed so clear that *day, and how the greenery that met my eyes became, in my own mind, the greenery of the trees and the bright foliage I left behind at Gunn's Run. How I longed for the scent of the Caribbean Sea that lapped along our shores at home.*

I was drunk with memories of our island, even as I told myself that I would be fighting for the mother country where I was born and have taken up arms against her enemies.

Over here, no one even knows I'm English. For all purposes, I am considered an outsider, and strange as it might seem, it is the Jamaicans whom I have met over here who have embraced me as one of their own.

Aynsford Collins, a fellow Jamaican, has proved to be a brave and faithful friend.

There have been times when, under fire, Aynsford and I, in staunch defense amongst allied forces, stood side by side in deep, muddy trenches, like blood brothers as we sprayed the advancing enemy with our bullets, meeting fire with fire. Those are the moments when one feels closest to God, those moments when one is within a hair's breadth of death. I have found that one becomes more human and less humane on a battlefield, though death and suffering rage around us. I don't know how often I have seen fellow soldiers blown to bits and incapacitated by bombings and machine gun fire. Though when first I saw such despicable things, I was as sickened, as were many of my comrades. The sight of bloody guts, slimy gore, and splintered bones in clumps of flesh scattered for miles over these foreign fields and valleys serves to remind each of us that such carnage is as a result of the ominous doom we ourselves inflicted on an enemy. Often I have to remind myself that all those scattered entrails and dismembered limbs were once young men who lived and breathed alongside us as soldiers. Even as we dug trenches, hiding the evidence as it were, our minds could not find rest, as we, the harbingers of death, have not forgiven ourselves for our deeds.

I have been told that, as a soldier, I will develop a mindset able to bear the heavy losses and suffering that comes with circumstances of war; and in some instances, it is said, one even comes to welcome death. I have found that I for one am vulnerable and perhaps even soft, for indeed there is a difficulty in having to forgive one's self. What if our superior officers, lieutenants, and lance corporals are wrong? And how often am I to find myself crying out for God's mercy, asking him to keep us poor devils safe in the hollow of his hand?

Surrounded by enemy attack, one contemplates things that should never be contemplated. What if the prayers of the enemy soldiers are more earnest than my own? Is God watching out for the enemy's family as He watches over mine, and in the end, whose side is He on, if any? Or has He abandoned us all in this horrific monstrosity that we call war?

Not a day goes by without my thinking of you, my beloved mother, and my young sister Eliza, and often Maggie too. Each night when I cannot sleep, I say prayers for all of you, and pray that I will survive to see you again. How lucky Peter Chung is to be away from this hell, where each day could well be our last, and where death's seductive scent lives inside our nostrils and in the very air we breathe. I have had friends who were not as fortunate as I, for though I have received wounds, gashes and burns on these alien battlefields, and even at one time was temporarily blinded in a blast, I give thanks to God, and to our brave men. One such man is Aynsford, my friend, who risked his own life to drag me and two other men to safety just before there was an explosion near to where we were stationed. He and a handful of others surely will be among those recommended for a gallantry decoration.

When and if Aynsford survives this action and he ever comes to see you at Gunn's Run on my behalf, please treat him with the love, respect and humility that I know you are capable of, for he might well be my very last friend.

Chapter 16:
Following the Heart

Dear Mother,

I hope you are keeping well.

I know how much you must be missing Dunstan, for I miss him too. Has there been any word from him? I think of him often and hope that God will spare him.

But before I continue, Mother, I want you to know that I am writing this from a boarding house where I have been living for over two months. Lucas and I do not live together, although he owns a lovely home not far from where I am. He says he does not want anything to tarnish my reputation. Mother, he is every bit the kind and gentle person I always thought he was. He has been a perfect gentleman. You will be happy to know he has not compromised me in any way, though it is I who might have wanted more from him, which brings me to the very reason why I am writing this letter to you.

Mother, I am hoping you will be happy to learn that Lucas and I will be getting married in two weeks time on May 15th, my birthday.

We both want you to join us in celebrating our union. Lucas has invited his mother Constance, who will stay in Lucas' home for a few days. You could stay there too, unless of course you would rather make other arrangements. But it would make my happiness complete if you would only come.

Since Lucas is a Catholic, Mother, we have decided to be married at the St. Peter and Paul Church, situated here in Kingston.

Mother, I must confess that I have never been happier, and I hope that you will share in my joy.

I love you very much.

Your daughter,

Eliza

When Eliza wrote that letter, she thought better of mentioning that she was working amongst Kingston's poor. She expected that her mother would be repulsed by what she would imagine about the work and would become overprotective of her child.

Eliza did not even mention that she had initially stayed with Maggie's relatives, or even about her stay at the hotel. For it would seem that she had learned that in life there were often things that were best left unsaid. Perhaps that was why she also did not mention her recent visit to see Aunt Phyllis and Uncle Aston.

That day when young Ivan, the lame boy, had hurried off with the shiny shilling in his hand, Eliza had held her head high with pride, for Ivan was the first to share the news of her engagement. No doubt word would spread, and she felt that soon enough all of Kingston would know about her commitment to Lucas Paynado.

She had walked into the haberdashery with confidence in her stride and was somewhat relieved to find that the stock had hardly changed, and she was not disappointed.

"Is you that, Eliza?" Uncle Aston said in disbelief, looking up from his ledger to see young Eliza looking flushed and radiant, running her slim fingers over the bedding, cutlery and glass dishes as though remembering every item with fondness.

"We did think you forget about us." Uncle Aston laughed as he came and took both her hands in his. "You look so well. How is things?"

"I'm well, Uncle Aston," she said, "and I have so much to tell you."

"Phyllis, come quick, look who come to see us!" Uncle Aston shouted, his voice quivered with such pride that Aunt Phyllis hurried from the kitchen and, to her astonishment, found Eliza in the shop. It had crossed her mind many a time that Eliza would never come back to see them, yet here she was, on the contrary.

"How nice that you come back, Eliza," Aunt Phyllis said, embracing the younger woman, with tears welling in her eyes. "You look good and is just the other day I hear from Maggie. She's coming to visit us again. We feel glad cause we really miss having young people like you in the house."

"I'm getting married," Eliza said shyly, squeezing both their hands. "Lucas Paynado and I are getting married very soon."

Aunt Phyllis grinned broadly. "Congratulations," she said, holding Eliza at arm's length. "Just look at you — you turn big woman now. Does Mr. Paynado know how lucky him is to get a pretty girl like you? Not that he not handsome himself, but is just that me never did expect ..."

"Come, come, Phyllis. Look how Eliza so happy,"

Uncle Aston said. "Congratulations are in order. It don't matter one bit that him is black-skinned and she is a white girl."

"Yes, is true," Aunt Phyllis said, peering intensely at Eliza, as though unconvinced that the match could be an ideal one. "And you know what?" she said finally. "You couldn't look any happier. I'm going have to admit that Mr. Paynado must be very good for you."

"Thanks, Aunt Phyllis, he is the best thing that has ever happened to me."

"Well," Uncle Aston said, "I must go to the storage room to get us a bottle of wine. It's the best we can offer on an occasion like this."

Reluctantly, Uncle Aston let go of Eliza's warm hand and retreated to the back of the store.

"Maybe you should wait until Mr. Paynado comes," Eliza said, but her voice trailed off, for Uncle Aston, in his eagerness, was already out of the room.

"Aunt Phyllis," Eliza said, "I was about to tell Uncle Aston that I left a message for Mr. Paynado to pick me up here after work."

"You mean to say he's coming here?" Aunt Phyllis said excitedly. "That's the first thing you should have told me. I can't believe that the well-known Mr. Lucas Paynado is actually coming to this shop! I'd better go straighten up the place."

"Don't go to any trouble, Aunt Phyllis. Lucas won't notice a thing," Eliza laughed. "Believe me, he has seen worse, and I should know."

"So where you getting married Eliza?" Uncle Aston asked, returning from the storage room bearing a large bottle of Madeira red wine in one hand and a tea towel slung over the other.

"It don't matter where she getting married, Aston,"

Aunt Phyllis said, sounding fussy. "The point is that she is getting married, and that's that. Anyway, let me go rinse out some wine glasses, cause Eliza just tell me that the famous Mr. Paynado is on him way here."

"Wait, Aunt Phyllis," Eliza said as she gently held on to Aunt Phyllis' hand in order to detain her. "First, I'd like to invite you both to my wedding. Please come, because if you only knew how Uncle Aston's good deeds have inspired me... this gesture of mine, is my way of saying thanks."

A week before the wedding was to take place, a small announcement appeared in bold type in The Gleaner:

Lucas Simon Paynado, Kingston's PNP affiliate, takes pleasure in announcing his engagement and upcoming nuptials to Eliza Lydia Gunn of Saint James. No further details have been released at the present time.

Word of the upcoming wedding quickly spread across the island, and especially amongst Kingston's working classes and the poor.

The morning the announcement appeared, one Jenny Abbot, a brown-skinned forty-year old woman from Ocho Rios read the announcement, and a cruel smile played on her lips. "Who the hell Lucas Paynado think him is?" she grumbled out loud. "Is how come him don't know that I love him, and now just look at him bold as brass getting married and all."

Hers was not the only sentiment of resentment, for almost every woman who had at some time set her cap for Lucas was gravely disappointed by the news. When it was discovered that Eliza was white, the tongues wagged even more; and it was widely assumed that Eliza must be rich and that Lucas was after her money.

There were those in Kingston's inner social circle, however, who were in the know. They wished the couple well and though the wedding was to have been a small affair with no grand celebration, those in that inner circle provided food and planned a celebration. It was well known amongst them that Lucas Paynado had come from the humblest of beginnings and had no family that could have provided for him.

Huge pots of curried goat, rice and peas, potato salad, bowls of tossed salad and coleslaw arrived at the church hall on the morning of the wedding — testament to the respect garnered amongst Lucas Paynado's peers.

Lucas' secretary Jane recommended a dress shop on King Street to Eliza and, because Jane's uncle was the store's manager, Eliza was given a discount on a wedding dress that had been gathering dust in the shop's storage room.

It was a washerwoman who worked at Eliza's boarding house who took on the daunting task of washing by hand the delicate silk, lace and netting fabrics of the long white dress and veil. When it was finally ironed and hung up, Eliza was convinced that that dress was the most stunning she had ever seen.

When Lucas heard about the meticulous ordeal involved in washing the dress, he couldn't keep himself from laughing out loud. "Remember when I used to do your washing Eliza?" he said. "It's a good thing that I'm not the one doing it now."

"You never washed a day in your life, Lucas," Eliza teased. "Everyone knew that it was those women at the river who did it for you."

Wilemina Gunn read Eliza's letter more than once and, with it in hand, went to find Constance, who still resided in the shack on her property. Unknown to her, Constance had refused to leave her, though more than once Lucas had invited her to share his home. No one could explain the loyalty Constance felt regarding Wilemina, though some people said that her gratitude to the English woman was only natural, since it was Wilemina Gunn who had given her a home when she had nothing but her son and the clothes on their backs.

As Wilemina walked quickly along the bushy path, she found herself remembering many things that had long passed. Jonathan might have walked here with Isilda before he met his death, she thought to herself, and dear Dunstan might even have played here as a boy. And sure enough, my Eliza must have found her way here too, for didn't she use to carry canisters of food for Constance? Most likely that was when she met Lucas.

She took note of the fields and fertile fruit trees, some of which she herself had planted, and it occurred to her just how isolated she was. She reflected upon the rising violence on the island, which had made the news, and thought herself lucky to have been spared. Perhaps, indeed she thought, Lucas Paynado did, after all, have a hand in securing the property from harm as a direct result of his connections. Not only must he have watched out for his mother, but all at Gunn's Run as well.

Constance was hanging out laundry when Wilemina found her, for she had recently boiled her clothing over coals in an old kerosene drum. Steam rose from the slews of wet and dripping clothes as she carefully hung them out on a makeshift clothesline just outside the shack. Though Constance's back was bent into the work, she looked up sharply, having heard the crackle of twigs under Wilemina's feet.

"Oh is you, Mrs. Gunn," she said. "I was wondering who that was walking bout on a fine afternoon like this."

"Yes, Constance, it's me. I came because of Lucas. No doubt you already know he's planning to marry my Eliza."

"Yes, Ma'am, I did get word bout that. Lucas send a man to come tell me, and then me go use the phone at the Chung's shop. Them have phone now, you know. So Lucas himself tell me on the phone. That's why I'm leaving for Kingston tomorrow, and I going take these clean clothes. Lucas says he going buy me a nice new dress and a hat and shoes for the wedding, when I get there. No wonder I always did say that him is the nicest boy a mother could ever have. I am real happy for your daughter. You going to the wedding, Ma'am?"

Wilemina sighed deeply. Any words she had planned to say in disapproval of the wedding seemed to vanish like the steam that floated from the clothing hanging on the line. Constance's genuine sincerity and anticipation of the celebratory event touched Wilemina, who could almost feel the first crack in her frozen heart.

"I wouldn't miss my daughter's wedding for anything, Constance," Wilemina said. "I'm hiring a car to take me to Kingston in the morning, and I wondered if you'd join me."

"Thanks, Mrs. Gunn, that is real nice of you. I was going take the bus that pass through Hedley, but it is a lot of rigmarole, so if you mean it, Ma'am, I will take up your offer."

Ezekiel Samuels read the wedding announcement while breakfasting on the terrace of his home. The house, recently bought, was situated in the hills of St. Andrew and overlooked Kingston. From that vantage, Ezekiel could enjoy the distinct impression the location gave of living both in the city and the country, since his property was secluded and wooded, yet close to the city.

He read the announcement a second time, realizing that the Eliza mentioned might indeed be the Eliza Gunn he knew.

"So little Eliza is getting married," he said out loud, though no one, not even his lone servant, was there to listen. He went to stand at the edge of the terrace, looked down at the sprawling city below, and wondered about Eliza's whereabouts. It occurred to him that she might well be at Gunn's Run, or even in the city, and he promised himself that he would visit Lucas Paynado's office that morning to find out. He had never met Lucas but often saw his photograph and his name mentioned in political situations in the paper. But he had never once associated the bright young man with the Gunns of Gunn's Run.

He thumbed through an old copy of The Gleaner until at last he found what he was looking for. There it was: a captioned photograph of Lucas Paynado speaking to an audience of farm workers. "Paynado talks politics", it read.

"I wonder what Wilemina must think of all this?" Ezekiel said aloud, noticing, as though for the first time, Lucas' dusky complexion and smoldering, long-lashed eyes. He found himself remembering how happy Eliza had been as a child when surrounded in the schoolyard by her black-skinned schoolmates.

"I suppose this was to be expected," Ezekiel said, finishing his coffee and tossing the rest of his toast to some hungry sparrows. The whole day lay before him and, having made plans for the morning, he was more than anxious to get on with the day.

It was almost ten o'clock before Ezekiel Samuels found himself at Lucas' Hope Road office. He had to reschedule some of his own appointments, with parents and teachers, regarding a small festival of storytelling and music, which he was organizing. Visionary that he was, Ezekiel had felt that there was a need to preserve the island's stories and songs for future generations. He planned to eventually compile them into a book, since many storytellers and music performers had come forward, knowing that the proceeds from the event would be channelled to provide monetary support for the Allies in Europe, and thus the Jews.

"Good Morning, Sir," the receptionist at Lucas' office said the moment she laid eyes on him. There was no mistaking the admiring glances she had sneaked his way, for Ezekiel Samuels cut a fine figure in his grey trousers, crisp white shirt, and red and blue tie, not to mention that he was the most handsome man she had seen in days. "How can I help you?" she asked.

Ezekiel smiled as he ran a hand through his dark hair which, despite his approaching middle age, still had the youthful tendency of flopping over one side of his face. "I was wondering," he said, "if there is any chance that I might speak with Mr. Paynado."

The receptionist fumbled idly amongst the loose papers on her desk, perhaps as an effort on her part to prolong the interaction with Ezekiel. Then at last, meeting his eyes, she returned his smile. "Who should I say is here, Sir?"

"My name is Ezekiel Samuels. Mr. Paynado doesn't know me, but I would be much obliged if you would please tell him that I'm here about the wedding."

"Very well, Sir."

Ezekiel had no longer than a three-minute wait before Lucas Paynado himself, dressed in a smart business suit, came out from his office to meet him. Ezekiel couldn't help but be impressed with the young man's manners, good looks and decorum, for Lucas greeted him warmly and offered him a cigarette from a silver cigarette case.

"I'm Lucas Paynado," Lucas said. "Allow me to light that for you. I don't smoke myself, otherwise, I would join you."

Ezekiel's grip was firm, pressing Lucas' hand. "Thanks, but I don't smoke either," he said.

Lucas laughed as he directed Ezekiel into his office, and already the two men felt camaraderie between them.

"I actually cultivated the habit of having that cigarette case handy," Lucas said with a grin, "because, when I first started working, I worked under an old Englishman named Bancroft Chambers who taught me everything he knew. Mr. Chambers used to say that there was nothing warmer than a good cigarette among good men. He left the island, but I never once let on to him that I never smoked. Have a seat, Mr. Samuels. There's more privacy here in my office."

"Congratulations, Mr. Paynado," Ezekiel said, sitting down across from Lucas. "I understand you are getting married to one Eliza Gunn. I read the announcement in The Gleaner and have been wondering, ever since, if the Eliza mentioned is the daughter of Wilemina Gunn?"

"Yes, Mr. Samuels, Eliza's mother's name is Wilemina. Are you acquainted with the Gunns?"

"Yes, Mr. Paynado, though you might not have known me. I was originally from Hedley and have been friends with the Gunns for years. I unfortunately became quite out of touch with them over the past few years. Lately, I have found myself wondering quite often about lovely Wilemina. I felt privileged to have known her and her husband Jonathan Gunn. He was as fine a man, as you could know. You might already have heard tell, Mr. Paynado, that Jonathan Gunn met a brutal end on those cliffs, not far from their home. Does Eliza still live there, and what about her brother Dunstan? I remember he was a good student; I hope he has turned out well."

As Ezekiel spoke, Lucas realized that the man's carefully chosen words betrayed hidden longings. What is he not saying? Lucas wondered, and in his mind he worked out the pieces of the strange puzzle that resulted from the very things that Ezekiel had not said. Is it possible, Lucas wondered, that this man sitting across from him, who speaks so disarmingly, was once, or still is a man in love?

"Mr. Samuels," Lucas said leaning forward conspiratorially and speaking quite low to prevent his words from being carried to anyone else except the man before him, "Mrs. Gunn is well, and I should know, because my mother lives on the property in a shack that was built there some years ago. That's where I first met Eliza. At first I thought she would be just a little white brat from the backra house, who wouldn't want to have any thing to do with us. But she used to bring food for me and my mother. I hardly even dared look at her then, for she was just a child of eleven or so. But the funny thing is, Mr. Samuels, every now and again, I used to catch her staring at me, and I was foolish enough to think that she was secretly laughing at our poverty. But I was wrong, Mr. Samuels. Eliza is both compassionate and kind. She got to know my mother and myself quite well, because sometimes she would spend hours with us as she played with her dolls. I was in my teens then, and a little bit wild, I suppose; but one day, almost like a revelation, I knew that someday I would marry that girl. I told myself that I had no choice but to get away from the property and improve myself. You see, Mr. Samuels, I knew even then that I would have to earn the right to one day ask her to be my wife."

"But what became of your mother, Mr. Paynado? How did she manage alone?" Ezekiel Samuels asked, leaning into the delicious story and listening.

"Oh, I occasionally went back to see my mother, of course, and I often sent her a little something whenever I could afford it, though I knew she was provided for at Gunn's Run. I have never failed to keep her informed of my whereabouts, and about what I was doing to improve myself. But I warned her to keep her mouth shut about me, and I took great precautions to stay out of sight of the Gunns, especially Eliza, and as the years passed, I knew she was growing up too. But one day, as fate would have it, I ran into Mrs. Gunn in the bushland. It was quite rainy that day, but she seemed quite fearless on encountering me, a strange black man barring her way in that isolated place. You see, Mr. Samuels, I had grown into a man and she must not have recognized me, and there was no way that she could have known that, basically, I'm harmless. So, as she didn't know that, I couldn't help but admire her courage."

"Well, well, well, Mr. Paynado. What did Wilemina do then? Did she figure out who you were? She can be quite astute, you know. I have often wondered if she had seen through me, for I am a very private man."

"Mr. Samuels, I had better explain that I had gone to

Hedley that day to speak with a group of men assigned by me to watch the Gunn's property. I was just returning from making sure that that job was being done, when I encountered Mrs. Gunn. I must admit to the fact that I had recently began to make something of myself, and that must have been what caused me to be cockier than I usually am. I remember that, after I told her who I was, I went as far as confessing to her that one day I was going to marry Eliza."

"Yikes! That must have thrown her for a loop." Ezekiel laughed. "I wouldn't be surprised if she thought you were about to rape her right there in the bush; then, the next thing she knows, you're talking about marrying her daughter. How did she react to that?"

"She laughed at me, Mr. Samuels, as though it was the most preposterous thing, and when I let it slip that I was the reason they were all safe from violence at Gunn's Run, Mrs. Gunn laughed at me again in total disbelief. But little did she know that the black boy she once knew had pulled up his socks. It is a long story Mr. Samuels but, in my travels, as I said before, I was lucky enough to be taken under the wing of the entrepreneur Bancroft Chambers and his late wife Gertie, who lived here in Kingston and had no children of their own. Their generosity financed my education, taught me always to be well mannered, to dress well, and to speak with conviction. When Gertie Chambers passed away a year ago, she left a three-bedroom house she owned on Cargill Avenue, for me in her will. I remember, every morning when I got up, she used to always say, 'Look at the man you see in the mirror, and go make him proud today.'"

"So, Mr. Paynado, what did you say became of old Bancroft Chambers?"

"He's still alive, Mr. Samuels, but he left the island. He lives in Panama now, where he's retired to a cattle farm he owns there. I would safely say that he is still a real champion for the underprivileged."

"So I see, Mr. Paynado, so I see."

Chapter 17:
Happening Over There

Even as Lucas Paynado spoke, German forces across the Atlantic had been suffering heavy naval losses, though they remained more determined than ever to gain control of more European nations. Both Britain and France had hastily sent troops to join the Allied forces at the front in an effort to prevent further invasions. However, many of their campaigns were riddled with bad planning, and the troops found themselves exposed and vulnerable without benefit of air cover and adequate supplies. As a result, many Allied soldiers were killed or severely injured in the resulting near-massacres, as Germany managed to gain an upper hand.

Though British shipping, as well as Britain herself, was considered in mortal danger, Dunstan Gunn and Aynsford Collins were amongst the fortunate few to have survived some of the deadly confrontations. There was talk of sending home some of the beaten, battle-weary men with the hope of recharging them and attending to the more seriously wounded.

However, many British troops who planned to cross the channel from the French coast were alarmed to find legions of German patrols and tanks advancing through rural France. It was of little comfort to learn on the wireless that Britain would be sending a few additional squadrons and RAF fighters. It was also well known that Sir Hugh Dowding, head of Fighter Command, opposed that tactic, for he felt that Britain would have needed four times the defense that they could actually send. In the end, he was successful in convincing the War Cabinet minister that it was more feasible for squadrons to operate over France from British bases.

However, after four days of journeying towards the French coast, a ragtag, exhausted troop of famished soldiers that included Dunstan Gunn thought they were lucky to have found what they had assumed was an abandoned farmhouse. Rations had run low, the journey was burdensome, and night was falling. Therefore, it was decided that the men would share a meagre meal and rest in the house for the night before commencing on their cautious journey through the European countryside.

The young lieutenant in charge, Gavin Powell, was first to notice that the door to the farmhouse seemed to be have been left purposely ajar. Brandishing weapons, he organized a search outside the building and, on finding the ground floor of the house deserted, decided that all was well.

Having entered the house, the men gathered around a long wooden table in the kitchen and were about to partake of rations when they were surprised to hear muffled sounds coming from a large bin in the kitchen's storage area.

"What the hell is that?" one of the men hissed.

"Could be a rat," said another.

"I hope to God it's not one of those damn Nazis!" said Aynsford, who had kept his weapon close at hand.

With guns at alert, two of the men went to investigate and on lifting the lid on the bin, they found, covered in grain, a trembling old man who must have been the farmer.

No language was necessary to understand that the old man had been hiding from someone or something dangerous. None of the troop spoke French, and therefore none of them were made aware of the full extent of the old man's fears.

The farmer eyed the uniformed men suspiciously and perhaps even more so, since some of them were black-skinned. But he seemed to relax, realizing that the soldiers meant him no harm. He stuck his hand inside the grain bin and retrieved a bulging cloth sack containing two bottles of homemade wine, a loaf of bread, and some cheese, all of which he willingly handed over to the soldiers.

The grateful men ate in silence, hardly noticing that the old man, who did not partake of the meal, preoccupied himself with nervously watching the doors and windows.

The men, six of whom were Jamaican nationals, were well aware that there was going to be at least a half a day's more journeying to the docks, where boats would transport them over to England. It wasn't any wonder that they surmised that the good wine and food might well be their last meal before reaching England.

"Dunstan," said Aynsford from across the broad oak kitchen table, "you probably wouldn't have guessed it from my foolhardiness, but I had military training in Jamaica before I came over here. But back home, you'd be hard-pressed to know that a war is going on over here because even in Kingston, many people feel distanced from war. It is a case of life going on as usual, if you ask me."

"That might be true," a Jamaican soldier named Alexander Douglas said, "but don't forget that they have all kinds of island-wide shortages and restrictions that affect everybody."

"Where did you get your training, Aynsford?" an English private asked as he broke off a piece of the cheese.

"Well, we all know about the military presence at Up Park Camp in Kingston," Aynsford said, "but I was trained up in the hills of Newcastle. It is not easy to get up there, because getting there involves a long, difficult climb on a steep, narrow, winding mountain road. But despite all that, there are civilian houses along the way, precariously perched at the very edges of those dangerous cliffs. Everyone up there is accustomed to seeing uniformed men in the vicinity. They wouldn't bat an eye if you or I walked by."

"I was trained there too," said Rudolph Clarke, a mulatto. "There is a POW camp there too, though none of you, besides Aynsford, might know about it. But I remember an instance when a young Italian POW managed to escape confinement and got lost in the wild bush up there on the mountain. Even civilians got involved in the huge search for him."

"Yes, yes," said Aynsford, joining in with a laugh, "and I hear that most of the people who live on that mountainside are either mulatto like us, Rudolph, or are even white. They say that the Italian POW must have mistaken those Jamaican civilians for Europeans when he encountered them, because they say that he tried to speak to them in every language you could think of. People still laugh about how he was babbling away in foreign tongues, but to no avail."

"So did they ever catch him?" Dunstan grinned as he eased his chair back. From his angle, he was able to glance momentarily out the kitchen's one window and noticed how dark the night sky had become, and he felt as though something ominous was in the air but not wanting to sound foolish, he did not mention it to the other men.

"Yes, he was caught all right," Aynsford said and laughed, "but here's something that might amuse you. Some of you might not know how hot it is in Jamaica. Well, let's put it this way: It is very, very hot there. I heard stories that many a British officer at our camps back home would attempt to fire up the Jamaican soldiers by referring to them as 'lazy buggers', especially if they marched too slowly under our relentlessly boiling sun. However, it was those sorry men who had the last laugh when their disciplinarian superior officers, unable to bear the intense heat, would faint flat out in front of their men."

"Okay, men, enough of this revelry," the lieutenant said, silencing the men's laughter and furtively eying the staircase behind him, perhaps imagining a warm bed awaiting him upstairs. "I suggest we all get a good night's rest before setting out again first thing in the morning." He headed for the stairs, but the old farmer stood stubbornly in front of him and barred his way.

"What's he on about?" the lieutenant asked in exasperation. "Go see what's up there, Private Gunn. You too, Hastings. But be careful."

Slowly and carefully, Dunstan and Private Lloyd Hastings ascended the stairs, guns at a ready. At the top of the landing, they found three doors and quickly investigated the first of the rooms, only to find nothing except an old sewing machine, a bale of rough cloth, and some spools of thread. Storming the second room, Privates Dunstan Gunn and Hastings found not only that the floor was covered in blood stains but that there was a double bed, heavy with quilts, that had been carelessly shoved around the room, judging by the deep, bloody scratches on the floor made by the bed's metal legs.

They approached the bed cautiously and pulled back the thick quilts, stunned to find an old woman lying dead in a pool of drying blood. Half of her face was blown off, and she was naked from the waist down. No doubt she had been repeatedly raped.

Once back out in the hall, the two privates realized that the reason they had not seen bloody boot prints on the landing was because someone, perhaps the farmer, had taken the trouble to wipe them away. They immediately investigated the third room and found a dead Nazi officer lying face down in his own blood, a pitchfork protruding from his back.

"There's a dead woman up here, and a dead Nazi officer too!" Dunstan shouted to the others downstairs, and the farmer who thus far had used no words either in French or even in English, finally broke down, and the words that came from his throat seemed to come from a long way off. "Nazi," he said. "It was Nazi."

The following morning, just before dawn, the soldiers packed up their belongings and readied for their long trek to the coast.

"We should perhaps bury the dead," the young lieutenant said. "The farmer is too old to do it on his own.

Some of us should keep going, while three or four of you could remain behind to do the job. It shouldn't take long. You might even be able to catch up with the rest of us within an hour or so, if you move quickly.Which ones of you will volunteer to remain behind?"

"I will," said Dunstan Gunn.

"Me too," said Mick Johnson, a Scottish national.

"And me," Aynsford Collins said, joining them.

Last to volunteer was Trevor Edwards, a young farmhand from the midlands in England.

It was to be the wisest decision those four men ever made, for later that morning, a mere three miles away from where the farmhouse stood, the troop on route to the coast was ambushed by a large Nazi contingent in a wooded copse. The British troop was outnumbered, and every last man was massacred.

Dunstan and the other three privates were unaware of the fate met by the rest of the troop. They buried the two bodies and were putting away their digging implements in readiness to leave, when they saw the farmer hurrying across the very field where his wife was buried. He was waving his hands and screaming something in French, when suddenly he was hit in the back by a sniper's bullet. The four soldiers watched in stunned horror as the intensity of the fatal blast lifted the old man off the ground, only to have his lifeless body fall splayed, in his cultivated field.

A troop of Nazis descended on the farmland, perhaps to search for their missing man, the man whom Dunstan

Gunn had found murdered upstairs in the farmhouse.

Not a shot was fired. The four soldiers were taken prisoner, staring down the barrels of enemy guns.

Chapter 18:
A New Home

Maggie arrived in Kingston by train on the afternoon of May 12. She had been ill while travelling and was told by a fellow passenger that if she kept her head between her legs, the nausea would pass. But finally unable to hold back any longer, she hung her head out the window. A blast of warm air greeted her as she spilled her guts outside.

She had never felt so ill, and she couldn't wait for the train to finally come to a stop in Kingston.

Uncle Aston met her at the station and though he had said not a word, he thought she looked wasted and poorly.

"How was the trip?" he asked, avoiding her eyes as he took her suitcase.

"It was fine," Maggie replied, even as she felt bile gathering in her throat.

"So, Maggie, you hear that you friend Eliza getting married in a few days time?" Uncle Aston asked, the two of them walking side by side towards the large arched doors that led outside.

"Is that true?" Maggie replied. But though she sounded calm, her heart leapt, for she felt that she should have been the one who was getting married. "No, Uncle Aston, we didn't hear anything," she said. "Eliza must be busy with the planning."

"Well, Maggie, Eliza herself came to our shop and invited me and your aunt to the wedding. You should come too."

"Oh no," Maggie said, growing more fearful, thinking that if Eliza saw her, she might learn her dreadful secret. No doubt she would realize that Dunstan was the father and then everyone else would know too. "She would have asked me if she wanted me to come, Uncle Aston."

"Nonsense, Maggie, me and Aunt Phyllis are going to the service. You going have to come with us."

The bile in Maggie's throat grew increasingly bitter as it threatened release. Maggie suddenly slumped against her uncle, weakened by a wave of nausea.

"I'm not feeling too well, Uncle Aston." She sighed and clung to him for support.

"What's wrong with you, Maggie? You not all right?"

Maggie made it only to the pavement outside the station before she heaved over with a bout of vomiting. "Here Maggie, use my kerchief and wipe you face. You must be eat something rotten. You want some water?"

Maggie quickly wiped her face in the broad handkerchief, but her mouth was particularly rancid, and she knew that the time for hiding her condition was at an end. "Uncle Aston," she said hesitantly, "it's not because of anything I ate. It's because I'm pregnant."

"Oh no, you poor, poor girl," Uncle Aston said. "Does your mother know?"

"Nobody knows. I've been too ashamed to tell anyone."

"So that is why you come here, Maggie?"

"Yes, Uncle Aston."

"So, Maggie, you plan to go through with it and have the baby?"

"I want to, Uncle Aston."

"Good Lord, what we going do now, Maggie? Who is the father anyway? Is he Chinese?"

"That don't even matter now, Uncle Aston."

"Don't matter! I don't know what's wrong with you young people these days! Nothing seems to matter! If I did know who him is, I would a tell him to get him backside here and take responsibility."

"Uncle Aston, please don't get so worked up. The father doesn't even know I'm pregnant. I didn't tell him."

"So then, Maggie, don't tell me that it is that sailor man I did hear bout. Lord have mercy, cause if we can't let you mother know, it look like is me and you Aunt Phyllis who going have to help you out. Anyway, I don't want you to worry, because worry could make you lose the baby. I will tell your aunt about it for you."

"Thanks, Uncle Aston, I really appreciate everything, but please forgive me, because I can't tell anybody who the father is, not now anyway."

"Suit yourself, Maggie, but a day might come when all of us might need to know."

Chapter 19: A Day to Remember

Lucas Paynado, dressed in beige cotton slacks and a white shirt rolled up to his elbows, had been waiting on his front veranda for nearly an hour when a hired car drew up. It was not entirely unexpected, since Constance had called to let him know that she would be arriving by car. However, she failed to mention that she would be accompanying Wilemina Gunn.

When Lucas approached the car, he was more than surprised to find Mrs. Gunn sitting in the front seat beside the driver.

"Let me take care of that, Mrs. Gunn," Lucas said as Wilemina attempted to pay the driver.

"Good day, Mr. Paynado," the driver said, peering out at him. "I been hearing bout you all across the island. They say you is a real champion of the people. It was a privilege to drive you mother and you future mother-in-law. So since it is for you, I going only charge half the regular fare."

"Thanks," said Lucas, "I'll continue to do my best to serve the people, and I am much obliged that you have brought these two precious passengers here safely. But I feel that in due respect in these hard times, especially for those in your position, it would be wiser if I paid the full fare, if only to express the full extent of my gratitude."

"Thanks, boss," the driver said, "I did tell a friend of mine that you is a man of principle, and it looks like I was right."

Lucas paid the fare and opened the car doors for both women. "Would you like a cool drink?" he asked, addressing the driver who had gone to collect the two suitcases from the car trunk.

"No thanks, boss," the driver replied, "I can't really stay, because I need to go pick up another fare up in St. Andrew."

"Well, thanks again," Lucas said, and he shook the driver's hand. "Here's a little something extra for your trouble." He smiled and discreetly slipped the driver a five-shilling note.

"Welcome to my home," Lucas said, embracing his mother warmly and lightly touching Mrs. Gunn's hand. "There is a cool jug of lemonade waiting inside, in case you are parched from the long journey. How was the drive? Was it all right, Mama?"

"I'm a little tired," Constance said, "but he was a good driver. He stopped often so we could stretch our legs, and we even get coconut water to drink. I glad Mrs. Gunn was kind enough to allow me to drive down with her, and I thank her."

"Lucas," Wilemina said, "I suppose I should let you know that I'm actually only just popping in to say hello. If you don't mind, I've made arrangements to stay at The Winchester Hotel, not far from here. Is Eliza here by any chance?"

"No, Mrs. Gunn, Eliza's at the boarding house. She's probably doing some last-minute packing and getting ready for tomorrow. But please come inside, let me show both of you around."

"This look like a nice big house, Lucas," Constance said, brimming with pride as she followed her son up the concrete front steps.

Once inside, the two women were pleasantly surprised to find a well-furnished living room with carpeted floors and soft couches, and at the window a profusion of potted plants drenched in sunlight.

"Oh, it's so nice here," Constance whispered. "Son, you really keep a nice home. Just look at these nice things."

"Thanks, Mama, the dining room is behind those wooden arches," Lucas said, absently waving his hand at the adjoining room.

"Now, that is just beautiful," Constance said, admiring the dining room, with its china cabinet, padded mahogany chairs, long, dark dining table, and curio shelf. "I did think places like this was only in magazines."

Wilemina Gunn's admiration was wordless. She could well imagine Eliza living comfortably there in Lucas' home. She feasted her eyes on the lace-curtained rooms and could almost see Eliza in her mind's eye, moving from one beautiful room to another like a spectre while occupied with one task or another. So caught up was she in her imaginings that she hardly heard the exchanges between Constance and Lucas.

"Mama," Lucas said, "I knew you'd like it here. The furniture is genuine mahogany; isn't that what you said my father's furniture was?"

"Yes you're right, Lucas, but you was so little when I did tell you, I never did think you'd remember bout it. But how you manage to keep everything so tidy and clean all by yourself?"

"Mama, I have a maid who comes three times a week to help out with the cooking and cleaning."

"Oh my, it sound like you is a real big shot now. No wonder everybody refer to you as Mr. Paynado."

"Lucas, all the bedrooms look real comfortable. Later on, me going lie down for a little while," Constance said. "I wonder which room I going stay in."

"The room with the violets is yours, Mama. The one with the roses is for me and Eliza. She loves roses."

"You think of everything, Lucas, but you always was that way. You haven't changed from the sweet boy you always was. Well, Mrs. Gunn, thanks again for everything. Lucas says he going take me downtown later to pick up my wedding clothes. But he should take you to see Miss Eliza first."

"That's an excellent idea, Mama. I'll take Mrs. Gunn over there right now. I shouldn't be long."

Though Wilemina had not said one word while touring the house, the moment she sat down in the car with Lucas she was more inclined to be entirely open with him. It wasn't lost on her that occasionally Lucas glanced over at her, perhaps noting how much Eliza resembled her. She took a deep breath and felt her hand tremble as she slowly reached across the car seat and lightly rested her pale fingers on his arm.

"Lucas," she said softly, a slight quiver in her voice, "I ought to tell you this: I really owe you an apology, don't you think? You might not know it, and really you couldn't, but I've resented you ever since that day long ago when first I got the slightest inkling that Eliza might be interested in you. You see, Lucas, I've always imagined wonderful things for my children and, in Eliza's case, I thought perhaps that a young prince like the ones in a fairy tale on a white charger would come to take her away one day. I also imagined, incestuous as it might sound, that the prince would be every bit as fair-skinned and as blonde as our Dunstan. Never once did I imagine that the prince would be a Negro, or even someone as dark-skinned as you. I'm not sure what my late husband's thoughts would have been on the matter, but I rather have to admit that I've come round to thinking that those thoughts I just mentioned are thoughts I should best keep to myself. There is no doubt that you love my daughter, and she has said often enough that she loves you. But from what I have seen, myself, of your beautiful home and even your well-mannered interaction with people such as our driver, and the respect such persons obviously have for you, I can tell that you've come an awfully long way, Lucas Paynado. Surely, you will go even further. Please accept my blessings, and please take good care of my darling Eliza along the way."

Lucas Paynado slowed the car to a halt and buried his face in his hands and, though the skies were full of squawking sea birds and the air was rife with the harried cries of Kingston's slum children, the sound of Lucas' soft crying was the only sound Wilemina Gunn heard.

Dunstan Gunn and the other captive men were taken on a route march. The march lasted two weeks and crossed into as many European countries, though occasionally stops were made by the Nazi squads to herd the POWs like cattle into deserted buildings. The buildings were, in actual fact, designated temporary stopovers, and it was here that Dunstan Gunn and Aynsford Collins found themselves amongst dozens of other prisoners from Canada, America, Australia, New Zealand, the West Indies and Britain.

At first, both Dunstan and Aynsford welcomed the fact that they were amongst others who spoke a common language. However, they were soon to discover that they were routinely monitored, not only by English-speaking Germans who cleverly infiltrated into their numbers, but also by hidden Nazi bugging equipment.

"Dunstan, there's a microphone under the table!" Aynsford whispered urgently after running his hand under one of the meal tables in a stopover house. "Remember, don't say a single word out loud about anything remotely military. Play along with me, and pretend that all is normal."

In all likelihood, there was no necessity for Aynsford's concern regarding unwittingly passing on military information, for the famished men at the tables seemed more preoccupied with talking about food. Many of them spoke longingly about the meals they were accustomed to in their homelands, while others expressed common disgust regarding the ration of a slice of dried, sour-tasting rye bread, the one bucket of water to be shared by dozens of men, and the thin soup that left no doubt that it was little more than water.

As a direct result of the bland starvation diet and the endless marching, many of the exhausted men were physically reduced to shadows of their former selves within weeks.

At the end of two and a half weeks of this monstrous routine, the men reached the final leg of their journey. They were loaded onto box cars on a train and told only that they would be taken to an undisclosed POW camp in eastern Germany.

On arrival at the compound, the men were split up into groups and assigned small huts with about a dozen or more men to a hut. It was miraculous that Dunstan and Aynsford remained together. Every man was assigned a bunk and a locker as well as a number, and one latrine was to be shared by several men.

According to regulations laid down in the Geneva Convention, the men would be allowed to write home and were entitled to receive clothing and food parcels through the Red Cross organization. But from compound to compound, these rules were never strictly adhered to. Some compounds had more severe food restrictions which resulted in theft, and there were tighter restrictions concerning letter writing.

Regardless of the differences from one compound to the next, every POW was under constant threat of being slaughtered by their guards. Escape was never far from a POW's thoughts, though signs were posted to the effect that escape from a POW camp was no longer a sport. The guard dogs, barbed wire fences, and military presence around the compound were a constant reminder that there was no possibility of escape.

Dozens of men met their deaths trying, though some had come up with ingenious escape plans. Some POWs managed to build a glider in secret, others tunneled under the fences using the most basic of equipment, while others yet fashioned clever disguises that resembled Nazi uniforms, including briefcases and boots. But although most of these attempts were unsuccessful, failures did not prevent the desperate men from continuing with their efforts.

An Australian POW, one of the men who shared the bunk with Dunstan and Aynsford, was the first of the new arrivals to start writing home.

"I'm Ryan," he said that first morning. "I need to write my lady, but who knows if my letter will reach its destination. I'm told that more than half of the contents of our letters are cut out with razor blades. It's the Nazi way of censoring letters. So what's the point of my bothering to write? I reckon it's just because I need to keep my brain turning over. I've been a POW long enough to have seen men killed for little or no reason by these guards. If I were you mate, I'd set about writing home while you can. Where are you from, anyway?"

"I'm Dunstan and my buddy over there is Aynsford; we are from Jamaica," Dunstan said, nodding at Aynsford as he spoke. "You might be right, Ryan. I should write home, because no one there knows what has happened to me. Who knows what my family might be thinking."

"Well, I need to write my sister Roslyn," Aynsford said. "We have always been close and I know she would be worried about me. She's my little sister, but sometimes you'd think she was my mother, though we are only three years apart."

"Hey," Dunstan said, "you've never mentioned your sister before. How come?"

"Well Dunstan, not only am I very private, but the thing is, I never thought it would interest you."

"Come on, I've told you about my family at Gunn's Run, haven't I?"

"Well Dunstan, I did so much listening, you left me no time for telling." Aynsford laughed. "But seriously Dunstan, I didn't want to talk about my sister. It makes me too sad. We were inseparable, Roslyn and I. We used to climb the same trees and even play cricket together, and she could use a slingshot as well as I. Not too many Jamaican girls are like her Dunstan, not many at all."

"How old is she?" Ryan asked, looking up from his letter with renewed interest. "She sounds somewhat like my niece Lorraine in Australia."

"She's twenty now," Aynsford said, "but she's still a bit of a tomboy. Here, have a look; I have a photo."

Aynsford pulled out a ragged photo from his pocket, and his fingers shook visibly as he passed it to the two young men.

"Not bad," Ryan said, staring at it longingly. "Looks like she is as light-brown as you Aynsford, and she might even have your hazel eyes, but she is a real beauty. You're mixed blood, aren't you?"

"As a matter of fact," Aynsford said, "my father was Irish-Jamaican and my mother was a Negro."

"Yeah, I could see that," the Australian said. "We've got a few mixes of our own back home. It's become quite a bit of a problem, if you ask me."

But who asked you? Dunstan thought to himself.

"Are you sure this is your sister?" Dustan grinned as the photo was handed to him. "Ryan's right about one thing, your sister's quite a beauty; not like you, my friend Aynsford, not like you at all. But to be honest, I've come to believe from what I've seen in Jamaica, that it is the mixing of the races that creates such exotic beauty."

"Speaking of beauty," Ryan said, "I've heard rumours that there's going to be some German girls coming into camp tonight and for a few cigarettes some of us might be able to bribe a guard to guarantee us chaps a turn with them. What do you say lads, have you any cigarettes to hand over?"

"Mrs. Gunn," Lucas said as he parked his car on the street in front of Eliza's Beechwood Avenue boarding house. "I'll wait out here for you because according to tradition, I mustn't see the bride until tomorrow. And another thing, would you please tell her that a Mr. Ezekiel Samuels came to my office recently. He seems to know your family quite well, and I have taken the liberty of inviting him to the wedding."

"You've met Ezekiel? My word, Lucas! I have not been in touch with him in years! How is he? I rather hope things are going well for him. How nice of you to invite him. I dare say Eliza will be pleased to know." Wilemina's words came out in a rush, and her heart pounded frantically, though she hoped Lucas would not read anything from the small smile that played at the corners of her lips at the mention of Ezekiel.

Eliza Gunn was packing the last of her small things into an overnight bag when she heard an unfamiliar knock at her door.

"Who is it?" she inquired, snapping the bag shut, somewhat exasperated, since she had been daydreaming about her upcoming honeymoon in Bath, St. Thomas, where the natural mineral water baths were reputed to be the finest in the island.

When there was no reply from whoever it was at the door, Eliza rose slowly. "Are you still there?" she asked nervously.

"Yes, I'm here," came the reply but though the voice was somewhat familiar, Eliza was not at all sure who it might be. It sounded to her as though someone was doing their best to disguise their natural voice. Could it be Lucas? she wondered and feeling bolder, she opened the door a crack, peeked out, and was startled to see her mother standing in the hallway outside.

"Mother!" she cried out. "How wonderful that you've come!"

She ran into her mother's open arms, and the two women shared a long embrace as their mingled tears flowed freely.

"How did you get here, Mother?" Eliza finally asked, leading her by the wrist and taking her into the sparse room she called home.

"Darling Eliza, it was your Lucas who drove me here, and he's waiting outside."

"He's here! So he must have known all along that you'd be coming."

"No, darling, he was just as surprised as you when I arrived at his house with Constance in tow."

"So you've seen the house, Mother?"

"Yes, darling, Lucas was kind enough to give us both a tour."

"So what do you think?"

"He seems to be exactly as you said. He's kind, polite and well-mannered. Yes, I can see why you fell in love with him. He's rather handsome too, isn't he, darling?"

Eliza's laughter spilled out and echoed in the small room. She felt all at once liberated, amused and shy. "I can't believe I am hearing you say that, Mother." She laughed. "But what I meant was, what did you think of the house?"

"Oh! It's really a lovely home, darling, and well looked after too. You're sure to be happy there, wouldn't you say?"

"I'm so glad you're here, Mother. I had been feeling quite alone, and there are so many things I have to do to get ready for tomorrow. And, Mother, Lucas and I are going away for our honeymoon. It's only for a week, but I'm so nervous, Mother. I've never been with a man before. What if I do all the wrong things?"

"Darling, that's the one time in life when even the wrong things will seem right." Wilemina laughed and discreetly changed the subject. "I see you've allowed your hair to grow, darling; it looks rather attractive. You'll make a beautiful bride, won't you?"

"Thanks. Are you staying at the house, Mother?"

"No, darling, I thought I'd stay in a hotel not far from there. One needs time to get used to this sort of thing. Wouldn't you say?"

"I guess you're right, Mother, but you know, of course, you are always welcome there."

"Yes, darling, I know, and I'll be back here first thing in the morning to help you to get ready, if I may."

"Oh, I'd like that Mother, but what am I to do about 'something old, something new, something borrowed, something blue'?"

"Don't worry, darling, I thought of that too. Here's a gold chain your father gave me. It's quite old, ancient in fact. The stone is a moonstone; it will look absolutely stunning against a white dress. You are wearing white, I presume?"

"That's so lovely, Mother; and yes, I am wearing white, thank you so much."

"Well, darling, for 'something borrowed' you could borrow this nice lace handkerchief that I always keep in my handbag."

"Oh, Mother, I have always wanted that handkerchief. It was Granny's, wasn't it?"

"Yes, darling, it's the one thing I have of Granny's. She didn't approve of your father at all; she said he wasn't good enough for me, amongst other things, of course. And I swore, back then, never to be like her. I hope you don't tell me different, darling."

"Surely, she was wrong about Father. Daddy was quite wonderful; I think about him all the time. Remember how he used to enjoy going to the Chung's shop, and how he used to sit smoking by the sea?"

"Yes, darling, I remember; and I really miss having someone to share things with. There has only been a brief word from our dear Dunstan, and I can only hope that the good Lord is keeping him safe. But, darling, we shouldn't dwell on sad things, should we? Let's just think about the happy occasion coming up tomorrow, shall we?"

"Mother you are right, and nothing makes me happier than the fact that you are here, and that tomorrow I'll be eighteen and married to the man I love."

"That's wonderful, darling, and I'm sure you've bought lots of new things, which will take care of the 'something new'. But I have a little surprise for you for the 'something blue.' Don't laugh too hard, darling; it's meant as a joke. I bought you a pair of lacey blue panties, and a blue rose for your garter belt. Here, have a look."

"Mother, they are just darling." Eliza laughed. "I'm going to wear both of them. Thanks so much. I wonder what Lucas will think when he sees me in this, it's barely even there, is it? You are naughty, aren't you, Mother?"

"Maggie, I don't want to be nosey or anything, but how far along are you?" Aunt Phyllis asked tentatively, as she set about altering a smart-looking formal outfit she bought at the Syrian shop next door for Maggie. Her clever alterations emphasized Maggie's growing bosom, but the loose flow of the material somehow bypassed and disguised Maggie's thickening waistline. "There, Maggie, how's that?"

"I'm about three months Aunt Phyllis, but I feel as big as a house."

"No, Maggie, no one would ever know. Just look how nice you look. Tomorrow, me and your Uncle Aston going walk into that church with you and show everybody how gorgeous you are in this new dress."

"Thanks, Aunt Phyllis. You're right, it is beautiful with all this velvet and lace."

"Yes, indeed it is, Maggie, and I did notice how Mrs. Lazarus and her son were admiring you when you put it in front of you in the shop."

Maggie laughed for the first time. "Yes, I remember," she said, "and Esau was acting as if he'd never seen anything like it. But you know what I think? He just wanted to make a sale."

"Maybe not, Maggie, maybe not, cause you don't know how pretty you are. Men will be attracted to you, pregnant or not. I bet that sea captain was attracted to you as well."

"Oh, Aunt Phyllis, stop it. That sea captain didn't mean a thing to me. Anyway, how could you know about men being attracted to pregnant women, when you've never been pregnant yourself?"

"Well, Maggie dear, let's just say it is something I've noticed. But my dear, don't be so flip about that sea captain. It's been three months since you saw him and since I'm good at arithmetic, I would say one and one makes two, if you know what I mean. Anyhow, I'm going to lend you your late grandmother's string of pearls to wear tomorrow. She brought it over from China all those years ago, and she would have been proud to see you wearing it at a wedding."

Chapter 20:
What Memories Are Made Of

Dear Maggie,

I am writing this from behind enemy lines. I am being treated well, so please don't worry. It is difficult for me to have to write this in a letter, but please don't wait for me, Maggie. There is no guarantee that I will ever return home. It would be selfish of me to hold you to a promise that we made so long ago. At least to me it seems like an eternity has passed since that day under the banyan tree. Every day here could well be my last, though I live in hope. There is every possibility that I will never see you again.

May you find the happiness you deserve with someone who can love you freely and be with you. You have my blessings.

Yours truly,
Dunstan

Dunstan set aside his pen and reread the letter, and was satisfied that it said everything that he wanted to say. He didn't want to make mention of feelings, since that might upset Maggie unnecessarily. Strangely enough, being far removed from her, he was no longer as sure of being in love with her. Under his present circumstances, he knew there was no future for them.

Unknown to Dunstan, it was approximately at that same time that confidential information was sent from the War Office in England to the army headquarters at Up Park Camp in Kingston, Jamaica. The wired information was to inform soldiers' families that their sons were either missing in action or deceased. Dunstan Gunn's name was amongst those on the list as being MIA and presumed a casualty. The War Office had no evidence that he and the others who stayed behind at the farm in France were not amongst those that the Nazis ambushed and massacred. The bodies of the rest of the troop were subsequently burnt by their marauders.

A letter of notification was to be delivered to Gunn's Run, and it was only by chance that Chunty had gone over to watch the property and she encountered the military man who arrived with the information.

"Is Mrs. Wilemina Gunn home?" the uniformed man asked, coming out of his vehicle.

"She's not here at present," Chunty replied, coming down the steps to meet him. "She gone to her daughter wedding in Kingston. I'm the one keeping an eye on the house."

"Do you know when she will be returning, Ma'am?"

"Could be about two more days time, Sir."

"Right, then I'll leave this letter with you. This is rather urgent business, so it is very important that Mrs. Gunn gets this personally. I would have come back here myself, but it's rather off the beaten track here, isn't it?

Ezekiel Samuels was amongst the first of the guests to arrive at the church. Dressed in a dark morning suit that set off the rich colour of his hair and a pale pink orchid in his lapel, he stood at the back of the church, mesmerized by the austerity and the beauty of the stained glass windows. In his mind, he wove wonderful stories concerning the wild flowers overflowing the vases on the altar and how joyfully they seemed to praise God with their bright faces. In contrast, the single red rose at the end of each pew brought to his mind thoughts of loneliness and isolation, and he couldn't help but think of Gunn's Run. With his head bowed reverently in front of the lifelike statues that honoured the saints, he trembled with anticipation, for soon Wilemina would walk beneath the shadow of those very images.

He fell on his knees in the last pew and prayed for the success of the upcoming nuptials. "Dear God, please smile down on the union that will take place here today. Bring Lucas and Eliza much happiness, and may they bear fruit and love and offer praise to you for the rest of their days. Though I am a Jew, amidst these sacred Christian surroundings, I cannot but feel the closeness of you, my God, in every fibre of my being. I praise you, my Father, and ask you to be with us all who gather here today."

In the midst of his prayer, a sudden commotion originated outside the building, and it attracted his attention. He immediately went to investigate, and he came upon a crowd of well-wishers who, in light of their impoverished appearance, must have come from Kingston's slums. They were standing outside the churchyard behind the wrought iron fence, and they were beating on empty tin pans and blowing home-made whistles. They were the very people that Eliza worked amongst.

"Lady Eliza!" they chanted over and over, their voices growing louder the longer they had to wait to see her.

Eventually, a young priest, Father Brennan, a native of Chicago who would officiate at the marriage, came out from the rectory, his rosary jangling at his hip, and in his own quiet soft-spoken manner, restored order amongst the well-wishers.

There was a sharp cry as a flock of seagulls flew overhead. Ezekiel turned his eyes toward the endless blue of the skies, and it reminded him of home and the sea. But there was no salt in the air, for the air was drenched with the scent of the wild roses and violets that lined the church steps.

It will be a day to remember, he thought.

It wasn't long before cars belonging to Lucas' political acquaintances began to arrive. Immediately behind them was a lone black car and when it pulled up, everyone saw that Lucas Paynado and his mother were inside. Lucas, who looked particularly handsome and distinguished, wore a tuxedo and a stark white orchid in his lapel. A cheer went up from the people behind the fence, and the beating on the pans commenced.

"Lord, give me strength, him look so good, and to think him was one of we own," a woman commented.

"Just look at him! Him look like royalty!" a man cried out.

"An' him handsome caa done," said a young girl.

"No wonder Lady Eliza love him!" shouted another.

And to their delight, Lucas Paynado took the time to stop for a moment to wave at them in greeting, acknowledging their presence. His gesture was met with loud drumming and whistles, for no doubt the handsome, well-mannered, black-skinned young man met with their approval. Constance, too, was greeted with cheers when she emerged from the car, smartly dressed in a new green silk dress, white gloves, hat and shoes.

"She is him mother!" someone shouted. "Oh my, she look stoshus. Just look at her."

But Constance was shy as she hid behind the brim of her hat and waved, only to be met with a barrage of drums and whistles.

Uncle Aston and Aunt Phyllis arrived with a group of smartly dressed guests and blended into the crowd entering the church without fanfare. And Maggie, looking especially radiant dressed in her new outfit, drew catcalls and whistles from the other side of the fence.

Aynsford Collins' assignment was to help unload stacks of bulky cloth bags in a building inside the prison compound referred to amongst the POWs as "the laundry house". He considered himself lucky to have been given a task, for he was soon to find out that there were POWs in camp with time on their hands who, as a result of boredom and apathy, would run at the barbed wire fences with suicidal intentions, knowing full well that the Nazi guards would shoot them dead. Many men gave up as a result of the despair and hopelessness of their situation. Waking up each day with an assigned task was somewhat of a blessing.

Both Aynsford and Dunstan knew from personal

experience that once in a while, groups of POWs were chained to each other and were expected to run down dirt roads with vicious guard dogs chasing after them. The men who couldn't keep up with the others were prodded with bayonets and hit on the head with rifle butts to keep them moving. The Nazis would then make sport of them by allowing some of the men to run toward wooded areas, openly urging and goading them to escape, knowing full well that what awaited the POWs in the woods was death in the form of machine gun fire.

Ever so often, a truck would arrive at the laundry house to take clothing away to an unknown destination offsite. Another truck would arrive with more clothes, as well as stacks of empty bags.

It was while working in the guarded laundry house that Aynsford first encountered Edith Werner.

A young German, Edith Werner was one of the few female guards stationed in the laundry area. From the beginning, she had seemed to Aynsford to be different from the other guards, not only because of her youth and her attractive auburn hair, but because the first time he had seen her, she had smiled discreetly at him. At the time, he wasn't at all sure if he was indeed the intended recipient of that smile but, since then, he kept his eyes averted whenever she was around.

The laundry house was a large building usually stacked to the rafters with soiled clothing. Aynsford heard it said that many items of the clothing had once belonged to former prisoners, Nazi soldiers, and dead Jews. He was further informed that the clothing was destined to be burnt in incinerators rather than to be laundered. In spite of rumours, he was never quite sure of the exact purpose of the existence of the laundry house.

The empty canvas bags Aynsford unloaded were as

large as potato sacks. They were stacked one on top of the other on one side of the room while other POWs, including Dunstan Gunn, were responsible for various types of sorting. The room was well guarded, though it reeked from the scent of death, urine and war. It was no wonder that the POWs inside were obliged to wear face masks.

The trucks that came to take away and deliver the laundry were always manned by Gestapo drivers accompanied by a Nazi soldier, who also wore masks while on duty.

One afternoon, when Aynsford went to unload the laundry bags, he noticed that Edith was the guard on duty distributing masks, and he was obliged to request a face mask from her. She barely looked at him, though she stood up and beckoned to him to follow her as she waved absently at the stacks of clothing, and nattered away in German. Aynsford had no choice but to follow, though he was quite oblivious to whatever it was she was saying. However, once out of visual range of the other guards, Edith turned to him, removed her mask and smiled, and Aynsford knew then that the smile was meant for him.

"My English not good," she whispered, coming nearer. "I speak with lips, okay?"

No one was more surprised than Aynsford when she suddenly drew him close and kissed him passionately on the lips.

"I like you," she said and might have said even more, were it not that they both heard footsteps. Edith reluctantly pulled away and replaced her mask, and not a moment too soon, for one of the older male guards appeared, seemingly from out of nowhere.

"Yes, Helferin Werner," he said, approaching with a Luger at his hip. "It's a good idea to take laundry from back here." He smiled menacingly. "They are getting filthy, eh? This man can get some more bags ready."

Edith's eyes never once met Aynsford's as she saluted her comrade smartly and walked away.

The memory of the kiss lingered for the rest of Aynsford's day.

That evening before curfew, Aynsford found Dunstan standing near the fences, staring longingly into the distance. "Dunstan," Aynsford whispered. "Escape is impossible ... but you won't believe what happened today."

"What?"

"You know that guard Edith?"

"Sure, everybody knows her," Dunstan replied, also whispering.

"She kissed me, Dunstan. We were in the back of the laundry house. Can you believe it?"

"Good Lord, Aynsford, that's dangerous! What's she up to?"

"I don't know, Dunstan, but I've never been so spooked in my life, especially since another guard almost caught us."

"What! Aynsford, you could have been a dead man! You're going to have to be careful from now on."

"You're damn right, Dunstan, I don't even want to go near the laundry house, but I have no choice, do I?"

"Not a word to anyone else, Aynsford. There are infiltrators everywhere. I even heard that there is someone here in camp destroying mail intended for the Red Cross. So even the letters we wrote home might not have gone through."

Chapter 21:
Turning Points

When the car carrying Eliza and her mother arrived at the church, it was met with huge cheers and joyful drumming. Ezekiel Samuels went out to meet the car and was taken aback by Eliza's stark beauty, for he had been remembering her as being a child, and here she was a full-grown woman. Her hair fell in shining ringlets about her face and, despite her covering veil, Ezekiel could see her painted lips, her sky-blue eyes, and her smooth cheeks, which were pink and flushed with excitement.

Her beautiful white gown, nipped in at the waist, showed off her figure and, at her throat, was her mother's smoky-white moonstone, which emphasized her virginal attractiveness. She is as lovely as a princess, Ezekiel thought.

When Eliza heard the welcoming roar from the crowd behind the fence, she turned to look at them and smiled, and then she waved enthusiastically, holding tightly to her bouquet of pale pink roses and white orchids. What a welcome it was: thunderous cheering, clapping, drumming and whistles!

Wilemina Gunn emerged from the car wearing a pale-blue lace gown that clung to her slim frame. Her blonde hair was partially hidden under a matching blue hat ornamented with pale-white roses. She looked radiant and far younger than a woman approaching middle age. Ezekiel had never seen her look as lovely.

"Wilemina," he said huskily, taking her hand, and she smiled up at him and trembled.

"Please give my daughter away," she whispered hastily. "She has no one else."

Ezekiel nodded acceptance, brimming with pride.

The noise from the gathered crowd grew louder and all at once, above the din, a bloodcurdling scream rang out. Ezekiel turned round quickly and through the corner of his eye, saw a figure running forward.

He was startled to see a brown-skinned woman brandishing a cutlass, charging towards Eliza, the bride-to-be. Without a second thought, Ezekiel ran and barred the woman's way. The woman lunged at him but missed her target when Ezekiel, who was bigger and stronger than she was, managed to wrestle her to the ground and quickly disarm her, but not before she slashed him through his thin jacket sleeve.

Everyone was screaming and in the confusion that ensued, the angered crowd behind the fence rushed into the churchyard, some of them managing to assist Ezekiel in restraining the deranged woman. The wedding guests inside the church rushed out to see what the commotion was about, and it was fortunate that four plainclothes policemen were amongst them. It took two of the policemen to handcuff the woman, who ranted and raged before she could be taken into custody.

"Is me, Jenny Abbot!" she shouted maniacally, "that should be the one marrying Mr. Paynado, not that white bitch!"

"Mr. Samuels," Lucas panted as he rushed to thank Ezekiel. He was trembling visibly, and there were angry tears on his cheeks. How close he had come to losing Eliza, he thought; how fragile were his dreams!

"I am forever in your debt, Sir. I am so lucky that I invited you to the wedding. What you did for us is amazingly brave. Thanks and thanks again. You are an extremely brave man," Lucas said, enthusiastically shaking Ezekiel's hand.

"Perhaps you're right, Lucas," Ezekiel replied, a smile playing on his lips, "but perhaps I'm also very foolhardy — you take your pick."

"Are you all right, Mr. Samuels?" one of the policemen asked. "Did you get hurt?"

"Oh no, I'm fine. I'm sure it's nothing more than a scrape."

"Oh my God, Mr. Samuels, I thought she could have killed one of us! I'm so grateful. You've saved my life. I hope to God that you're all right."

"Eliza, I'm grateful too."

"Ezekiel, I don't know what I would have done if any of you were hurt. You are all right, are you, darling?"

Ezekiel was both surprised and pleased to hear Wilemina refer to him as "darling", though he made nothing of it, for he knew that one does say strange things when traumatized.

"Wilemina, I'm only glad that I was here and able to help."

The two policemen who remained behind managed to restore some semblance of order before discreetly speaking to Lucas.

"Did you happen to know that woman, Mr. Paynado?"

"I've never seen her before in my life," Lucas replied truthfully.

"We thought as much," one of the policemen replied. "The woman's obviously deranged. She will be admitted into the mental hospital or even imprisoned because, no doubt, that was an attempted murder."

"Everyone please join us inside the church!" Lucas Paynado called out to all those who had assembled outside, still nervously discussing what had happened, and what nearly could have happened.

"We have a wedding waiting to take place!" Lucas shouted again. "I would like everyone, even those of you who were standing outside the fence, to come and join us inside the church for our celebration. There is so much I have to be thankful for."

As people streamed back into the church, Eliza Gunn leaned on the good arm of Ezekiel Samuels. There were blood stains on his other sleeve, a benchmark of his courage, as he proudly accompanied the beautiful bride down the long aisle. The organist struck up the chords for

"Here Comes the Bride", and Lucas Paynado's heart pounded as loudly as the drums that had welcomed Eliza. Could it truly be happening? he wondered. Had he overcome all the odds? He stood near the foot of the altar, unaware of how handsome he was, a nervous smile flitted across his eager young face as he watched for Eliza. It seemed to him as though he was reliving a recurring dream in which everything was surreal and the impossible was becoming possible.

A muscle worked in his jaw as he looked past the assembled congregation. He was, all at once, intoxicated with the sweet scent of the roses and the vision of Eliza. How he longed to actually hold her in his arms as, with bated breath, he waited to receive her. How slowly, it seemed to him, that she floated on Ezekiel's arm, to find her way to him.

The solemn vows were exchanged amid rapt silence and, at the pronouncement, cheers rang out joyfully in the church. And when Lucas, trembling like a boy, lifted Eliza's soft veil, he saw that her face was luminous with longing. He took her in his arms and kissed her deeply, and the organist immediately began to play "Faith of Our Father, Holy Faith". There was thunderous applause, and those who could, raised their voices in song.

"Lucas, I love you so much," Eliza whispered.

"You are my life, and my love," Lucas replied.

"Your daughter is married," Ezekiel said, coming to stand near Wilemina. "How do you feel about that?"

"I'm taking things in stride, Ezekiel. I'm rather happy for Eliza; it's what she wanted, isn't it? Lucas has no choice but to be good to her, for he knows I'll be watching. I meant that as a joke, Ezekiel; please don't look so serious. But right now, I am more inclined to be concerned about that arm of yours. Is it really all right?"

"To be honest, Wilemina, it has been throbbing all through the service. I suppose I should get it looked at, shouldn't I? But first, let me congratulate the happy couple."

"May I accompany you, Ezekiel?"

"Oh thanks, Wilemina, but that won't be necessary. I know a doctor who practises nearby. I'll come back directly."

"Ezekiel, I was actually wanting to know if I could accompany you to congratulate the newlyweds."

The celebration went long into the afternoon, though Lucas and Eliza left the reception directly after cutting the cake. They were gracious and grateful, and said so, even as they piled their suitcases into the hired car that would take them to Bath. But just before the car sped off, Eliza, with great merriment, gathered all the ladies around her and threw her bouquet. Everyone laughed when one of the secretaries caught it.

Wilemina had been mingling in the crowd and came upon Maggie. "How wonderful to see you, Maggie. It's so nice that you came, it really is. You do look splendid, don't you? I don't know whether it is because of your new dress or your hairstyle, but you seem to be absolutely glowing, wouldn't you say?"

But she hardly heard Maggie's reply for, all the while, she had been keeping watch for Ezekiel; and suddenly there he was, across the room. "Maggie, I'll talk to you later," Wilemina said, hurrying away.

Ezekiel must have seen her too, at that very moment, for with great strides, they met each other in the middle of the crowded room.

"So what did the doctor say, Ezekiel?" Wilemina inquired.

"The good news is that there's no need for stitches, just an ointment and a bandage. However, I will need to rest the arm."

"Well, Ezekiel, since you won't be dancing, how would you like to pop round to the hotel where I'm staying? We could have a drink and catch up, couldn't we?"

"I'd enjoy that, Wilemina; we do have a lot of catching up to do."

Ezekiel ordered two rum punches at the hotel bar before he and Wilemina headed to her room.

"There's more privacy in my room than at the wedding reception," Wilemina said. "I also have a small balcony if you should feel inclined to enjoy the fresh air, and there's a marvelous view of the Blue Mountains. Unfortunately the hotel patio is rather full of pretentious types. Why, one gentleman wanted to know why I'd bothered to choose Jamaica over Hawaii for a holiday. I rather set him straight when I told him that I live here."

"How long will you be staying here, Wilemina?"

"Tomorrow night is my last night."

"It's too bad you didn't come to stay with me."

"You have your own home now, do you, Ezekiel?"

"Yes, Wilemina, it's a little ways out of the city, up in the hills. It has wonderful views."

"Really, that sounds rather splendid; I'd love to see it sometime. Though at the present moment, there is nothing I would enjoy more than being with you right here, Ezekiel Samuels."

"I feel the same way about you, Wilemina darling, and, as a matter of fact, I think we had best lock your room door. I don't think either of us will want to be disturbed."

"I couldn't agree more." Wilemina laughed, throwing her hat and her purse on the bedside table.

When Eliza and Lucas arrived at the hotel in Bath, they were met with flowers from the management, and whisked through formalities at the front desk. A bottle of chilled champagne with two glasses on a tray awaited them at the reception counter.

Lucas grinned when he saw the tray and playfully attempted to tug Eliza down the carpeted hall. But she, excited as he was, grabbed both glasses and the bottle before Lucas swung her into his arms and then finally over the threshold to their room. He uncorked the bottle and, with their hands intertwined, he and Eliza drank to their lasting love and happiness.

"I want you more than anything, Mrs. Paynado," Lucas said.

"And I you, Mr. Paynado," Eliza murmured, feeling somewhat intoxicated, not from the wine but from the essence and headiness of finally realizing her dream of being Lucas' bride.

Slowly, he unfastened her many buttons with as many kisses. "My God, you are beautiful, Eliza!" he gasped, gazing at her standing before him. Feverishly, she in turn removed his clothing, surrendering to him through joyful tears. And she felt feather-light in his arms as he backed towards the double bed and slowly, skillfully pulled the covers around them.

Chapter 22:
Milestones

Since Constance had to remain behind in Kingston to watch Lucas' home until his return from his honeymoon, Wilemina accepted a drive from Ezekiel. It would mark his first visit to Hedley in years.

With Wilemina's blonde head on his shoulder, Ezekiel navigated the country roads with extreme caution. He had never felt such happiness. There was no denying the joy that Wilemina brought into his life. How strange it was, he thought, that this beautiful woman, a non-Jew, had always been, since the first day he saw her, the one person who made him feel complete. He had spent the previous night in her arms at the hotel, and he was extremely grateful that she was everything he had hoped she would be.

They stopped at a small inn near St. Ann's Bay and enjoyed a light lunch of lobster and greens before walking down to the beach holding hands, sharing a kiss under the mangrove shelter.

"How I missed the sea!" Ezekiel whispered in her ear. "There were so many times I would have wanted to come back to Hedley but couldn't have faced it, thinking you didn't care for me."

"Ezekiel darling, perhaps I wasn't ready then, but no doubt you know how I feel now. I expect you will stay the night; will you?"

"I'll stay forever if you want me to."

When Ezekiel's car drew close to the house at Gunn's Run, he cut the engine and stopped for a moment to admire the house in the distance. "Imagine, I helped to build that." He smiled. "It was quite an accomplishment, and it is still quite a beautiful home, isn't it?"

"I love Gunn's Run, Ezekiel darling. I used to think I would never leave. But I have come to realize that one is ruled by circumstances; don't you agree? Let's hurry inside, we have the whole place to ourselves."

They emerged excitedly from the car, like two young lovers, and held hands as they ran towards the house, anticipating more precious time together. Then, Wilemina noticed, with some surprise, that Chunty was sitting as still as a statue on the veranda.

"Hello, Chunty," she called excitedly. "The wedding was wonderful. Eliza was so beautiful, wasn't she, Ezekiel? Chunty, I saw your Maggie. I have to tell you all about her and her dress. But look who's here — it's Ezekiel Samuels."

Chunty came down the steps one careful step at a time, clutching that damned letter in her fist. There was no welcoming smile on her face, for though the letter was still sealed, something of the solemnity of its contents must have seeped into her soul, for her eyes were downcast and saddened.

"This came for you, Wilemina," Chunty said, sounding hollow. "I have a feeling is bad news."

"Oh, Chunty, I hope to God, it is not what I think it is. I wanted to be so happy today."

Later that afternoon, a long-distance telephone call came to the Lazarus' shop in Kingston, and Maggie was sent for. The call was from Chunty. Esau, Mrs. Lazarus' only son, was alone in the shop; his mother had gone to do the banking, leaving him in charge.

"The phone's there," Esau said, waving his hand towards the back of the counter as he busied himself with dusting the mannequins and rearranging the displayed clothes, and keeping his eye on Maggie. He didn't know exactly why it was, but she had seemed particularly disturbed when he had gone to fetch her. Something inside him felt protective of her, and he wanted to shield her from anything that might make her unhappy.

Maggie knew nothing of his thoughts, but her mouth was dry and her hands trembled as she took hold of the telephone receiver. "Hello, Mamma," she said nervously, as though already anticipating the worst.

"Maggie dear, I have bad news," Chunty said. "Please sit down if you can."

"What is it, Mamma?" Maggie asked, an icy wave of nausea washing over her.

"A letter come, Maggie. You not going like what it say."

"Mamma, you're frightening me. Just tell me what it says."

"Dunstan Gunn, your good friend, is dead. He died in the war."

Maggie felt her stomach heave, and her legs buckled under her. The phone fell with a clatter, and Esau came running.

Maggie had no idea how long she had passed out. She did not even know that Esau Lazarus had reassured Chunty that her daughter would be alright, for the next thing Maggie knew, Esau was cradling her and hushing her in his arms, as if she were a baby.

"Esau," Maggie said when finally she opened her eyes, "I want to die. I just don't know what else to do now." With great sobs came her tears, which Esau gently wiped away with his handkerchief.

"Did someone die, Maggie?" he inquired, bending his head closer to her trembling lips.

"Yes, Esau, someone has died, and now I have no reason to live."

"Come, come, Maggie. You mustn't say things like that."

"Esau, for God's sake," Maggie blurted out. "I'm pregnant, and the baby's father has died. You'd say the same thing if you were in my position."

"Are you pregnant, Maggie? Because if you are, you don't look it at all!"

"Yes, Esau," Maggie sobbed, "I am, and I might as well admit it, for it won't be a secret much longer, whether I live or die."

"Oh, you poor, poor thing," Esau said, shaking his head sadly. Maggie looked into his eyes and saw that behind his thick glasses, his eyes were green, and there was compassion there. She noticed too, as if for the first time, that his honey-coloured hair was already receding, though he was no more than twenty-five; and she felt that the hands which held her were strong, despite his gentle soul.

"Esau," she said, "I don't know what I might do with myself now. I'm beginning to feel that I didn't love the baby's father enough. He was a wonderful friend, but I feel I ruined things by being impulsive. I allowed him to have his way with me, and now he is gone. What is going to become of me now? Oh God, I might as well die."

"Maggie, please don't worry. I don't even want to know the name of your former lover. It is you I'm concerned about; I want to help in any way I can."

"Esau, all I can think right now is that I want to die. Things would be so much simpler for everyone."

"Maggie Chung, just you listen to me. You do have things to live for, that baby for instance and, Maggie, it doesn't matter to me that you're pregnant with another man's child. I've always had my eyes on you. Even Mamma noticed. I can help you, Maggie, if you'll let me; just don't cry anymore, promise me."

"Esau, what exactly do you mean?"

"What I'm saying is I want to take care of you, marry you if that would be a solution. You're probably thinking, 'Who would want to marry stupid ole Esau?' But Maggie, I'm no fool. I know full well that you don't love me — if only I could have been that lucky. But there is enough love in me for the both of us. Will you let me kiss you, Maggie, before Mamma comes back?"

Maggie wiped her tears and turned her cheek so that Esau could kiss her there. "That will be all right for now," he said. "Mamma mustn't know anything about your pregnancy, though. It is best if she thinks it's my child. Which makes me wonder — was the father dark-skinned or light?"

"He was white, Esau, and my aunt and uncle already know about me."

"Do they know who the father is?"

"No. They seem to think it's a sea captain I met last time I came to Kingston. But I swear to God it's not him!"

"Well, Maggie, they still could think the baby is mine. I'm a light-skinned Syrian, my hair is fair, and even the timing sounds right."

"You would do this for me, Esau?"

"Why not? I love you. Did you think I was going to sit at Mamma's knee for the rest of my life? Now dry your eyes, Maggie, and give me a proper kiss."

POWs had started to fall ill in the prison camp, mainly because most of their drinking water had become contaminated with sewage. Some of the men lost over thirty pounds in weight, and it was not uncommon to come upon men looking like skeletons. It was said that dysentery was spreading fast; it was no wonder that the latrines, which were actually large metal tanks with a two-by-four running across the top, were constantly occupied. Some of the men even began to have fears that because of their weakened state, they might easily fall into the sewage below them. Nothing was safe from contamination, for even the bunks they slept on were quickly becoming infested with bedbugs; and those men who chose to sleep on the floor instead were soon to find that there were cockroaches everywhere.

One afternoon, Dunstan, feeling particularly wasted, went to sit on one of the bags in the laundry house. He felt as though he was on his last legs, for food was scarce and good water was in short supply.

He was taken by surprise when Edith Werner came over to him.

"You all right, soldier?" she asked. "You need to eat?"

Dunstan turned his head away from her, feeling too weak to respond.

"Here, drink," she said, handing him her own cup, in which there was a little beet soup.

Dunstan drank deeply and hungrily, and nodded his thanks.

"You mustn't be sick," she said as she walked away.

That evening, Dunstan whispered to Aynsford what had happened, and Aynsford grinned. "She's a good person, Dunstan. I told her that you are my buddy. She and I met at the back of the laundry house, by accident I think, and she spoke to me. She wants to help, and she gave me this."

"What?"

"It's two small pieces of chocolate. Here, have a piece."

Dunstan sucked on the chocolate square, savouring the taste. "I might never taste chocolate again," he said, "but that small piece was the best I have ever had."

"I agree." Aynsford smiled. "It's Swiss chocolate. Anyway, when we were at the back of the room, Edith held my hand for a moment — I thought I had died and gone to heaven. She is the enemy, I know, but I can't help how I feel."

"Keep that up, Aynsford, and you'll be a dead man all right."

"She told me to keep tabs on the delivery trucks, the days and times of their departures and arrivals. I think she is on to something but isn't saying anything; and this afternoon, she went off in one of the trucks with the Gestapo driver, and I've never seen her do that."

"She's probably going to give him the jollies, if you know what I mean, Aynsford."

"No, I don't think so; the guy was too old."

"Aynsford, you ought to know how many women over here get raped. If it is not the Germans doing it, it is the Russian soldiers. Some of those German guys could be as old as my grandfather, but I'm sure they get their jollies too. Did you notice those escapee women on the road the other day with the fronts of their dresses wired together?"

"Yes, I saw them. Some of them had their entire dress front weirdly tied with cord, and it gave me the creeps."

"That's because the guys who raped them cut a slash down the front of their clothes to gain quick entry — that's why. These are the kind of animals we're dealing with over here, Aynsford."

"I know, Dunstan, and I even heard talk that we might be sent to another camp. This one's had it. Just this morning, two POWs sick with dysentery were shot outside the fence."

It was a bright morning, teeming with the sounds of roosters and yelping stray dogs, that Maggie Chung arose too early, slipping out of the shop with intent to meet Esau Lazarus on the pavement outside. Uncle Aston was already off to mass, and Aunt Phyllis, oblivious to Maggie's movements, allowed herself an extra forty winks before having to face the day.

Maggie wore the same dress that she had worn to Eliza's wedding, adding only a new stylish black hat ornamented with red roses. She looked beautiful, though her eyes were still puffy with tears. She didn't have to wait long, because Esau did not disappoint her. She saw him almost immediately; he was standing tall, wearing a dark-blue suit with a matching tie, and his hair was slicked back. He isn't that bad looking, she thought, as he pushed his glasses up on his nose. He approached her and smiled.

"Good morning, Maggie," he said and seeing that tears welled in her eyes, unfolded his handkerchief and dabbed at them. "You look wonderful," he whispered. "Let's hurry. The register office is open; I checked the hours yesterday."

"Esau, I'm not sure I'm doing the right thing," Maggie said, lagging back. "Maybe I shouldn't be marrying you. It's not fair."

"Nonsense, Maggie, it is our baby now. Give me a kiss. Everything will be fine."

His kiss was warm and he seemed more than eager to please her.

"Okay, Esau," she said weakly, as though finally resigning herself to her fate. "We'll have to get it over with before everyone else is up."

They had to wait interminably in the register office, longer than they had anticipated, for first they had to wait for the arrival of the Justice of the Peace, who, they were told, was always late. Ahead of them was a young black soldier on a day pass, waiting to marry his sweetheart, though neither he nor his love looked any more than seventeen. Next to go in would be an old, overweight East Indian baker reeking of coffee and cinnamon and sweat. He seemed quite conceited, boasting openly about his sexual prowess with a highly pregnant young brown girl beside him, who hung her head in embarrassment. Then there were Esau and Maggie.

Esau held Maggie's hand tightly, as though he was afraid that she yet might take flight but when they were called into the office, he squeezed her hand lovingly.

"This is it," he said, hardly betraying his nerves. "No turning back now."

All at once, Maggie felt light-headed. There was a rush in her ears that reminded her of the banyan wind and, inevitably, Dunstan Gunn; and then there were fresh tears.

"Sweet Maggie, don't cry," Esau said, his soft lips kissing away her tears. "This is the best decision you could have made — you'll see — for I will never love anyone else."

They were married at ten forty-five that morning and came out of the office into the blazing sunshine at five minutes after eleven.

"Mrs. Lazarus," Esau said with a grin as he brandished the marriage license in his hand, and gazed lovingly at his new bride. "I booked a room for us at the Myrtle Bank Hotel. It is only for a day, but I wanted you to have something special to start off our marriage."

"Thanks," Maggie said, though her words came out hollow. How unreal it all felt, and how final …

They arrived at the hotel by hired car and, without fanfare, slipped into the reserved room that overlooked stately Middle Eastern–looking palm trees in the very heart of the Caribbean city.

Esau immediately closed the ornate curtains to diminish the sun's fierce glow, while Maggie sat stock still on the bed, her heart racing. What am I doing here? she thought to herself. But Esau came to stand beside her and leaned into her ear.

"Consider this the moment of our baby's conception," he said with a grin. His happiness was so infectious that Maggie, who had been full of remorse, was transformed and moved by the enormity of the young man's tremendous generosity.

Esau gently put his arms around her, leaned down and kissed her lips. "My sweet darling," he whispered, and it surprised Maggie when she found herself hungrily kissing him back. Hours slipped by in the reserved room, where they made love again and then again, Esau proving himself an attentive and tireless lover.

"Dearest, sweet Maggie," he sighed as, finally exhausted, she fell asleep in his arms.

Maggie awoke to Esau's gentle kisses at six-thirty that evening and was amazed at how natural it felt to surrender herself to him again. She would have remained thus, had she not glimpsed an alarm clock on the bedside table.

"Esau, it's late," she said. "My aunt and uncle must be worried. I'll have to go to tell them about us."

When Maggie arrived at the shop, Uncle Aston was busy with a customer but on hearing the door jangle, he looked up and saw her. Her cheeks were aglow, and there was an unaccustomed sparkle in her eyes.

"Where you been, Maggie? Why you so dressed up?" he inquired, hardly able to conceal his concern. "Your aunt and I were worried, and Mrs. Lazarus came over to tell us that Esau is missing too. We wondered if he was with you."

Maggie grinned broadly, hardly able to restrain herself from blurting out the news. "Please call Aunt Phyllis, Uncle Aston. Esau's gone to get his mother. We have something to tell you."

Hearing Maggie's voice, Aunt Phyllis came rushing into the room at the precise moment when Esau arrived with his mother in tow.

Unmindful of the customers, Maggie went at once and took Esau by the hand, to the astonishment of her uncle and aunt, as well as Mrs. Lazarus.

"Listen, everybody," Maggie said brightly, "this might surprise all of you, but Esau Lazarus and I went and got married this morning. We didn't want any fuss and bother, so we decided to do it this way."

"What!" Aunt Phyllis exclaimed. "And you never tell nobody! What is this world coming to? Imagine keeping something this important a secret. Does Chunty know? Is that why she called the other day?"

"No, Aunt Phyllis, I haven't told Mama yet. I still have to call her. Show them the license, Esau. Look, Aunt Phyllis, it is official, all signed and dated."

Mrs. Lazarus was so surprised by the turn of events that she blew her pink nose in her handkerchief and cried huge tears into her work apron.

"Oh Lord, my late husband Ahmed should have lived to see our baby Esau grow into a man. People say my Esau is a mama's boy, but they're wrong, because not even I knew that my boy was getting married. I suspected that he secretly loved Maggie, but I never in my dreams thought that she would have him."

There was such excitement in the store that Esau ran next door and came back with a bottle of rum and a bottle of Johnny Walker, and Aunt Phyllis hurriedly went to find glasses so that all present, including the swelling number of customers, could drink a toast to the couple.

"So is he the father then?" Uncle Aston whispered in Maggie's ear.

"He will be a good father," Maggie whispered back. "He loves me very much."

"So are you going to stay here with us, Maggie?" Aunt Phyllis asked, holding tightly to her niece's hand.

"No, Aunt Phyllis, tonight we will be staying at the Myrtle Bank Hotel and, tomorrow morning, Esau will be taking me to his home next door, above the store."

After all the congratulations and the laughter, Esau and Maggie Lazarus took their leave and returned to the Myrtle Bank Hotel to spend their first wedded night together.

Chapter 23:
A New Life

Six months passed before Maggie received Dunstan's long-delayed letter through the Red Cross service. She barely finished reading it when tears spilled from her eyes. The words Dunstan wrote must have been his last thoughts, she said to herself. What an unselfish man he must have been. No doubt was in her mind that since writing that letter, Dunstan Gunn had died. She gave in to the flood of tears that ensued and alternately prayed for Dunstan's soul and thanked God for having found her Esau Lazarus to love.

Wilemina, too, at about the same time, received a copy of Dunstan's capture card. For each POW was required to fill out a capture card that included their photograph, and the information would be sent without need of postage stamps, through the Red Cross, to their next of kin. The information on the card was dated long before the notification she received concerning his passing, and Wilemina felt that, from the dreadful war, that photograph was all that was left to her of her dear son. Not even Ezekiel Samuels' kisses or Eliza's phone calls could console her.

Though miles apart, both women, Wilemina and Maggie, arrived at identical conclusions, for each assumed that Dunstan Gunn was dead.

"Sweet Maggie, are you all right?" Esau asked full of concern, as he came into the flat upstairs from his mother's shop, to find his wife sitting at the lunch table, weeping over the letter.

"It's nothing," Maggie replied, crumpling Dunstan's note and stuffing it into her shirt pocket. "You should know that, these days, the slightest thing just makes me want to cry."

"You sure that's all it is, Maggie? Here I was thinking that I wasn't loving you nearly enough."

"Oh, Esau, no one could love me as much as you do."

"How's our baby? Has he been kicking a lot today?"

"Esau, it could be a girl, so don't go assuming it is a boy."

"I know, I know, Maggie, all I really care is that the both of you are all right. And you know something else? Whenever I see you, all I want is to love you more. Do you suppose that, with so much of me inside you, the baby might come out looking like me?"

"Oh, Esau, you're being silly." Maggie laughed. "Our baby won't have your green eyes or your wonderful lips, or even your honey-coloured hair. Though I think its eyes might be almond-shaped like mine, don't you?"

"You could be right, Maggie, but I still think there will be something of me there. And another thing, did you know my mama's starting to realize that you are actually nine months pregnant, and not six?"

"I know, Esau. It's because I didn't like deceiving her any more than you do, so I sort of hinted to her that I got pregnant nine months ago. And since she knows that I was visiting Kingston then, your mother jumped to the conclusion that you and I had relations back then. She even said that she thinks you'd be too embarrassed to admit it. Where is she, anyway?"

"She just left for the market, the one near Parade. I closed up the shop and came upstairs for a cuddle. Do you think we will have enough time for anything else?"

"Oh, Esau, you are so funny. Don't you see how huge I am?"

"Sweet Maggie, when did that ever stop me from wanting you?"

"Esau Lazarus, I never thought anyone, including you, could find me attractive at this enormous size."

"My sweet Maggie, don't you know how ravishing you are?"

"Esau Lazarus, you know I can't resist you when you say things like that." Maggie laughed. "We have less than an hour before your mother comes back. Come in to our bedroom — I'll show you how much I have come to love you."

A week would pass before Maggie Lazarus' eight-pound, seven-ounce son, William Samuel Alexander Lazarus, was born after twelve hours of labour at the Kingston Public Hospital. Maggie's water had broken at home and contractions had set in when Esau, with his mother, who was never too far behind, took her to the hospital. She was immediately taken to the labour room, under the care of Dr. Hector Sturridge, a fresh-faced young doctor, and two nurses.

Judging from the serious expressions on the nurses' faces, Maggie surmised that they might be distant, and methodical. She was not far from wrong, for when the pain began to come in waves and she screamed for Esau again and again, neither Dr. Sturridge nor his nurses would allow Esau into the room. Isolated from her husband, Maggie was terrified; she wept openly and loudly, wracked in intense pain. Was it God's way of allotting his punishment, she wondered.

She would not allow herself to think about Dunstan Gunn, not even when the serious-faced nurses smiled and announced that the baby was coming at last.

"He is blonde, like his father," they cried, both nodding in agreement as their mouths opened in surprise.

The baby let out such a wail when it was slapped that the sound of it clutched at Maggie's heart, and she swore there and then that no one would ever dare hurt her son.

They laid the newborn on her chest and Maggie, full of love, saw that he was squirmy, pink-cheeked and fair. His eyes were almond-shaped, like hers, but his hair was the colour of a pale yellow rose that had started to turn brownish.

Esau and his mother were the first visitors allowed into the room.

"Mama, look at your beautiful grandson." Esau grinned, walking over to stand beside the bassinet. "He is a true Lazarus, isn't he? And look at our Maggie, how radiant she is."

"Oh, he's adorable, Esau." Mrs. Lazarus smiled, weighing and measuring the baby boy with her brown eyes. "He reminds me of your grandmother Elham Lazarus," she said with pride. "You didn't know her, Esau, but your baby's eyes are hazel, just like hers, and his hair looks like it will be as blonde. Your Maggie has done us so proud, Esau; just look at his cute little fists, and those perfect little toes."

"Sweet Maggie, I hope you get all the rest you can, for Mamma was saying that, with strong lungs like his, William will be keeping us up all night when we bring him home. Let me give you a kiss before you fall asleep; I want to thank you for our son."

"Yes, Esau, I'm really worn out, but it was worth it just to see that look in your eyes."

Esau smiled and adjusted his glasses and despite the presence of his mother, leaned down and kissed his wife fully on the lips, and momentarily held her tight.

"Esau darling, you'll be glad to know my mother's coming on the morning train to give us a hand," Maggie whispered before she closed her eyes and gave in to exhaustion.

Chunty was driven directly to the hospital the moment she stepped off the train.

"So what him look like?" she eagerly asked her sister Phyllis.

"Chunty dear, to me he looks more like the father."

"What Phyllis means," Uncle Aston said grinning as he pulled the car over to park it, "is that him don't look Chinese like us."

"Well, Chunty dear," Phyllis said, "we mustn't forget that the daddy is a Syrian and them blood strong like ours."

"So, Phyllis," Chunty said, an edge creeping into her tone, "when Maggie did come here that first time with Eliza, you didn't know she was fooling round with this Syrian guy?"

"Maggie is a grown woman, Chunty, and this 'Syrian guy' as you call him, is her husband. I saw the licence myself, and he's from a very nice family. We've known them for years."

"Nice me eye ..." Chunty began, but Uncle Aston cut her short.

"So what about Peter? Any word about babies yet?" he asked bursting into the conversation, deliberately changing the subject. "Is Peter able to do anything anyway?"

"Oh him," Chunty replied, the ghost of a smile on her lips, "he and Rita seem to be trying day and night. Sometimes I have to laugh to myself, cause them think I'm too deaf to hear all the noises them making. But no, so far, nothing to report."

Edith Werner was standing outside the laundry house when Aynsford saw her. She was looking perturbed though, and when he approached she changed her stance and appeared more officious. Perhaps her change of attitude was for the benefit of anyone who might be watching, namely the sentries who were posted at intervals all around the compound.

"Soldier," she whispered, for she never called Aynsford by name, "it is bad news. Many in camp are dying. We will have transfer to other compounds. Some of us will be parted. You and me perhaps."

Though long expecting the coming upheaval, Aynsford was still taken by surprise, for he had come to accept the routines assigned to fill his daily existence. How often had he heard talk from incoming POWs, transferred from other compounds, about gross indignities and inhumane treatment dealt to them elsewhere. He had even written his beloved sister letters of farewell, letting her know that there was no sense in her expecting his survival when there was death in the cards all around. But Roslyn Collins never received even one of her brother's letters. Unknown to the sorry men, most of their correspondence was burnt almost as quickly as they were written, and the few letters that went through took months to arrive at final destinations.

Aynsford, known for his decency, humility and level headedness even on the battlefield, was all at once shaken by the spectre of the inevitable changeover, for surely death awaited him somewhere down that road.

"So it could mean that I wouldn't see you anymore?" he said, his words charged with the disappointment of the forecast.

"Yes, it is so, but soldier, I have plan."

Edith proceeded to quickly explain, in her German-accented English, that she had deliberately and regularly slept with the old Gestapo laundry truck driver in order to gain his confidence. Recently, he had even allowed her to drive the truck herself, as long as he was by her side.

"I do that for you, soldier," she said, and in her eyes Aynsford saw what he believed to be a complete lack of emotion.

"What do you mean, you did it for me?" Aynsford replied bitterly, repulsed by the thought of the aging bulky Gestapo driver and the spry, young Edith in compromise.

"I want we escape together," she said, hope sparkling in her eyes.

"But what about my buddy Dunstan?"

"Dunstan too," she quickly added, knowing full well that Aynsford never would consider leaving without his friend.

"Tomorrow evening, I put pill in driver's drink. Okay? You and your buddy hide in laundry bags. I get you loaded on truck; we drive away, just like that."

"But what if the driver wakes up?"

"No, no. I give him strong pill tomorrow. He won't wake for hours. Okay?"

"Okay, I'll tell my buddy about the evening pick-up."

It was six months since their honeymoon, and Lucas Paynado was still reeling from the shock of what could have happened to Eliza at their wedding. He had thought long and hard about his life, and found himself always coming back to the same decision. Therefore, when one of the secretaries came in search of him one Monday morning, she found him already clearing out his files.

"So is the next headline about you going to be 'Paynado Quits' or what?" she asked jokingly, never considering that Lucas Paynado had it in him to give up.

"Yes, Jean, I suppose you're right," Lucas replied with a solemnity she had not expected. "I've decided to leave politics."

"What! But why, Mr. Paynado? You are so good at what you do. You can't be serious."

"Jean, I couldn't be more serious. This kind of public life is not good enough for me anymore, not when it means people I love, especially my wife, could be in danger. You see, when people start seeing you in The Gleaner and other newspapers in association with something as passionate as politics, they start to think that they own you. Some people even go as far as to create imaginary lives that include you. I am known as a man of principle though unfortunately, there are some out there to whom I am nothing more than an object of sexual desire. This is the downside of exposure, Jean. I can never forget that my beloved Mrs. Paynado was almost murdered because a deranged woman knew who I was, because she read about me and had seen my photograph often in the paper."

Jean Campbell came to stand beside Lucas Paynado's desk, stunned and reluctant to say goodbye to an upcoming party affiliate with a mind as astute and sharp as Lucas'. She could not ever remember a time when he had ever sounded as sincere as he did just then. Attempting to prolong their conversation, she slowly, though somewhat reluctantly, began helping him to pack the two carton boxes he had placed on the chairs. It was a long while before she could even bring herself to speak, for she herself had often thought that Lucas Paynado had brought a certain savvy and sexiness to the campaign that surely would have attracted votes.

"But what do you plan to do with your life, Mr. Paynado?" she finally asked, fully aware of the finality that rang in Lucas' previous statement. "Do you realize Mr. Paynado, that with your looks, the newspaper will dog you whatever you decide to do?"

Lucas looked up sharply, exasperation burning in his eyes. How often were people going to be judging him, he thought, solely from the point of view of his appearance?

"Let them dog all they want, Jean," he said, his words fluid and his thoughts clear, "but in the end, it won't be me that photographers or journalists will be interested in. For if I have my way, they will be clamoring for photographs and stories that will prove the reality of the causes I will be supporting. Believe you me Jean, this new campaign of mine is designed to expose, illuminate and defend the little man. It will create a greater social awareness of those in the lower classes, including our destitute, our sick, and the hungry, for whom everyday is a struggle. Let those journalists bring their cameras, Jean; soon they will see that this is not a beauty or popularity contest. I plan to make my cause an eye-opener so that the invisible suffering in this country of ours will become entirely visible. Tell those reporters Jean, to get their damn cameras ready!"

"Lucas Paynado," Eliza sighed as he held her in his arms that evening and told her about his decision, "I am so proud of you."

She had not batted an eye in response to his revelation, though she pressed even closer to him. "Darling, you are indeed a man of the people, in every sense of those words. But don't you go forgetting that right now you are mine."

She smiled, letting her pale hands explore him and Lucas, in response, lovingly kissed her throat and invited her lips to find his.

"Eliza Paynado, my darling," he said softly, as at last she turned to face him, "with you as inspiration, I am sure my decision comes as no surprise. I suppose you already know that what I want is for us to work day and night alongside each other, in every sense of those words."

When Chunty arrived at the hospital, most of the fire in her had gone out, for the words her sister had said rang true. Phyllis is right, she thought. Maggie is indeed a grown woman. It's just that all these years, I have been assuming she would end up with Dunstan Gunn. Life is indeed full of surprises.

The medicinal stench of disinfectant and carbolic soap was overwhelming as Chunty practically raced down the hospital hall, willing her bulky frame to press on.

"That's her room there," Uncle Aston said stopping at one of the closed doors. "We'll wait outside and give you a chance to be together with your daughter and your grandson."

"Maggie," Chunty called cheerfully, pushing the door open and entering the room, "your mama is here."

But Maggie was not alone. Mrs. Lazarus was standing by the window, holding the baby and cooing over him. Maggie, sitting gingerly at the edge of the bed, was obviously still in some discomfort.

"Mama." Maggie smiled, her tired eyes brightening. "Come see the baby, I mean, your grandson."

Mrs. Lazarus, with baby blankets draped over her arms, stepped one careful step at a time across the room and stopped in front of Chunty, her eyes fierce with possessiveness.

"I'm Ingrid Lazarus — much obliged to meet you," she said, extending her free hand. "You must be Chunty Chung. This beautiful boy is our very own grandson."

Chunty leaned in, and the baby was gently passed over from one grandmother to the other.

Chunty felt the weight of the child in her arms and felt her heart brim over with love, so much so that she had to catch her breath as she smiled. Slowly, she peeled away the little sheet that practically covered half of the baby's face, and tears welled in her eyes, for the baby was more beautiful than even she had expected.

"He looks like my late husband's mother, same colouring," Mrs. Lazarus said, her eyes glowing with pride and memories.

"He looks just like Maggie!" Chunty sighed as she turned away and went to sit in one of the three chairs in the room, holding her grandson. "I see that one of the baby's given names is Samuel. It's after my late husband,"

Chunty said with pride, reminiscent of an animal marking its territory.

"Well, my son Esau gave him the name William, because he says it is the name of a conqueror, and he says this William will conquer us all."

"Where's your husband, Maggie? When I going meet him?"

"Mama, Esau just went to get me some water," Maggie said, stiffening her legs and hardly able to change her position. "He will be back in a minute, and you'll probably think that the baby looks just like him."

"Are you okay, Maggie? I can see you're still in pain."

"It's not too bad, Mamma, but I'm really thirsty all the time."

"Maggie dear, I did bring some callaloo soup to build up your strength. It look like you going need it."

As Chunty spoke, Esau came rushing into the room, carrying a jug of ice water and a drinking glass.

"Maggie dearest, I got as much ice in the water as I could." He grinned. "I had to bribe a nurse to get it, but for you, I'd do anything." And seeing Chunty there, he quickly rested his burden on the bedside table and immediately went to shake Chunty's hand. "I'm Esau," he said with a smile. "You must be Maggie's beautiful mother, for she looks just like you. What do you think of your grandson?"

There was something disarming about the bespectacled light-haired young man, Chunty thought, not just because of his easy smile or his good manners, but because her Maggie was obviously the very centre of his world.

"Yes, Esau, I'm Maggie's mother. It's a pleasure to meet you, and Maggie is right." Chunty paused and smiled. "I'm inclined to think little William looks a lot like you."

Over in Europe, cold weather had started to set in again, and there was snow in some of the low-lying regions where there should have been the first signs of spring. Forecasters were saying that driving could be treacherous as a result of storms. Dunstan Gunn and some fellow POWs had started to help themselves to items of warmer clothing from the laundry house. At first they had been uneasy about doing so but as the weather worsened, they felt it was a necessity. Even the guards seemed to turn a blind eye, for the one or two items taken made no real difference to the huge mound.

Unfortunately, both the clothes and the men had already become riddled with lice infestation, and there were no facilities for proper baths. Conditions worsened daily and besides dysentery, some of the POWs had begun to break out in boils. It seemed that things could not get any worse.

Dunstan Gunn was fortunate that the worst he had suffered was lice. His hair had recently been shaved, and that managed to alleviate much of the discomfort, though lately he had to do his best to try to shake out lice and the accumulated filth from his clothing.

"Dunstan, we could get out of here tomorrow," Aynsford whispered one morning after inspections, for every morning the POWs were checked and accounted for.

"This nightmare could be over for us as soon as that, if you'd agree to escape with me," he said more urgently.

"What do you mean, Aynsford?"

"Edith will help us."

"How?"

The two soldiers huddled together in the cool wind, each in his own way dreaming of escape and what freedom might mean, as Aynsford recounted the plan proposed by Edith Werner. Shaky though it seemed, it was their only real hope and, in the end, both men felt willing to place their trust in her. There was no one else in a position like hers that they could even think of trusting.

"Sounds like it could work," Dunstan said, "though it is disgusting to think what Edith might have had to do to make that old bastard jolly."

"Personally, Dunstan, I try not to think about it at all. I try to concentrate only on the plan. And it occurred to me that to be on the safe side, we could also ask that English POW named Smithy to supply us with some false documents. That's what he does most days, forgery. He's pretty good at it too. He's made a crawlspace below his hut, and that's where he goes to do it. It gives him purpose, he says. Someone told me that he can even forge letters well enough to pass as typewritten. He has a stack of stuff hidden somewhere. For a few cigarettes, Smithy will do anything for us."

"Yes, well, that's a good back up contingent, Aynsford. I've got tons of cigarettes myself."

"So it's a go then, Dunstan?"

"Yes, I don't see why not. Otherwise, we could be stuck here forever."

"It's almost a year Dunstan, and I haven't even heard one word from my sister. She probably thinks I'm dead."

"I'm in the same boat, Aynsford — no word from home either. I hope to God everyone is all right."

Roslyn Collins did indeed believe her brother had died, and the Collins household had not been the same since Aynsford no longer ran things. He was an efficient and methodical worker, though he often presented himself as being first and foremost humorous. No wonder he was well missed, even on the job.

There were only two persons left in the Collins household besides Roslyn, for her aging grandmother, the seventy-odd-year old Sylvia Collins, who adored Aynsford, still lived there, as did Roslyn's forty-five year old uncle, Joseph Rudd. It was seven years previously that Rosalyn and Aynsford's hard-working parents had lost their lives in a freak boating accident on the Rio Grande River.

As a result of that accident, the orphaned brother and sister had become inseparable, and now Roslyn was thought to be the only surviving heir. At age twenty-one, she felt obliged and responsible to help to run the pickle and preserves company her parents had founded, Collin's Culinary Preserves, which was well known throughout the island and despite continued shortages, locals were still inclined to invest in the hot-pepper sauces and pickled peppers the company made famous.

Fortunately, Uncle Joseph was in his prime, a disciplined and experienced worker. He knew every recipe inside out and every vat like the back of his speckled hand. Such was his dedication that there wasn't a day when he did not take work home with him. His life was ruled by measurements and weights and thoughts of importing and exporting.

With sharpened taste buds, Uncle Joseph could assess when ingredients needed to be adjusted to make them better than the best, and he allowed no margin for error. He personally saw to it that his workers used only the finest quality Scotch bonnet peppers, cane vinegar, mangoes, tamarinds, onions, carrots and garlic — with no substitutions.

Uncle Joseph's passion for work might have caused him to be quite a one-track mind, for his head for business prevented him from caring deeply about anything else. His orphaned niece Roslyn worked as his secretary, though it was she, as owner of the business, who often had to stand in his defense against disgruntled workers regarding wage cuts and long hours.

Even if Roslyn Collins had not been as young and attractive as she was, she still might have been admired for her generosity of spirit and her ability to remain calm, even in the worst of situations. Her one fault, according to Uncle Joseph, was that she was a woman. "Women shouldn't run companies," he often grumbled. "Women belong in the kitchen."

Perhaps it was Uncle Joseph's disciplinarian nature that influenced Aynsford in his decision to join the army, which led to his travelling to England and fighting in the war. Uncle Joseph was of the opinion that, as a child, Aynsford was far too high-spirited and spoilt and in dire need of discipline. However, whatever Aynsford's reason was for leaving home, he was often to regret leaving Roslyn behind. He never spoke of his connection to Collin's Culinary, and even Dunstan Gunn, the best friend he'd ever had, was left in the dark.

Roslyn Collins was notorious for keeping journals, and one of her journals was completely devoted to her brother. It wasn't because she was in the least morbid, but because she felt that it was her way of keeping his memory alive. Most mornings before work, she would sit at her desk and scribble notes and letters to him.

Dear Aynsford,

It's too bad you couldn't be here to enjoy this beautiful day. There is sunshine coming in at the window, which I have opened a crack so that I can hear birdsong. As you know, our uncle feels that outside noises distract the mind; therefore, if I hear him coming, I will be obliged to close the window. But you would have loved the scent of ripening mangoes on the trees outside, though some of them, the best ones, will end up in our rich dark sauces. Remember how as children we used to climb those trees and peep into the factory to see Mama and Papa, head to head, at work in this very office room where I now sit, chained as it were to this desk.

My days are spent here Aynsford, day after day. There is no one in my life, though I am certainly of age, for Uncle would not approve of anyone. He seems to feel that every man is only interested in stealing the business away from me, or wants to have his way with me. Granny and I have become quite dependent on each other for company. Every day I bring tales to tell her, just little things, nothing too serious, and she likes it. She says I should sit under the trees to have lunch, but I feel that Uncle would not like it, for that is where the workers are to be found at that time of day, and you know how strictly he abides to the division of the social classes.

Hope your day is more special than mine.

Your beloved sister Roslyn

The evening that Edith's plan was to be executed, the laundry truck arrived at the compound on schedule and as usual, the old Gestapo driver came out to stretch his legs while the new batch of laundry was being loaded. He went as was his custom, to the room where the guards often congregated to converse over tea or coffee. Edith Werner had a metal thermos of tea waiting for him and a stack of homemade biscuits.

The weather had worsened; there was blowing snow along the roads, and the driver was already somewhat exhausted from the navigation. He welcomed the tea and the small talk with the guards as a diversion, though what he really looked forward to was to have the young Edith in bed with him.

While the guards were occupied in conversation, Aynsford, crouching low, managed to slip between some of the laundry bags without being seen. He was soon followed by Dunstan, who managed to pull some extra bags around them to further avoid detection. They were well aware of it when some twenty minutes later, Edith and the driver, whose name was Markus Bettermann, came out from the tea room. Edith made a point of stopping to call to a group of the POWs to find out if the loading was completed, and if Dunstan and Aynsford could have seen Markus Bettermann, they would have realized from his gait that his legs were already unsteady.

"Perhaps, you should drive Edith," Markus Bettermann said wearily as he approached the truck. "The bad weather must have worn me out, though I would still like us to stop at a farmhouse, further along the route, to enjoy each other, okay?"

"I'd like that," Edith replied, laughing girlishly as she swung herself and a duffel bag into the driver's seat.

"Your breasts are beautiful Edith. May I?"

"Oh, Markus, you'll have to wait, for here we must behave as professionals."

"Yes, you are right … you will wake me when we get to the farmhouse?"

"Naturally, Markus. As soon as we are out of these gates, you can have a snooze. No one will see you, and I'll keep watch — all right?"

Crouched up beneath the laundry bags, Dunstan and Aynsford heard every word of the conversation, though they could make no sense of what was being said. Further more, their hearts were in their throats; every moment was precious, and each word could well be as potent as a gunshot blast.

The truck shook under the weight of the new occupants, and the laundry bags shifted somewhat. The two hidden men were greatly relieved when one of the POWs, perhaps the Australian, threw a few more bags into the truck and miraculously the load settled back into place and the engine purred and spluttered to a start.

"We are on our way," Edith said out loud, in English, as a few bedraggled POWs, including Smithy, stood within earshot and watched as the truck laboriously moved towards the gate.

Once there, they were delayed when two new guards meticulously went over Edith's documents and maps while two rookie guards, who were either bored or eager for action, grinned and began to stick bayonets into a few of the exposed laundry bags. Edith became extremely agitated, and she jumped out of the truck to confront them.

"Stop that, you idiots!" she commanded. "You will damage the clothes."

"What does it matter?" one of the guards replied with a laugh. "There's more where that came from."

"The sales from these clothes are helping to fuel our economy," she replied tersely. "The money we make after they are washed and sold is fueled back into our government's coffers. Do you really think that Germany is that rich? If we are to win this war, we need financing, however we can get it. Stop being such children and behave like the men you are supposed to be."

Edith's officious manner must have had effect, for the guards backed away from the truck and proceeded to open the gates.

"What's the matter with the other driver?" one of the guards asked, noticing how much Markus Bettermann was beginning to slump over.

"He's in pain, it might be dysentery," Edith replied sounding concerned. "He could have picked up something from the prisoners."

"I'm all right, no need to be concerned," the old Gestapo driver said groggily, though he was hardly able to keep his eyes open or prevent his words from coming out slurred.

"Take him to see a doctor in the nearest town," the guard said, waving the truck on.

With Edith at the wheel the truck proceeded, despite the weather, at top speed towards open country. Ten minutes into the journey, the Gestapo driver was fast asleep, his jaw hanging slack as his head bobbed against the back of the seat.

Chapter 24:
Loyalties

It was the same week when baby William came home that Uncle Aston finally installed a telephone. He had it to say that he had not realized its necessity until it came. Chunty sent word to the shop in Hedley to let the family know the phone number, and later that evening Peter, who had been busy when she called, finally got back to her.

"Hi, Mama. Peter here," he said. "How's Maggie's baby? Was it premature? What's he like? Is he Chinese-looking at all?"

"Hold your horses, Peter!" Chunty replied. "You not going ask bout Maggie? Well, Peter, the both of them are fine, and as for little William, well, he look Syrian to me, though his eyes shape like Maggie's, and he is real big too."

"Please tell Maggie I sent my love. I know she's busy right now, and Rita says to give the baby a kiss for her. Anyway, Mama, tell me what you think of her husband. Is he nice? Funnily enough, I thought she was going to marry Dunstan; they were so close. But she must have really fallen hard for this guy; she didn't even know him that long before they married."

"He's real nice, Peter, and there's no doubt in my mind that he adores Maggie. I kinda glad the baby look like him, cause him is real sweet. I know I mustn't speak ill of the dead, but I feel this guy make a better match for our Maggie than Dunstan Gunn. Because I was inclined to think she did feel that the Gunn them was better than we. You should see how she and her husband always making moon eye after each other. No doubt Maggie is sensible enough to see that this guy's love is exactly what she needed in life."

Thick snow blanketed the countryside, and the further the truck went, the worse the weather became. Edith, knowing the terrain, drove for several hours nonstop on back roads, covering great distances without running into patrols. Small villages with half-timbered houses, fortified towns that overlooked narrow cobbled streets, castles, farmer's fields, and occasional glimpses of majestic rivers were mere blips on the dark horizon as the truck raced by. However, when petrol began to run low, Edith was greatly relieved to approach a familiar, deserted, wooded terrain. Once inside the wood, she emerged from the truck and came round to the back end.

"Soldier, better get out here," she said. "There are things I must do, and I need assistance."

She removed a rolled camping mattress from the back of the vehicle and lay it down under the trees. Then, from her duffle bag, she took out a pair of her panties and a bra, and with the help of both Dunstan and Aynsford, lugged the old driver from his seat, to lay him down on the mattress with the dirty underwear over his face. Next, she opened his waistband and his fly before covering him with a thick blanket. She then slipped into a civilian overcoat and a thick wool hat and a scarf, after which she and the two soldiers rolled the truck down an embankment, where it crashed against a clump of tall alpine trees. Then, together, the three conspirators set off through the trees on foot.

"Won't he die out there in the cold?" said Aynsford.

"Only if he's lucky," Edith replied with a chuckle, "for as we speak, a band of resistance soldiers comes to meet us. They'll find him first — he is well dressed for weather, is he not?"

"So why did you leave your underwear?" Dunstan inquired.

"It's my signal, soldier. But also I want that old toad to think that with his fly open, and my underwear there, he had had his way with me. Or is possible he will think it was one of the resistance soldiers who did so before he could?"

"Now I get it," Dunstan said. "You want him to think the truck had an accident, or something like that, and that you disappeared after being raped by someone, or even after having had relations with him."

"That's exactly it, soldier. But whatever he thinks, he will not find us."

Less than half an hour later, a dozen or so armed men involved in the resistance arrived on the scene of the staged accident. They immediately bound and gagged the old Gestapo, who by then was slowly awakening to find himself surrounded by guns and Edith missing. It was embarrassing for him to find her underwear over his face, and even more so when he discovered that his fly was open to expose his genitals. One of the armed men made a show of swinging the panties in front of his nose, to taunt him, while another, hidden among the trees, disguised his voice well enough to sound like Edith's as he screamed for help in German — for the Gestapo driver to hear.

Meanwhile, three or four of the armed men clambered down the incline to unload a few of the bulky laundry bags from the truck, to lighten the load. Then they refilled the petrol tank and heaved the vehicle back up the embankment. The keys were still there, as planned and, when they started it, the engine immediately turned over. Six of the men jumped into the back of the truck, while another man drove with the bound Gestapo at his side. It was too dark for anyone to notice that there was a gun pointed from the back of the vehicle, trained at the older man's head.

The snow was beginning to pack down in earnest and footprints would be easily obliterated, though that was not enough to prevent the five remaining men from setting off with great speed to catch up with Edith and the POWs.

Baby William was pampered by both grandmothers, and he was the talk of Barry Street. Chunty made a habit of taking him out in an old pram first thing in the morning, and his Syrian grandmother would do the same in the evening. Passersby always stopped to admire him; some even gave small tokens of affection, including fruit, and on occasion homemade booties. Some nights, little William slept above the haberdashery in a cot set up for him there so that he could be with Chunty in her room. Other nights, he hovered between Maggie and her vigilant mother-in-law. His bottles were sterilized and filled anywhere between the two kitchens, for there was always Cow & Gate milk powder, in one or the other, to be prepared for him.

Between the doting grandmothers and his granduncle and aunt, there was plenty of time for Maggie and Esau to work in the store alongside each other and enjoy precious time together.

"So when is your mother going back home, sweet Maggie?" Esau asked one morning just after opening the store. "It's not that I want her to go, of course, but I was wondering just how long our lives will be this ideal."

"Oh, Esau, I know you. What you really want to know is how long we should expect to have all this glorious time to enjoy each other?"

Esau grinned and continued to neatly fold some recently arrived blouses and foundation garments. It was his habit to present every loose garment as attractively as possible in boxes. Once the item was sold, he would often keep the box to use a second or even a third time.

"You know me too well, my sweet." He smiled. "It frightens me sometimes, but come, let me give you a kiss. No one is in the shop yet."

Maggie slipped behind the counter to join him, still tagging the socks she was getting ready to put on display. Esau came up beside her and mischievously ran his hand up her skirt. "Come, come, Esau darling," she said with a laugh, "you know you shouldn't do that in here."

"So do you want us to go upstairs, Maggie?" he asked, removing his glasses and rubbing his eyes as if in disbelief. "It's too bad we've just opened the store but as a matter of fact, I don't see any sign here that says 'No Wife Kissing Allowed'. Do you?"

He grinned boyishly, as he proceeded to dramatically swing Maggie backwards, to plant a soft, lingering kiss on her lips.

"Maggie, my sweet, it's almost coming up to the time when the doctor said we can start doing rudeness again," he whispered with a smile. "I can hardly wait; can you, sweet Maggie?"

Before Maggie could reply, there was a jangle at the door as someone came into the shop, and it startled Maggie, who was still in her husband's arms when she turned to see who it was.

She was wide-eyed with surprise when Eliza Paynado walked in accompanied by Lucas.

"Maggie," Eliza said excitedly, "how good to see you. Just look at you both. This must be your husband. Would you believe I only just found out that you are married? Congratulations. You should have told us, Maggie; we would have come by sooner. What a dark horse you are. Well, I certainly hope that this gentleman here is your husband."

"Yes, I'm Esau Lazarus, Maggie's husband. Much obliged to meet you both," Esau said, stepping from behind the counter to shake their hands. "You just caught us cuddling — we could cuddle all day if we had the chance."

"So I see." Lucas laughed.

"Esau, meet my husband, Lucas Paynado," Eliza said. "Lucas and I actually just stopped by briefly to see your family next door, and Uncle Aston told us the news. He said you even have a baby boy already! How did I miss all this? I would have loved to have seen your baby, but I understand from Aunt Phyllis that Chunty took him out for his morning walk. He must be such a sweetheart, isn't he? So who does he look like anyway, is it you, Maggie?"

"No, not at all. Everyone says he is more like Esau."

"Well, Esau, I'm glad Maggie found someone like you, for you seem to be every bit as romantic as my Lucas."

Dunstan Gunn was standing against a thick fir tree, with his muffler pulled up over his face and his fur-lined collar turned up, for the weather was turning colder. Aynsford and Edith, equally bundled up, were sharing a cigarette, and its dim glow in the dark reminded Dunstan of a beacon. How often had he seen beacons from his window as a child, and dreamed of adventure. The darkness in the surrounding forest was so thick and heavy it reminded him of being in a cave, and his thoughts flew home to Gunn's Run. The sound of the wind whistling through the large tree trunks in the European woods inevitably brought the banyan to mind, and he almost choked from the rush of memories of his much missed home.

"They will find us anytime now," Edith said, tossing her cigarette butt into the snow. "Did you bring more cigarettes, soldier?" She turned to Dunstan. "There might be time for another smoke."

"Unfortunately, I don't smoke," Dunstan replied. "I only collected cigarettes to use for barter."

"Like for girls who come into camp — you think we don't know?" Edith said, spitting out the words like venom.

"Yes, I suppose so," Dunstan replied bitterly. "One has very few moments of pleasure in a prison camp, wouldn't you say? Those girls brought a little fun, nothing else."

"Yes, you might be right, soldier. For as guard, we made sure nothing sexual happens with prisoners. But you must not forget also that as guard, we were also restricted to staying in the worst camps."

"You probably did us a favour, Edith," Dunstan said, remembering how those girls willingly had their way with the obnoxious guards, who could afford to pay them in marks. Then those same girls, their mouths bright with red lipsticks would tease the prisoners with their suggestive pouts and hip wiggling, to tempt them into parting with cigarettes.

"Most likely, those girls were riddled with venereal diseases. I was lucky not to have had relations with them. But all that aside, Edith, I have to thank you for getting us this far away from the depravity that we had to live with for so long. Still, it sometimes is difficult for someone like me to get past the fact that you are a German guard."

"I might have been guard then, soldier, but not now. Would it ever be possible you think of me as a woman?"

"I don't know, Edith, but it doesn't matter what I think. Aynsford likes you, and I trust him implicitly."

"Aynsford." Edith smiled, using his name for the first time and testing out the sound of it on her tongue. "Tonight, he and I could be together, soldier." But she turned away swiftly, having heard a twig snap in the woods behind them. Her trained fingers slowly moved to caress the trigger on her revolver as she stood at the ready and waited.

"Hold it!" a voice shouted from the dark. "It's us, the Grey Foxes. We have a van waiting on the other side of that bridge up ahead."

"Niles, you startled me," Edith replied, quickly putting away her weapon as her friends approached stealthily. "Your van, can it take us to the Belgian border tonight?"

"Don't see why not. Everyone will fit in the back. Just don't make a sound; there might be road blocks along the way. Josef and I will drive in the front seat, and if anyone asks, I say he is my apprentice electrician."

All was as it should be in the pickles and preserves factory. The machinery hummed with the same comforting drone and precision as it had done for years, and every worker, like those in a beehive, saw to it that their tasks were done and executed well.

Sunlight streamed in at the windows as Roslyn Collins, with her brown hair tumbling about her shoulders, bent her head over the reams of figures her uncle had assigned to her for checking. There had been no opportunities that morning to make entries in her journal, though she did think of her brother, wondering what he would have made of her present circumstances.

She had only just completed the first row of figures, when a jarring scream from the factory floor startled her.

"Mr. Rudd collapse!" someone shouted, and Roslyn immediately dropped everything and ran out into the plant.

"Uncle Joseph!" she cried out, seeing her uncle prostrate on the floor, his eyes rolled back, and his tongue heavy and shaking as though trying to impart information.

"Run, someone, please call a doctor!" she shouted, kneeling down and managing to cradle her uncle in her arms. "Please let him have some air. Don't all crowd around so. Will someone please open a window; it's too stuffy in here."

Roslyn felt her uncle's weight in her hands and was surprised at his frailty, for his arms and his bones were as sticklike as a bird's. His heavy, laboured breathing alarmed her further, though she spoke to him as gently and as lovingly as a mother to a child.

"Please don't worry, dear Uncle. I'm here; I'll make sure nothing bad happens to you."

When the doctor finally came, Roslyn accompanied him to the hospital with her uncle and learned that he had suffered a stroke.

As her uncle rested comfortably, she was encouraged by the hospital staff to return to the factory, for there was nothing that she could do to help except to pray and stay out of the way. Though quite shaken, she reluctantly returned to work, if only to try to appease the fears of her employees. But she surprised herself, for she walked through the factory with her head held high and instilled such confidence as she accepted the workers' good wishes, she couldn't help but feel that she had taken over the reins.

She set about seeing to it that the day's production continued in a smooth vein, in much the same manner as her uncle would have done. She taste-tested and examined the new batches of sauces from each vat and recommended the appropriate spices to brighten up any that didn't quite come up to the Collin's standard. At the end of that first difficult day, she returned to the hospital and finally had an opportunity to speak with the doctor on duty.

"Your uncle has had a massive stroke, Miss Collins," Dr. Graham Middleton said gravely. "I'm afraid his right side will likely be paralyzed, though we will have to wait to see if he has also lost his ability to speak. Meanwhile, we will have to keep him here at the hospital for bed rest.

Lucas Paynado threw himself into his work amongst Kingston's poor, and his dream of working with Eliza was fulfilled. Side by side, they laboured amongst the masses who found their way to the poor house. He even began to entertain the idea of renting a larger building on North Street to try to accommodate the hordes that could not be accommodated in the original house.

It was because of his past political connections that he was successful in drawing public attention to the plight of the poor, and newspaper articles began to appear regularly as donations poured in. However, after some months, public opinion became weary with the focus the press was taking and demanded more uplifting newspaper articles. The problem, they said, was entirely too large to handle by so few, and Lucas Paynado began to feel that his initial efforts were in vain.

"Lucas darling," Eliza said one afternoon over lunch, "I never thought I would ever say this, darling, but don't you think that if you were still in politics, you might have had more influence in channelling government funds to our cause?"

"Eliza, I have been thinking the exact same thing lately. For though I am doing good in the eyes of God and the nation, without funds I cannot extend myself to meet the overwhelming demand for sustenance. I don't know how many people we had to turn away today. It really sickens me, darling, for we shouldn't have to be doing that. Something is morally wrong with our society, and perhaps I have to conclude that it is impossible to address it properly from the position I am in."

"But, Lucas darling, have you tried getting back into the party?"

"Yes, darling, I have. I must admit that I should have consulted you first. But the doors were so firmly shut in my face that there was no need to mention it. I can't really see my way into getting back in. You see, darling, I have been labelled a quitter."

"Perhaps there were some internal jealousies over your successes, darling. There are always vultures everywhere, waiting to pick one's bones, wouldn't you say? Why don't you approach the other political party, the JLP? Mother was always a firm admirer of Mr. Bustamante. I remember how she used to read articles about his letters to Buckingham Palace. She said that those letters enlightened the British Parliament about Jamaica's true social situation. From the sound of things, Lucas, Mr. Bustamante, whom I should mention also started out from humble beginnings, would empathize with causes such as ours. And with your political savvy, darling, who knows, that party might well need men like you."

"Wouldn't they consider me a turncoat, darling? The worst thing, Eliza, is to be labelled."

"Lucas, it's a chance worth taking. As it is, you have nothing to lose. Why don't you set up an appointment? Speak with them. I'm sure that ultimately what both parties want is whatever is best for our country, and if I know you, darling, so do you."

Wilemina Gunn was more isolated than ever at Gunn's Run since Constance started visiting Kingston regularly and Chunty was away helping with baby William. Even Wilemina's lover, Ezekiel Samuels, was mostly in Kingston, except for weekends, having not completely made up his mind to give up his Kingston residence and move back to the country. So, most days, besides the young ginger labourers, Wilemina was quite alone on the property. There were days when the silence would have been deafening if not for the roar of the sea and the cling cling, ground doves and bananaquits that nestled in the nearby poinciana trees. Once in a while, she would find herself talking when no one was there to listen and occasionally, she almost could hear other voices. For there were voices from the past whispering in the sun-filled rooms. First, there was Isilda, once again fussing over the children, then Jonathan, with his "cheery-byes" as he contentedly headed for the grocery shop; and, recently, Dunstan too threatened to join in the chatter — she swore that, if she listened well, she could just about hear him.

It was not as though no one knew she was alone, for most of Hedley knew her circumstances and were protective of her. But then there were always the undesirables who roamed the island's countryside searching out persons in exactly Wilemina's situation to prey on.

One Friday afternoon, as she was sitting alone on the veranda, Wilemina noticed that in the distance, a black-skinned young man was approaching the house by way of the beach. He carried a sharp cutlass but she saw no danger in it, since she innocently assumed that he was sent to help with the ginger. She remained at her post in her rattan chair, a gift from Ezekiel, and waited. However, when the man boldly mounted the broad wooden steps, she was immediately alerted by his rough confrontational manner as he approached her. From that proximity, she saw that his red-rimmed eyes were seething with rage and that his grip on his weapon was firm. Though filled with terror, Wilemina dared not move a muscle to retreat.

"Good afternoon," she said, hoping to defuse his deep-muscled anger, for even his biceps seemed to bristle with resentment.

"Shut up, white bitch!" he spat out, brusquely brushing past her to enter the house. "Where you money is? You better find some money, bitch, or me going kill you!" To emphasize his point, he growled obscenities and banged on the very table where Jonathan Gunn had occasionally had his afternoon tea.

Wilemina rose fearfully, her heart stopping, though somehow she found the courage to walk towards her room. But the moment she approached, the young man grabbed her roughly and slammed her forcefully against a wall with his powerful hand. He proceeded to forcefully squeeze her breasts as he ground his knee between her thighs to hold her there firmly, bringing his lips closer to hers.

"Please, don't!" Wilemina said, defiantly turning her head aside; and meeting his eyes, she saw such a wild look there that she knew without doubt that such words would fall on deaf ears, for already he was fumbling with her long skirt.

"Bitch, I going give you something you should a get long time now."

Wilemina, with no weapon, no telephone, and no possibility of help arriving soon, felt her very thoughts reel in anguish and turmoil. In desperation, she blurted out words that surprised even her.

"You'd better stop, you bloody idiot! Don't you know I am Lucas Paynado's mother-in-law?"

Those words must have been like a gunshot blast, for when the crazed young man's eyes met Wilemina's again, he reeled in sudden recognition. He shoved her aside like a sack of coconuts, grabbed his cutlass and ran down the steps, leaving deep footprints in the sand behind him.

The van carrying Dunstan Gunn and Aynsford Collins successfully passed through two roadblocks without incident. The patrols on duty examined Niles' and Josef's papers and accepted Niles' word that they were on their way to install electrical equipment in a town near Stuttgart.

"Is your van carrying equipment?"

"Yes," Niles replied, "my apprentice and I must rush; there was an explosion. Where are we now anyway?"

"Near Wurzburg."

"Gut, I must hurry then."

As soon as they were given the go-ahead and waved on, Niles turned to Josef, who had sat stock-still beside him through the questioning, and smiled.

"We are near Wurzburg, Josef — not too far to go now, is it?"

Chapter 25:
Ute Nurman

Just after dawn, the van with the soldiers neared where Niles assumed was Stuttgart, for there were miles of farmland and fields in sight. Unsure of his exact location, he stopped the vehicle and went to stand on a rise, using his binoculars to survey the terrain. Up ahead, he could see that the land dipped into a deep, wooded valley. Dunstan and Aynsford were lucky that Niles had not continued driving for, not far from the valley, up ahead, was an enormous roadblock buzzing with dozens of armed Nazi patrols. Niles wasn't sure, but he felt that somehow his presence might have been detected, perhaps from the early morning sunlight glinting off of his binoculars.

He hurried back to the truck and quickly alerted the others. "Your journey ends here, Edith," he hissed. "Quick, you and your friends hide in the fields. Only Grey Foxes must be in truck. We can easily pass for electrical construction crew. We have equipment. I come back for you here later."

Edith, Dunstan and Aynsford waited for hours in the melting snow, hunched behind haystacks and farm equipment, until it became clear to them that neither Niles nor the van would be returning for them. They were ravenous, and that evening they resorted to eating raw cabbages and a few potatoes found under the mounds of hay.

"Some German farmers keep provisions under hay," Edith had said, so they searched under a couple of haystacks and were lucky to find cabbages, potatoes and onions, some of which Edith stuffed into her bag.

As evening wore on, they decided to head out on foot, away from that region for fear of further roadblocks. After two hours, they found themselves in a thick, dark alpine forest.

They gathered the driest sticks they could find and lit a small fire, and huddled beside it until morning. Aynsford, who awoke early to search for land mines, was fortunate enough to find a partially frozen stream instead, and Edith used the butt of her revolver to shatter the thin layer of ice.

"I have cups," she said, pulling two tin cups from her duffel bag. "We can warm water for drinking."

"Edith, do you have any idea where we are?" Dunstan asked.

"Perhaps near Black Forest," she replied, "I'm not sure — I don't know this region that well."

"Didn't you read any of the road signs?"

"Soldier, you forget that I was hiding in van too."

"Wherever we are, its darn cold," Aynsford added. "What wouldn't I do for a warm bed?"

"Me too," Edith said, eyeing Aynsford suggestively.

"Perhaps we should follow the stream," Dunstan said as hunger gnawed at his gut. "We would at least have drinking water. If we returned to the road, we could be walking targets."

"Don't you think Nazis might be here in this forest?" Aynsford said, taking a sip of the freezing water.

"Aynsford," Dunstan said grinning sardonically, "Nazis are everywhere. We are in Germany, aren't we? Moving on is the only chance we all have for survival."

"Our patrols are always on lookout for runaway prisoners and Jews," Edith replied gravely. "They might already be searching for you and also for Gestapo driver."

That afternoon, they came upon an abandoned shed in the forest. It looked as though it had been recently occupied, for there was an old blanket left lying on the floor.

"It looks like hunter has been here," Edith said. "See the hooks on wall to hang equipment and over here, with dried blood stains, is where he hung his catch. Perhaps he was hunting deer or wild boar. It must have turned too cold to stay here."

"Perhaps," Dunstan said with a shrug, "or else this was one of the places where Nazis hid with captured Jews."

There was a considerable change in the weather. It seemed warmer, and the snow began to melt; and that night and the night after that, all three of the companions slept huddled together in the shed under a blanket. For a few days, they survived on old potatoes and shriveled cabbages they had pilfered from farmers' fields. But despite the melting snow, after three days of rough living, they decided to move on.

Thoroughly weakened, they hiked through a forested mountainous region, and Edith began to wonder if they were closer to Switzerland rather than the Belgian border. The going was rough, though they didn't dare return to the flat lands. Towards the end of three days, they noticed a considerable change in the weather, and they were able to loosen their scarves and unbutton their thick jackets.

Then one clear morning filled with birdsong, they were taken completely by surprise when a woman dressed in light clothing came walking towards them from out of the trees. She was perhaps around thirty and as muscular as a field worker, though her mouse-brown eyes darted suspiciously when she encountered Edith. Glancing at each other, the two women sized up each other as though each was trying to decide if the other was a friend or a foe. In the end, it was Edith who broke the ice and smiled, perhaps realizing what a ragtag, bedraggled, filthy party they must have made, especially with the two men already almost fully bearded.

"Guten Morgen," Edith said in greeting, "I'm Edith. These are my friends, Aynsford and Dunstan."

"Come with me then," the girl replied in German. "I am called Ute."

"Do you speak any English?" Dunstan asked hopefully.

"Yes, my English is good."

Ute, as it turned out, lived alone in a small wooden house in the interior of a thick forest situated on the steep mountain slope. So well camouflaged was the house that it would have been almost impossible for the three travellers to have found it on their own.

"Eat," Ute said as they settled in her kitchen. "I have bread and soup. From this window here, I see you in forest," she explained, leaning against the kitchen's window frame. "I could see that you not Nazi pigs."

Edith said not a word but leaned into the soup with the others and drank hungrily. It was as if a great stone had blocked their gullets, for their throats were parched and dry and as the soup went down, the passages slowly cleared.

"Thank you," Dunstan said huskily, finding that he could only sip the broth, for after such a long drought, his stomach felt as though it had shrivelled. More likely, all three of them were suffering from the effects of dehydration.

"You need wash," Ute said laughing as, with her strong muscular arms, she brought a deep bucket into the room with a bar of soap, a razor and some rags. "I'll bring water and towels too."

Dunstan noticed a wide hot water kettle on the hearth and a large clay water jar on the floor nearby, and it occurred to him that it must have taken a great deal of strength and determination on Ute's part to bring water up to the house. He watched in admiration as she used a small saucepan to ladle water from both containers into the bucket. Then, without even batting an eye, she instructed each of the newcomers to strip down and wash, perhaps knowing that by then, all three were beyond caring about modesty.

When Edith stripped off her clothing and let down her hair, Ute cringed, not because of the younger woman's firm breasts or her shapely feminine thighs, or even the long auburn hair that caressed Edith's shoulders, but because Ute glimpsed the Nazi guard uniform that was under Edith's coat. Ute said not a word as she poured more water, which delighted the two men, who relished the opportunity to wash away some of the months of accumulated filth.

"You may wear my husband's clothes until I wash yours," Ute said, addressing the two men, "and you, Edith, can wear somewhat of mine."

"Is your husband here?" Edith asked, her eyes trained on the closed door of the lone bedroom.

"No, my husband Gunter was killed by Nazis," Ute replied, her voice suddenly harsh, and still hurting from the pain. "He was a Jew, my Gunter; we built this house as hiding place. One day, he was arrested in the village nearby — they put him on death train to Poland with many others."

"So he was taken to the concentration camps?"

"Yes Dunstan, I alone have been here since."

"Are you German then?" Aynsford asked.

"No, it was my husband who was German Jew — me, I'm Dutch."

The interior of the cottage was quite simple. There were no hidden rooms or closets; it was more like one large, all-purpose room with a fireplace and a small bedroom attached. That night, after the newcomers were clean and shaved, Ute took three thick quilts from out of a wood trunk and handed them out.

"You and Edith will sleep in bedroom," she said nonchalantly, nodding at Aynsford. "I will sleep here near door and Dunstan, you will sleep over there, near fire."

The only sound Dunstan heard that night was wind moaning in the trees, the screeching of a night owl, and the soft rhythmic sighing coming from the bed in the other room. It wasn't long before he drifted off to sleep, dreaming of home.

But Maggie Chung no longer entered his dreams as she had before the war tempered him. She had become part of his past and inhabited a place in his memory that he no longer visited. The boy that he was then no longer existed, for time and the experience of war had matured him into manhood.

Not a sound did he hear when Ute quietly slipped out from under her quilt to find him over by the stove. Quietly, she crawled in between his quilts and curved her muscular frame around him, to keep him warm. It wasn't until just before dawn that she silently returned to her own quilt, without having had any expectations from him or uttering even a single word to him.

The next day, Dunstan learned from Ute that they had travelled north rather than south, as they had thought, and that they were close to the Netherlands border. That day, to everyone's surprise, the weather again turned cold, and Dunstan and the others were even more appreciative of Ute's shelter. Days of freezing rains, snow and strong winds followed and made the mountain trails impassable. But the colder it became, the thicker were Ute's soups. She threw in more cabbage and beets and, at Dunstan's urging, used some of her flour to experiment with making soup dumplings like those in Jamaica. It was her hearty soups that kept them going through the long, dreadful last days of the winter weather.

The four companions grew remarkably close and in consideration of comfort, took turns sleeping in the bedroom or else in the kitchen area. Every night before bed, they would talk for hours in front of the fire, each ultimately discovering more about the others.

Aynsford often spoke about his spunky sister Roslyn and hearing his stories, Dunstan found himself already half falling in love with her.

"I only hope I'll be able to meet her in person someday," he said one night as he glanced longingly at the photograph Aynsford kept near the long kitchen table with his few possessions.

Dunstan often felt, gazing at her photograph, that Roslyn Collins was somehow able to share his thoughts — and what longings she stirred in him.

He was unaware of the growing hurt in Ute's eyes, since he did not realize how much he reminded her of her Gunter, and how deeply disappointing it was that he was not in the least attracted to her.

"Ute," Aynsford said, "when the war is over, and you are out of isolation, you will surely find love again." His words were filled with compassion, for he had seen the far away look in the older woman's eyes when she gazed at Dunstan.

"When the weather improves, I will need to go into the village again," she said with a shrug. "Is there anything you'd like, Aynsford?"

"Yes, thanks, as a matter of fact, I have a letter that should be mailed."

"Tell us about your family, Ute," said Dunstan, drawing up a chair by the fire to join the others in the warm camaraderie.

Ute sighed deeply; the very planes of her face seemed marked with memory.

"My father was dairy farmer," she said. "My mother worked with him. I was only child, but studied in Denmark, at university in Copenhagen. That is how I met my Gunter. We both wanted to be lawyers; we considered ourselves intellectuals. When we married, things were getting bad for Jews, but we never thought it would affect me and my Gunter, for he was blonde like me and we had each other. Then, when war broke out, Jews were hunted;

we came to Germany with help of underground to find Gunter's family. But they were already taken — his young brother Benedict, his parents, and even his old grandparents, all of them, taken to death camps. We made it here from Munich by telling many lies and using forged documents. And with help of a few good people, we were smuggled on trains and barges and even onto farms and into safe houses. Gunter thought we would be safe isolated here in forest when we built this house. Kind people gave us things — those kettles, the bed, and these quilts. Gunter made the chairs and table. Once in a while, we went to village for food, cheese, sausages, things like that. People were kind then; they gave us many old cabbages and beets for soup. Then one day Nazi's came and everything changed ..."

When Ute finished her story, her eyes swam with tears; she blotted them on her sleeve and refused to let them flow.

"And why are you Nazi, Edith?" she added, hatred burning in her eyes.

Edith was taken completely by surprise for she had discreetly disposed of her uniform and was not aware that Ute knew her secret. She searched for words, but could not come up with a coherent answer until she bit her lips so hard so she could almost taste the blood.

"Ute..." she said, restraining her emotions and curtailing words that might incriminate. "It was not my choice," she finally said and, with her fists clenched tightly, she continued. "We hated it, my brother Dieter and I. We were forcefully taken away from family and trained. You are wrong if you think I liked it. One day my brother spoke out, and he supposedly was killed in an accident involving explosives. But I know it was no accident — it was murder! I played along with their game so I could survive but all the while hoped one day to revenge Dieter's death. I have helped dozens of POWs to escape camps, but only now have I fallen in love with one of them. What greater revenge than falling in love with a mulatto. Nazis hate mulattos! Hitler wants the white race to be one hundred per cent pure, and he has sterilized hundreds of mulattos!"

"Edith, I might be wrong about you, but I will never trust a Nazi, not after what they do to my Gunter."

The four companions remained together in the hidden mountain house until the warm days of spring finally arrived in earnest.

Several months after her uncle's sudden illness, Roslyn Collins was still fully in charge of the daily operation of the factory. She hired a secretary-bookkeeper, and made herself available to help with the slightest problem. In Kingston's business community, she soon became known for her attention to detail and for her business expertise, but most of all, for giving a human face to the workforce. It surprised her whenever it was said that Collin's Culinary products had improved under her management, since she had continued to follow the same traditional family recipes and formulas to the letter.

"Is because the good Lord make her products turn out so nice," one of the workers had it to say.

"And she so good to us, who could fault her?" said another worker.

Uncle Joseph, who was confined to a wheelchair, kept his brain active from the sidelines by following the upturn path of the company's sales and production. He was more than proud of his young niece's achievements, and he continued to feel useful, since she often would turn to him for an opinion.

During the day, a hired household helper saw to his every need, and Roslyn would take over in the evening hours. The arrangement worked well, since the household help, Lottie Stevens, a friendly and formidable woman, was soon to become ensconced in their daily lives, becoming companion and friend to Uncle Joseph and Roslyn's grandmother.

One afternoon when Roslyn came home from work, she was surprised to find Uncle Joseph in his chair awaiting her at the front door. He was clutching an envelope with a German postmark and, because horrific news of the war had reached his ears, he was quite visibly perturbed by the letter's arrival.

"This came today," he slurred. "It's for you. Do you know anyone in Germany?"

"For me!" Roslyn said in surprise. "No, Uncle Joseph, I don't know anyone in Europe. Wonder who it could be?"

"Well open it; I've been dying from curiosity all day," Uncle Joseph said, managing a lopsided smile for, since the many hours spent with the charismatic Miss Stevens, his prickly edges tended to be smoothing over.

There was no mistaking that Roslyn's hands trembled as she tore the envelope open. A single sheet of folded paper fell out. She held it tightly, then unfolded it to read the only words written: "A.C. is alive, as is D.G."

She almost fainted, and she had to hold on to the arm of Uncle Joseph's chair for support, for the short note was written in her brother's hand.

It was Ute who mailed Aynsford's letter in the village when the spring weather turned warm, not realizing that the address on the envelope would have attracted the attention of the village postal worker.

"You know people in the West Indies?" the woman asked suspiciously.

"Yes," Ute replied, "family friends."

"And they are called Collins? Are they German?"

"They used to be called Kolens but changed their name there," Ute lied as she turned her head away so that the woman would not see the dishonesty in her eyes.

That night, when she told Dunstan what had happened in the village, a cold shiver, like a premonition, ran through him. "We mustn't send any more mail then," Dunstan said. "It is not safe; we might be in grave danger."

"Dunstan, my friend, if bad things happen, don't forget what I tell you a few days back about hiding. You must go to places near mountain that I showed you. Now I will give you list of safe houses here in Germany and Holland. Keep with you always, memorize it."

There were tears in Ute's eyes, and from her doting expression it was easy to see that even though her deep feelings were not reciprocated, she still admired Dunstan.

"I'm sorry it didn't work for us, Dunstan," she said gruffly, "but you are not my Gunter and will not be. It is clear you have feelings for Aynsford's sister. I confess I hoped you would like me a little."

"I'm almost afraid to think that Aynsford is alive, Uncle Joseph. What if he has truly passed away, as we had thought previous to this letter? I don't think I could cope with the disappointment and the grief. But the postmark on this letter says Unger; it's a small German town, I suppose, because I have never heard of it," Roslyn said nervously. "I'm going to check Aynsford's stack of letters because, as you know, I kept all of them, and I'm going to see if there is any D.G. mentioned. Perhaps D.G. is Jamaican; why else would Aynsford mention him or her?"

Roslyn Collins spent most of the evening quietly rereading her brother's letters and running her finger over every word with deep affection. There was a wan smile on her face as she read, yet she would not stop even for supper, choosing only to pick at some slices of pineapple, bending her head into the task at hand.

Somewhere near the end of the pile was where she came upon the name Dunstan Gunn, mentioned as one of the soldiers who went with her brother to stay at her aunt's house in London. Roslyn's hand shook with excitement. She was about to immediately shout for her uncle, but something intangible stopped her.

She put her finger on the name and said it over to herself: "Dunstan Gunn, Dunstan Gunn", and the sound of it in her mind seemed somehow significant, yet she couldn't decide why. "Dunstan Gunn," she repeated, and it seemed somehow to fit like the last piece of an unknown jigsaw puzzle. "What a distinguished name," she said. "I like the sound of it. Please God, bring Aynsford and Dunstan Gunn home safely."

"Uncle Joseph, Uncle Joseph," she finally called out, unable to contain her excitement. "I think I've found him! D.G. is mentioned in two of the letters in a row — come see!"

Together she and Uncle Joseph pored over the letters, and Uncle Joseph nodded agreement. "Yes, that must be D.G," he said, sounding almost as excited as Roslyn, though his forehead was deeply furrowed as he gave thought to the name.

"I heard that name Gunn recently," he thought aloud, "but where?"

"It sounds familiar to me too, Uncle Joseph … Oh, I know! Wasn't it the name of that blonde girl who married Lucas Paynado, who used to be with the PNP? Wasn't she a Gunn?"

"I think you are right, Roslyn. If I remember correctly, she was called Gunn. I think she was from somewhere in St. James because at the time, I was thinking that some relatives on your father's side with the same fair colouring had settled in Montego Bay. But they have long passed on now, of course."

"Uncle Joseph, perhaps I could contact Lucas Paynado's wife. Last I heard, she was working in the poorhouse. It would do no harm to ask if she has a relative named Dunstan."

Chapter 26:
The Rebound

Months passed since Lucas Paynado transferred his affiliation to the Jamaica Labour Party. He managed to keep mostly in the background of its operation, though keeping himself informed and avoiding high-profile situations. But fate had more in store for him than that.

One night, while assisting with a political campaign in Manchester, Lucas was called upon to stand in for the JLP candidate who had suddenly taken ill after a meal of cod fish and bammy. Lucas' reputation for rhetoric was well known amongst party affiliates; it was no wonder that he was conveniently enlisted to appease the restless, waiting crowd.

When he stepped on to the stage, he was met with a barrage of insults and boos and cries of "turncoat billy goat".

Undaunted, Lucas stepped up to the podium to bang

his fist on a large upturned wooden keg. The sound resonated like a call to freedom. He held his head high and reeled into his speech.

"I am not here to talk about the middle man, or the big man, or even the small man. I am here to talk about the people who reside in this constituency, the people who break their backs daily to put food on the table, the people who sweat and strain under the sun to try to make ends meet and earn even the smallest living, the people who go to bed hungry, the people who have nothing but rags on their backs, and the sick whose cries fall on deaf ears. I'm talking about the people who need assistance to send their children to school, the people who have no home except for the inside of a cardboard box, the people who walk barefoot in the hot sun and in the rain, and you the people of Manchester, who must demand freedom from your burdens and support from the good government of the Labour Party. We want to help you to carry on and get through each and every passing day. You are the people, my friends. You are *my* people ..."

By the time he came to the end of his speech, Lucas Paynado's ears rang with thunderous applause, loud cheers, and whistles. It was clear to all present that a potential new candidate was born, who, along with the party he was affiliated with, would lead Jamaica into a new tomorrow.

When Ezekiel Samuels came to Gunn's Run late that Friday evening, he found Wilemina waiting alone inside. She was sitting in the glow of a single candle in the living room. There was something unusually disquieting about her demeanour though when she saw Ezekiel framed in the doorway, she immediately ran to him.

Every detail of her ordeal came back to her as she shared her harrowing story. "It is only because I am Lucas' mother-in-law that I was spared from a brutal rape," she said hoarsely, trembling from the memory.

"How terrible it must have been for you, darling," Ezekiel said, kissing her lips and comforting her as he held her in his arms. "Everything will be all right, I promise. Did you contact the police? Are they going to do anything about that damn hooligan?"

"Yes, yes, darling, it was terrifying, but I knew that I ought to keep my head. I went through the bush over to Hedley and on the way, every sound startled me — twigs, birds, everything. I kept thinking that that brute was somewhere, lying in wait for me. Wouldn't you think so too? But I somehow made it to the village police station, and a constable returned here with me. It was rather good of him."

"So a policeman came out here to investigate?"

"Yes, and I dare say he assured me they'd keep an eye on the property, in case that brute returned."

"Wilemina, their keeping an eye on the property won't be good enough! The first thing we must do is to get a telephone installed here. And I am going to stay here with you, as of now. I will not leave any stone unturned until I am quite sure that you are safe."

He immediately busied himself with seeing to the locks on all the doors and windows.

"That's it, done," he said after an half an hour. "Every last one is in working order. First thing in the morning, we'll go to the telephone company. I will insist that they install a telephone out here. But, darling, are you quite sure you are unharmed?"

He felt her tremble against him as he ran his fingers through her hair, and she drew even closer.

"Ezekiel darling, how I longed for you to come home." She sighed. "Awful as my ordeal was, the worst of it was thinking I'd never see you again."

"Wilemina, I hope to God nothing like that ever happens again. It's a good thing I didn't see that hooligan; I swear I would have killed him, and I mean it! But I can't begin to forgive myself for not being here when you needed me."

"Ezekiel darling, I'm rather grateful you are here. I know how tirelessly you were working in Kingston trying to find a venue for your festival. But I dare say, have you given any thought to holding it right here at Gunn's Run, on the beach?"

"You know, Wilemina, come to think of it, that is an excellent suggestion. You do know, of course, that all proceeds will be going to help Jews in Europe, don't you?"

"Yes, darling, I know. I rather think that that cause would have been something my Dunstan would have supported."

"Yes, Wilemina, I am sure he would have, God rest his soul. We could discuss the details later. Right now, I'm more concerned with making absolutely sure that you are quite all right."

She smiled softly, though Ezekiel could see that her cheeks were radiant with tears. "You are so beautiful," he said, marvelling at how untouched by time she seemed. "From the first I saw you, Wilemina, my heart was yours. If only you knew how I longed for you, darling, though I was in no position to reveal my feelings. But fortunately all that has changed."

"Ezekiel darling, life gave me a second chance at happiness when it brought you to me, wouldn't you say?"

Roslyn Collins was sitting at her desk, with her office door closed. There was work to be done, but she couldn't get the letter from Aynsford out of her mind. She pulled a list of organizations in Kingston out of her drawer and found the telephone number for the Alms House amongst them. She began to feel foolish about wanting to call Eliza Paynado with such a flimsy piece of evidence but each time she said the name Dunstan Gunn to herself, it was as though something as powerful and seductive as a drug had taken hold of her. How can I be feeling this way about someone I have never met? she thought. I don't know a thing about him, least of all what he looks like.

Compelled by the strange attraction, she found herself awakening to a passion she had never experienced, for it was as though her very longings were driven by an unseen hand.

She dialed the number nervously and awaited an answer as the phone at the other end of the line rang four times.

"Hello. May I speak with Mrs. Paynado?" she asked, and it seemed an eternity passed before Eliza came to the phone.

"Eliza Paynado here. Can I help you?"

"Hello, Mrs. Paynado. You don't know me, but my name is Roslyn Collins. I'm calling from Collin's Culinary. The reason I'm calling is my brother Aynsford. He was away in Europe in the British army, and I received some letters from him that mentioned a friend, and I am wondering if you might be related to a Dunstan Gunn."

"Why, Dunstan was my brother, Miss Collins. But I am sorry to say that he was killed in the war."

"Was he, Mrs. Paynado? Are you sure?"

"Yes, my mother received the notification."

"Mrs. Paynado, do you think it would be possible for you to come to see me at my office? There is something I'd like to show you that might be of interest to you."

"Maggie!" Chunty called excitedly as she came bursting into the Lazarus' shop. "Maggie, you'd better come and hear this news."

"What is it, Mama? You are screaming so loudly you could wake William, and I just bathed him and put him down for his nap."

"Well, dear, I heard from Peter, and him say that Rita pregnant at last."

"Is she? Oh, Mama, Peter must be so happy. I'll call to congratulate them."

"Maggie, them did really work hard for this to happen, but don't say nothing yet, my dear, cause Rita not doing too well. She is three months gone, but Peter says she bleeds sometimes. So I going go back home to be with them — cerasee tea good for that, you know."

"Esau, Mama's going back to Hedley, so now our so-called free time is almost over."

"Maggie, my sweet, my mama will want to help even more with the baby, as you well know. So while she enjoys herself with little William, you and I can enjoy each other. As a matter of fact, she just took him out a few minutes ago, but he will be all ours when she brings him back. It's a good thing we set up a bassinet in the store."

"Esau, it's not busy here right now," Maggie said nervously. "My mama's gone back next door to pack. Would it hurt to close the store for an hour or so?"

"I don't see why not, Maggie. My mama probably won't be back before that; she told me that she took little William's bottle and some diapers."

Seeing the wan expression on his wife's face, Esau quickly went to the doors and, with keys jangling at his hip, he closed up the shop and drew the blinds.

"There, sweet Maggie, it's done. Now, perhaps you will tell me why you look so unhappy?"

"Esau, I don't know why, but I just want to be alone with you for a while. I have a funny feeling that something ominous is going to happen. Please hold me, Esau. I just hope nothing bad happens to anyone."

"Sweet Maggie, nothing bad is going to happen. Mama says that many new mothers feel much the same way as you do right now. Just you come to me; perhaps all you need is some good rudeness," Esau said, pulling out one of the large blankets they had brought downstairs to fold in the bottom of the bassinet. He surprised Maggie when he spread the blanket neatly on the floor behind the counter and proceeded to lie down.

"Esau," Maggie said, managing a laugh as she squatted down and joined him on the soft blanket. "Whatever happens as of today, I want you to know that I'll never love anyone but you, and I want you to promise that our secret concerning little William will be safe between us forever. One thing I never want is for our William to feel like he is a misfit, or to be called a bastard by anyone."

"But of course I promise, sweet Maggie. No one would ever dare to insult my son; they would have to get past me first," Esau said huskily, pulling his wife closer and folding the blanket around them. "You should know by this that you and William are my life, Maggie. I would do anything for the both of you."

"Even rudeness?" Maggie smiled, though she couldn't help remembering that the blanket around her was the same blanket Dunstan Gunn had brought to keep her warm that night so long ago.

"Especially rudeness, my sweet." Esau laughed.

It was a bright spring morning; dissonant birdsong permeated the deciduous German forest, and a fragrant breeze wound its way in and out of the trees.

Dunstan Gunn kept perfectly still, standing at Ute's cottage window and watching a herd of shy brown deer blend into the surrounding lush foliage.

He was surprised that despite the proximity of the terrible war, hosts of Yellow Flag and blue Hepatica flowers bloomed surreptitiously beneath the trees, creating an atmosphere of enchantment.

He let his eyes follow the forested slope down from the cottage to where it dipped into the valley below, knowing that behind the trees were hidden heaths, bogs and lakes. He had seen them when Ute had eagerly taken him there to point out the most suitable and secluded places for hiding.

He had also seen yellow floating heart flowers growing abundantly in those waters, and Ute had pointed out to him that, if he stood perfectly still, a fox, a boar or even an animal as rare as a lynx might approach.

How beautiful and dangerous a forest can be, he thought.

So captivated was he by his surroundings that he hardly heard when Ute approached him from behind.

"So we are alone," she said, coming to join him.

"Where are Aynsford and Edith?" Dunstan inquired, reluctantly turning away from the window.

"They woke up early, and Edith told me that they would go bathe in small lake on other side of mountain, near where I showed you."

"I slept late," Dunstan said stretching against the window frame. "I really should wash too; the lake water is warmer now. Just look at the weather outside."

But Ute glanced out only briefly, for her eyes were reluctant to stray from the long lines of Dunstan's frame, so mesmerized was she by his large-knuckled fists, his tight biceps, and his muscled torso.

"I'll join you at lake," she smiled, "but first I pick mushrooms in forest for supper. You go, I meet you there."

She wiped her broad hands on a clean towel and tied a kerchief on her head before collecting the basket she kept by the door.

"See you soon, my friend," she said brightly, pausing briefly at the door before setting out down the mountain path into blazing sunshine.

Dunstan watched from the window, feeling saddened, knowing how much she wanted to be loved. But in spite of that, he could not find it in himself to fall in love with her.

He saw when she neared the edge of the forest, and he was about to turn away when something glinting in the sunlight attracted, his attention. He watched mesmerized, as quite unexpectedly a Nazi officer emerged from the trees.

Filled with horror, Dunstan could barely prevent himself from screaming to warn Ute. He could barely draw breath as he stood frozen at the window.

The officer raised his weapon and fired a single shot. Dunstan heard no sound, and there was not even the slightest interruption to the birdsong.

But Ute was hit with such force that her body flew up in the air like a puppet, her basket careening the rest of the way down the slope. When she hit the ground, her body lay perfectly still, and Dunstan saw that there was a gaping bullet hole in her forehead.

In the face of such horror, it was only because of his military training that he had the presence of mind to grab his small bundle of papers from the kitchen table. All he remembered of that moment was that he ran madly out through the back entrance of the cottage.

He charged through the thick forest, furtively glancing behind as he ran, knowing without any doubt that the whole mountainside leading up to the cottage must already be overrun with Nazis.

Blindly crashing through the foliage, he half-remembered Ute's directions. He could almost hear her voice as he raced.

Camouflaged by the thick forest, shrubs, and banks of wild flowers, he finally approached the swampy bogs and heaths, and knew the lake was not far off.

He waded waist-deep through tall reeds and rushes just as Ute had instructed, and he could almost hear her still: "Don't run in the mud," she had said. "Enemies could follow your tracks, and there might be guard dogs too. Go through the bog, not around it, and hide amongst the reeds. No one will see you there. Stay there until it is safe — my Gunter and I once hid there."

Approaching the other side of the bog, he thought he heard a laugh, and realized it was Edith's laugh.

But when he reached the lake's shore, neither Edith nor Aynsford were to be seen, though he could still hear her seductive laugh. He followed the sound to where a woodland stream emptied into the lake and below the tall trees, he came upon a haven of lush ferns, green groundcover, and huge moss-covered rocks and boulders. It was cool and peaceful there, and it felt to him like a place of refuge, reminding him of the banyan grove back home.

Swiftly and silently, he walked alongside the stream, and he heard as it whispered, gurgled and bubbled urgently over the rock face, to charge over little waterfalls and barrel its way through the natural rocky terrace. Then Dunstan saw them.

Aynsford and Edith, fresh from their morning wash, were laughing together as they stood pressed against the soft mossy rock face. They were half dressed, drying each other's hair with a towel.

Dunstan ran the last few yards towards them. "Hide in the rushes down at the bog!" he hissed urgently. "The Nazis are here!"

Edith turned quickly, a testament to her military training, and saw him. She was wearing a skirt but was nude from the waist up, and her firm, jutting breasts were exposed. Her hair, which had grown longer, was heavy with rivulets of shining water that illuminated her face.

Aynsford, conscious of Dunstan's presence and Edith's partial nudity, threw her blouse to her and she pulled it on self-consciously, fighting with its buttons and grabbing her things as they all ran. Seeing her there, devoid of anything military and looking more like a goddess in a grotto, there was no longer any doubt in Dunstan's mind that Edith was indeed a woman in every sense of the word.

"What happened?" Aynsford whispered when they settled in amongst the reeds. "Where's Ute?"

"She's dead," Dunstan replied gravely. "I saw it from the window. She was going to gather mushrooms but she never even made it as far as the forest. A single bullet was all it took. I am sure that by now those damn Nazis are up at the house searching."

"They won't find anything of mine," Aynsford said. "Everything I own is here in my kit bag, not that I had much. And thank God Ute burnt those old prison clothes of ours."

"I burnt my guard uniform too," Edith said. "Nothing in the house will link us with her. As for my gun, I always carry it here in my bag."

"What about the razors we used to shave with when we were there?" Dunstan asked.

"I brought mine so that Edith could shave me here."

"I left mine," Dunstan said. "There was hardly any time, though I grabbed my papers and the lists Ute gave me; but everything else I used and wore belonged to Gunter and are left behind."

"Don't forget — we are all wearing Ute's and Gunter's clothes," Edith said wryly.

That entire first day, the three friends remained hidden in the bog and early that afternoon, a platoon of about thirty Nazi soldiers came unnervingly close to them to set up folding tables, at which they enjoyed a lunch of sausages and bread, washed down with hot tea. Every word they said was audible, for the sound carried easily in the open air.

"What are they saying?" Dunstan whispered, and Edith informed him that they were speaking about Ute. They said that though the woman lived alone, she had good food in the kitchen, for they found leftover soup, fresh-baked bread, cheese, and a few sausages. Some of the soldiers said that Ute must have had to wear men's clothing, since she was so big boned, and others of them regretted not having raped her before she was shot for though she was large and muscular, her face was passable.

Neither Dunstan nor the others dared move even a muscle until darkness fell and the soldiers again retreated into the trees.

"Are they all gone?" Aynsford asked, peering into the darkness.

"Yes I think so," Edith replied.

"Time to go then," Dunstan said. "We might make it to the border by morning if we travel all night. Ute told me where to go; I still have the scraps of papers she gave me, though she had me memorize everything. "

Once out of the bog, the three weary travellers set out westwards on foot. For hours, it seemed to them that they had let themselves into a darker and more foreboding forest but towards morning, the trees thinned out, and at the bottom of a slope they approached a river. Boats and barges were moored on the riverbank and up ahead, lit by lantern light, was a small hut filled with drinking men.

One of them, an old man, saw the three strangers approach, and he came outside to meet them. Always on the alert, Dunstan noticed that one of the man's legs dragged as he came towards them.

"Do you suppose he's carrying a weapon?" asked Aynsford.

"No, perhaps not," Dunstan replied, scrutinizing the older man more carefully. "He's probably arthritic."

"Need transportation?" the old man asked in German.

"Yes," Edith replied, "we need to speak with Tomasz Hafen."

The old German laughed gutturally as he turned aside to signal to one of the other men. "All the pretty girls want Tomasz," he said, shrugging.

When Eliza Paynado arrived at the Collin's Culinary factory, she was alone. She walked slowly through the plant, fascinated by the drone of the machinery, the deep vats, and the workers moving like clockwork from one station to another. All around was the wonderful aroma of spices.

"Can I help you Miss?" a rat-faced woman asked, coming up to Eliza, regarding her as lost.

"I'm here to see Miss Collins," Eliza informed her with a smile.

"Miss Collins' office is just through that door up there. You can't miss it."

But before Eliza could take another step, Roslyn Collins came out of her office to meet her.

Eliza couldn't help but be astonished, not only by Roslyn's youth but also by the air of confidence she exuded and the fact that Roslyn Collins was every bit as attractive as the smart clothes she wore.

"Good morning, Mrs. Paynado," Roslyn said. "It's good of you to come at such short notice. Please come and have a seat in my office."

"Are you the owner?" Eliza asked, wide-eyed, gawking at the maze of pipes, the machinery and the assembly lines. "I never dreamed there was a place like this here in the city."

"It's a family business, Mrs. Paynado. I'm in charge at the present time. Come with me — I have something to show you."

Once they were both seated inside the office, Roslyn Collins retrieved her purse from inside of her desk drawer. "Mrs. Paynado," she said huskily, "my brother Aynsford went to England for military training, and that is where he met your brother. It seems they became close friends. He and your brother even spent some time in London with an old aunt of mine. Aynsford was later transferred over to Europe, and his letters became sporadic, to say the least. Then there was nothing at all and after several months, we received notification of his passing. Needless to say, we were devastated." There were tears in Roslyn's hazel eyes as she spoke, and Eliza was moved by her sincerity.

"It was the same for us," Eliza said regretfully. "Dunstan's letters were rather spare, but he was never one for letter-writing. I always said he was better at thinking. When we received the notification of his passing, my mother and I were terribly shaken. Mother took it rather badly. Thank goodness I had my Lucas for support. But, as a matter of fact, Dunstan didn't even know that I got married. There are so many things I would have wanted him to know."

"So you married Lucas Paynado after your brother left the island?"

"Yes, I did. Dunstan would have wanted to be at the wedding. But I was so in love, and still am, that I wanted to marry Lucas sooner rather than later. I know people still wonder how I could have fallen in love with a black-skinned man, but love knows no colour barriers. But forgive me, Miss Collins, I'm straying from the matter at hand. What did you want to show me?"

"Well, Mrs. Paynado, I agree with you about love knowing no colour barrier. You might be interested to know that my parents had a mixed-race marriage; one was black and the other white. Despite that, my brother and I turned out just fine. Now here's the letter I wanted to show you."

Eliza bent over the envelope and, seeing the recently dated postmark, nervously pulled out the letter. It only took her a second to read it but when she looked up from it, her eyes were swimming with tears.

"So do you think they are alive, Miss Collins?"

"Yes, I do, because that is definitely my brother's handwriting. And, by the way, please call me Roslyn. I'm sure our brothers are not referring to each other as Mister So-and-so." Roslyn laughed.

"Please call me Eliza. It's funny, but I'm still not used to being referred to as Mrs. Paynado, as wonderful as it sounds to my ears."

"Eliza," Roslyn said, easing herself back in her swivel chair, "I was wondering if you had a few minutes. I would be interested in hearing a little about your brother. I've been somewhat curious as to just what kind of person Aynsford has for a friend. Before I met you, I couldn't even picture your brother Dunstan in my mind. I didn't even know that he has an English background. I must confess that I have become quite intrigued by him."

"Well, Roslyn, you might like to see this," Eliza said, passing her a photograph she took from her purse. "This is what he looks like. I honestly believe that next to my Lucas, Dunstan is the most wonderful man I have ever known. He and I were terribly close; he was always protective of me, and kind to a fault. I hope to God, Roslyn, that he is indeed alive."

"Eliza," Roslyn said, scrutinizing the photograph, "you didn't mention how handsome your brother is — just look at him. I suppose he must have had lots of girlfriends."

"Yes, Dunstan's a treat, isn't he? But no, he only had one girlfriend. She is Chinese but after he left, she fell in love with someone else, and she is now very happily married with a young son."

"Does Dunstan know?"

"I really don't know if he does, but I'm sure they must have corresponded. I know for sure that Maggie, that's the girl's name, has long gotten over him, for she and her husband are very much in love. I saw them recently."

Roslyn stared at the photograph again before returning it to Eliza. I'd never get over him, she thought to herself, knowing full well that she was already falling in love with him.

Tomasz Hafen came out into the night and was introduced to the three strangers. He was a large, muscular man with a thick patch of dirty blonde hair above his broad forehead and dark brows. Judging from the first man's comment, Edith had expected a handsome man, but Tomasz was nothing like that. His face was plain and if anything, his brawn was testament to hard work rather than to vanity. He smiled shyly when Edith requested passage on his barge and became quite animated when she mentioned Ute.

"Ute is my good friend," he said in his booming voice. "I do anything for her."

"Ute told me you speak English well," Dunstan said hopefully. "Perhaps she would have wanted me to be the one to tell you what happened to her."

"What happen to my Ute?"

"She was shot yesterday morning."

"My Ute is dead! Who would dare kill my Ute?" Tomasz demanded, his eyes bulging with rage.

"It was a Nazi officer," Edith said. "Ute was taken by surprise. She was going to gather mushrooms. All of us had to run, or they would have shot us too."

"Those murdering bastards have corrupted this country!" Tomasz said, his eyes burning with anger. "Ute and Gunter and I were close friends. She could drink like a man, then bake like an angel. I once told Gunter I would look out for her if anything happened to him. But she assured me she could take care of herself. What a beautiful creature she was," he said with a lump in his throat. "My one regret is that I should have convinced her to marry me."

"She never drank while we were staying with her," Aynsford told him, grasping Edith's hand.

"That is because she never let liquor pass her lips since her Gunter got taken," Tomasz replied, lowering his voice. "The day Gunter was taken, they had gone into the village. She was going to the doctor; then they were going to celebrate with beer — she thought she was pregnant. But while she was with the doctor, Gunter was taken from off the street. He was buying vegetables, and someone betrayed him. She couldn't help him. She never spoke of the pregnancy again, because she lost the baby. Now, tell me where are you three headed?"

"Well, Ute gave me this address in Holland," Dunstan said, handing Tomasz a small scrap of paper with an address scrawled in Ute's hand. "She told me it's a safe house."

"I know the place," Tomasz replied. "I've been there a few times, but this time I do it for Ute. We can leave in an hour; there is a false bottom in my barge. You must hide there for several hours. I take you the safest route."

Chapter 27 :
Unification

Lucas Paynado accompanied Eliza when she decided to visit Gunn's Run to tell her mother about Roslyn's letter. If there was ever a time that she would need the support of Lucas' strong arm, it would be then, she thought.

Everyone was waiting on the veranda, drinking tall glasses of lemonade. Ezekiel was in his favourite chair and Chunty, who was visiting, was leaning against the railing when Wilemina had come smiling down the steps to greet her daughter and her son-in-law.

"Darling, we shouldn't get too excited about this new development," Wilemina said after Eliza had spoken to her about the letter. "I couldn't stand it if we got all worked up and it turned out to be false. Don't you agree, Chunty?" But Chunty hardly heard a word, for she was bursting with news to impart about little William and the impending birth of her new grandchild.

It was already late afternoon, and a light breeze from the sea ruffled the faces of the double hibiscus flowers that grew alongside the steps. Eliza pulled up her chair beside Lucas' and, as they looked out to sea, she was filled with memories, reconnecting with and admiring the well-remembered landscape.

The sound of waves slapping against the shoreline, the haunting cry of seagulls, and the distant shouts of village children rendered her rampant with nostalgia, and she vividly recalled herself and her beloved Dunstan playing in the outlying areas of the beach.

"Lucas darling," she said, taking his broad hand, which she would have kissed had they been alone, "I really miss being out here in the country, don't you? We really should come more often; Dunstan and I had the most wonderful childhood here."

"Well, speaking of children," Chunty said excitedly, "I never know it was going to feel so good being a grand-mother. But the best part is that when the baby gets troublesome, you can pass them back to the parents. Eliza, you should hurry up and help your mother become a grandmother. What's keeping you?"

Everyone laughed, even Wilemina, who secretly dreaded such a possibility.

"Lucas and I aren't ready yet." Eliza smiled. "There are a few things we still want to do. But if Dunstan is alive, as that letter seems to indicate, I hope to God that one day he will present mother with a grandchild. Because in the midst of all the bad things that have happened here at Gunn's Run, including mother's recent brush with attempted rape, we certainly could use some good news."

"There is some good news, darling," Wilemina said conspiratorially, leaning towards the others, her eyes brimming with excitement. "Ezekiel is going to be living here with me from now on. And another thing is, I think we might try for a baby."

"A baby!" Eliza gasped. "You! Oh, mother, I can hardly believe that. I remember you once told me that a lot of decorum is expected of us as white people, so how would you explain this change of heart?"

"Darling Eliza." Wilemina chuckled. "I thought that you of all people would understand about love. You've said words to that effect often enough. Hasn't she, Lucas? Ezekiel and I love each other very much and, if we had a baby, surely it would be an outward sign of that love. Wouldn't it, Ezekiel darling?"

Ezekiel nodded in agreement, admiration burning in his eyes.

But no one was more stunned by the news than Chunty. "My, my, so you not going get married? My goodness I going have to tip my hat to you. You are brave, cause I know that if it was Maggie or me, we would a have to get married."

"Oh, Chunty," Wilemina said with a laugh. "You Jamaicans can be so old-fashioned. For whether we are married or not, Ezekiel and I will love each other just the same, no more or no less. Wouldn't we, darling?"

"Wilemina's right," Ezekiel said. "I have loved her for years, and nothing will change that, not death or marriage."

"I quite agree with what you are saying," Lucas said thoughtfully, "though in my case, I'm glad I married Eliza. Not only because people would have talked if I hadn't, especially with me being in the public eye, but when it comes right down to brass tacks, I love Eliza too much to let her suffer any kind of insults or reprisal. We didn't know each other fully until marriage, and that was good enough for us both. I don't think we would be sitting all cozy here at Gunn's Run if we weren't married. Do you?"

"That's true," Eliza said. "Sadly things are different for everyone. But if that's the way Mother and Mr. Samuels want it, then so it should be."

Dunstan, Aynsford and Edith, jammed together, sat knee to knee below the deck of Thomas Hafen's barge. The confined space reeked of fish and pickled cabbage, not to mention human sweat. Tomasz Hafen informed them that there was a pail, provided for bathroom purposes, attached to a pulley rope; but they should use it discreetly, and only when absolutely necessary. He also provided them with a thermos of hot tea and some thick slices of rye bread.

"This will help to tide you over until we get you to a safe house," he told them. "I belong to a clandestine anti-Nazi organization known as The Righteous Gentiles. We are a resistance group dedicated to the downfall of Nazis. There are many of us residing here in Germany; Ute was one of us. It is very dangerous because whenever we help persons such as you, we put our own lives in imminent danger."

He then proceeded to prime them regarding what would be expected of them aboard the vessel. "Not a word!" he said. "Try not to move too much. We must go through many dangerous checkpoints and controls before we get to the Netherlands. As you can see, I am transporting sauerkraut, bushels of fresh fish, cabbages and carrots, so there is no room for comfort aboard."

Though the start of the journey went swiftly, going along the fast-flowing river, there were three or four twenty-minute stops at armed checkpoints, and those below deck could feel the barge tip and sway as unknown persons came aboard to inspect the cargo. By morning, they had gone through many more of those heart-stopping episodes, and once there was even a long delay. But Edith informed the others that she overheard it being said that Tomasz was having a smoke with one of the Gestapo at their final checkpoint. She and Aynsford would have given anything for a smoke, though the few cigarette packages they still had were hidden on their persons.

By mid-morning, they crossed the border and having passed under a heavily guarded raised bridge, they were in the Netherlands.

The barge was secured and moored to the dock; Tomasz Hafen disembarked from the vessel without saying a single word to his passengers. It was an half an hour before he returned, loaded down with oilskins. He casually threw them over the rails and proceeded downstairs under the watchful eye of a Nazi guard.

"It's dangerous here," Tomasz hissed through a crack once he was below deck. "There are Nazis on shore. We have to change plans. But it might be better for you in the long run. A friend of mine, Helmut van Kirk, a seaman, is loading his vessel to leave port. He brought chickens and eggs and butter and milk in exchange for the right to fish in the North Sea; the Nazis gave him permission. He is almost ready to leave. But don't worry, he is one of us. His real intention is not to fish, but to set explosives offshore to stop Nazi boats from getting too far out to sea. The Nazis won't even know what hit them when Helmut is through with them."

"But how will we get to his boat undetected?" Dunstan asked.

"You'll be wearing fishermen's garb," Tomasz said before he went back up on deck. Up on deck, he shaded his eyes and searched the pier until he saw that the guard was a little way off and his back was turned. Tomasz immediately seized the opportunity to squeeze open his hidden trap door enough to drop some of the oilskins below.

"Put those on and cover your faces as best you can," he whispered. "There is a pair of men's pants for Edith too. She will have to tie them at the waist with the string I provided. Unfortunately, there is a vigilant Nazi guard right here on the pier. He must not see that Edith is a woman, or that Aynsford is not Caucasian. Helmut's boat is eleven boats away from mine on the left side. It is called Sonnenaufgang. If you have false papers, make sure you have them ready, just in case. Edith, you must pretend you are a young boy, and help the others to carry the rope and the fishnet that you will find up here on deck. It is heavy, but keep your heads down. Remember what I said, and good luck. I hope to God that wherever Ute is, she is watching over you all."

Early one evening some months after Eliza's visit, Ezekiel Samuels found himself lost in thought. He was feeling despondent as he paced the living room floor at Gunn's Run, going over final preparations for the festival. He had tried for hours to come up with an appropriate opening story, and nothing would come to him. He was about to give up when quite unexpectedly, a story filled with passion and intrigue came to him.

"Wilemina!" he called out excitedly. "Listen to this. Tell me what you think."

He went to stand at their bedroom doorway, and he saw Wilemina inside dressed in a silk, pastel-blue nightgown. It seemed to him as though she was being caressed by the last rays of the sun as she sat brushing her hair at the vanity. The fading sunlight glinted against the gold and silver of her curls and when she turned to face him, her blue eyes were startling.

A strange "otherness" came over Ezekiel. He had not had that feeling for the longest time, but it came to him in much the same manner it used to when he was a younger man filled with a story's passion. There was no doubt in his mind that he had recaptured something precious that he thought had been lost forever.

"I have been struggling to find an appropriate story, darling," he said huskily, half-engrossed in the vision of Wilemina before him and half in the compelling magic of his story. "And all along the story has been living right here with us."

"What do you mean, darling?" Wilemina smiled. "Please tell me; I love to hear your stories."

Wilemina stretched out a hand to receive him and patted the bed beside her. Ezekiel was so moved by the small gesture that he floundered. It was almost as if he was intoxicated. It might have had everything to do with Wilemina's seemingly undying beauty. Perhaps it was the sight of her pale, alabaster shoulders, or her rounded breasts that peeped out from behind the pale-blue lace, or it could even be the power of the magic that lived in his story. But Ezekiel felt somewhat diminished by something more potent than he had expected, and he had to lean against the doorframe for support as the story flowed freely out from him.

"There was an island far away, situated in white mists and clouds, and there amongst that magic lived a brave king named Jona and his fair queen Willa, who ruled the kingdom wisely and well for hundreds and hundreds of years. Yet they grew not a day older, even as the fair queen presented the king with two beautiful children, first a boy named Du, then a girl called El. And all was well in the kingdom.

"However, there was a knight named Ezel, who served under the king and who secretly loved the queen and for years and years managed to keep his illicit feelings hidden. He fought battles and dispensed with dragons all in the queen's name, until one tragic day when the brave king was killed in a fierce battle far across the ocean.

"Queen Willa cried great tears of grief and regret at his passing, but it was that faithful knight who dried them. What anguish there was in the castle, even as the young Prince Du rode off to avenge his father's death and fight great battles in the very land where his father the king was murdered.

"Years passed, and young princess El, who grew weary with awaiting her brother's return, crossed the moat and left the castle and found herself in a strange but beautiful land. Never again did she desire to return to her father's kingdom, for she willingly gave in to the enchantment of a strangely handsome young prince who wore great, black armour ..."

"Oh, Ezekiel darling, what a wonderful story. I think it's your best ever, don't you?"

"Thanks, Wilemina, but its unfinished; I am still working on it. I really have to put more thought into it. But I agree it could be my crowning achievement. I hope to have it perfected by the time of the festival."

Wilemina was about to elaborate, when the newly installed telephone rang out urgently in the living room. She watched as Ezekiel crossed the floor with great strides to answer it, and she held her breath, listening. At first she thought that Ezekiel's "hello" had sounded excited but even from where she was, she could see how tightly he clutched the receiver and was alerted by his hushed and discreet manner.

"Yes," he said. "Where? How many? Are they in good health? When will it be possible to see them?"

"Who was that?" a curious Wilemina asked the moment Ezekiel put down the receiver.

"Darling," Ezekiel replied softly, as though keeping his emotion in check, "the caller wants to remain anonymous. But the call was about something that might interest the both of us. I was just told that a small ship carrying Jewish refugees has arrived here in Jamaica at the port in Oracabesa, St. Mary. The arrival of such contraband cargo is being kept secret from the general public. But listen to this, besides the few crew members aboard, all the passengers are children, Wilemina! They are Jewish children who have survived appalling conditions over in Europe as a result of the war and also the many days at sea without proper nourishment and care. The caller is someone I know personally from having been involved with the Jews in Kingston. He was wondering if we would be interested in raising one of the children as our own. Only a select few Jamaican families are being solicited. What do you think, darling? Should we?"

"Oh, Ezekiel, how awful for those poor, displaced children! I couldn't bear to think that they could suffer anymore than they already have. I've heard such horrid things about refugees and evacuees. What a dreadful and terrible thing war is, darling! When can we see the children? We do have the space, and food to spare, don't we, darling?"

"Are you quite sure you'd want to do this, Wilemina?"

"But of course, darling. Why ever not? I have to admit that I have come to the conclusion that I'm not capable of conceiving again. Not after so long anyway. Eliza's more than nineteen, isn't she? Otherwise, judging from our frequent love making, I should have been pregnant by now, wouldn't you agree? Darling, we've been trying and trying, but it has amounted to nothing. I rather believe that being mother to a Jewish child would almost be the same as being mother to your child, wouldn't you agree?"

"Wilemina," Ezekiel said, tears and pride brimming in his eyes, "you are quite a remarkable woman, do you know that? No wonder I have such deep feelings for you. You are the only person on this earth who could have made me this happy. Darling, I was told that we can see the children first thing in the morning. It's not too far a drive to Oracabesa from here."

"Ezekiel darling, I'm beginning to think that, if Dunstan is indeed alive, as Eliza seems to want to believe, perhaps we should move into your house in Kingston. I rather think it might be better, not only for the child we intend to adopt, but for Dunstan too, don't you think? Gunn's Run is his legacy, and if by some miracle his life is spared and he does come home, I rather would like to think that this home is waiting here for him."

Dressed in black oilskins, Dunstan, Edith and Aynsford gingerly made their way across the pier, carrying the rope and the fishnet between them. They counted the boats as they made their way, though none of them said a word out loud, fearing that the Nazi guard might recognize them as frauds. Then, there it was, beside them — the Sonnenaufgang.

Dunstan was just about to position himself to mount the boat's ladder, carrying the bulk of the rope when, to his surprise, someone was at his elbow. He looked around to find that it was none other than the Nazi guard.

"Papers, please," the guard said in German with an air of authority, but Dunstan didn't flinch; he kept his wits about him. Thanks to his military training, and to Edith's coaching, those words had become familiar to him, and he quickly presented Smithy's false documents.

The guard moved not a muscle as he scrutinized the document, and it was another heart-stopping five minutes before it was handed back without comment. "What about you?" the guard said turning his attention to Edith. "Have you any cigarettes?"

Relief washed over Edith as she gladly pulled out their last cigarette package from her pant pocket, remembering to keep her head down. "Vielen dank," said the guard, waving them on.

"Bitte sehr," Edith replied huskily, sounding more like a boy.

It wasn't until they were on the deck of the boat that the three new passengers were fully aware of how large the Nazi contingent on the wharf was. It was easier for them from that vantage to ascertain that the Nazis were occupied with inspecting crew members as well as boats and barges lined up along the pier. Dunstan had the distinct suspicion that they were searching for someone or something in particular.

"More likely, they are searching for Jews trying to escape the country. We can only pray they do not decide to inspect us more thoroughly," Edith said, remembering her old occupation.

"Thank goodness we left when we did," Aynsford said, "because, by the look of things, it would surely mean back to the POW camp for us, or even worse."

Helmut van Kirk, the boat's captain, turned out to be a short, swarthy man with a twinkle in his eye. It was plain to see that he was amiable when he came from below to join them on deck; and with a quick handshake, he hurried them below.

"You speak German?" he asked nodding at Dunstan, but Dunstan shook his head. "No!" the captain exclaimed in surprise. "Does anyone of you speak German? I wanted to let you know that we are leaving immediately."

"Good," Edith replied. "I'll tell the others."

"Do they speak English?"

"Yes."

The boat pulled out slowly from the pier, to nose its way to the mouth of the river where the waters met the sea. It was more turbulent there, for the waters quarrelled and bubbled unreasonably as the boat proceeded, leaving streams of foamy water billowing behind.

"Thank goodness we are no longer on German soil," Dunstan said, grinning broadly. Watching from one of the portholes, he saw the land drop away inch by inch, as the boat distanced itself from the shore.

The further out they went into the North Sea, the colder the weather became. Occasionally, in the wake of the boat, birds Dunstan did not recognize with huge wingspans, would arc and dip over the rough waters, as though paying homage.

"This reminds me of home," Dunstan said, for his proximity to the sea filled him with nostalgia. "The salt air, the blue curve of the sky, and birds wheeling are all reminders of Gunn's Run; and if the wind were not this cold, I could easily have imagined that those were John crows flying over Jamaica."

"Dunstan, my friend, you have a great imagination. Sometimes you remind me of Roslyn. She was always one for making things better than they are. Yes, Dunstan, I miss home too, but do you know where we are headed?"

Aynsford held Edith's hand reassuringly, sensitive to the fact that, unlike himself and Dunstan, she was leaving her homeland behind.

"I don't know where we will be going," Edith said softly, "but we have been gone for more than an hour. My dear Aynsford, I think it is good for us to leave Germany."

Another half hour went by before the boat finally slowed, its engine shuddered, and it eventually came to a standstill, the only sound that could be heard was the sound of waves lapping furiously against its sides.

"We wait here," Captain van Kirk said, coming below to join his passengers. "I have rendezvous with other boat," he continued in broken English. "It is a British boat. I show their men where Nazi mines are so they can bring their boats through safely. Then we set more mines to humbug the Nazis. All this before I can go fish."

It was a good half hour or so before the expected British vessel loomed on the horizon. Though it was a small ship, its size seemed impressive when it sided up alongside the smaller Dutch fishing boat.

Captain van Kirk immediately radioed the vessel and announced that he had some English-speaking passengers aboard seeking asylum. It took some time before there was a response but when the reply came, it was in the affirmative. "Get your asylum seekers ready to come aboard," a British voice said crackling over the radio set. It seemed miraculous after all the three weary friends had been through, and they hugged each other in sheer jubilation.

In less than an hour, all three passengers were safely transferred to the British vessel and provided with warm blankets, hot tea, and sweet biscuits below deck.

Late that afternoon, POWs Dunstan Gunn and Aynsford Collins together with their former guard Edith Werner stepped off of the vessel onto English soil at Southhampton. Army officials were immediately notified and, after briefing, both Dunstan and Aynsford were admitted to the army hospital for various tests and prescribed rest, after which they would be able to secure their discharge from service.

Edith was invited to stay with Aynsford's aunt in London. Having heard their story, the authorities treated her like a hero, and Aynsford's aunt welcomed her like family.

"The first thing I must do," Aynsford said, "is call my sister Roslyn, and the second thing is marry Edith. This whole experience has really taught me something, Dunstan. I'm sure you know it already, but I had to go through all that hell to know how much I love Edith. There's nothing I want more than for Edith and I to spend the rest of our lives together."

"The first thing I will do," said Dunstan, "is send a telegram home to Gunn's Run. It seems that the salty wind from the Caribbean is calling me, and I can't wait for it to take me home."

"Hello, Roslyn. It's me, Aynsford."

"Aynsford, Aynsford, my brother!"

"Yes, your long-lost brother Aynsford, who's so lucky to be alive."

"Aynsford, is that really you? Oh, my goodness, how wonderful to hear your voice! God has answered my prayers. When your letter came, I never stopped praying."

"Roslyn, I'm coming home. I'm bringing a German girl named Edith with me. We are getting married here in England before we come home. I owe her my life."

"Oh, my goodness! Congratulations. What a surprise … I don't even know what to say, Aynsford, except that I'm very happy for you both. But may I ask — how is your friend Dunstan Gunn?"

"Dunstan is well. As a matter of fact, he is right here beside me. Why don't you say hello to him."

Aynsford quickly handed the phone over to Dunstan and grinned. "Say hello to my sister," he said, and Dunstan gripped the receiver and smiled.

"Hello, Roslyn."

"Is that you, Dunstan?"

"Yes, it's me. It is hard to believe that I'm actually speaking to you at last. It was as if you went through the entire war with me, did you know that?"

"What do you mean, Dunstan?"

"Well, your brother was always talking about you, so I feel as if I already know you. I hope I'm not being out of line if I say that I've fallen in love with your photograph."

"That's interesting, Dunstan, because your sister Eliza Paynado showed me your photograph, and I felt much the same way."

"What do you mean, Eliza Paynado? My sister's name is Eliza Gunn."

"Your sister got married, Dunstan. She's Mrs. Lucas Paynado now. He's a politician."

"Really. Well, I guess I'd better get ready for a few more surprises. But Roslyn, would you mind if I give you a call later? It seems your brother wants to talk to you some more. But I think you and I still have a lot more to talk about too."

The telephone lines between London, Kingston and Gunn's Run must have been burning up that first week, for there were dozens of calls back and forth across the Atlantic. Most notable were the long, deep conversations between Dunstan Gunn and Roslyn Collins. Those calls brought them closer together, despite the miles between them. No doubt, it was as if a raging fire had ignited between them, and each of them grew more desperate to finally meet the other.

"I can't wait to take you to see Gunn's Run, Roslyn; it's where I grew up. I would like to spend the rest of my life there, and perhaps even raise a family there someday. My mother lives there, now, with the man she loves. He's a Jew and a former school teacher of mine. She says they've adopted a little three-year old Jewish girl named Ruth, and they are moving to a larger home in Kingston in a week or so. The Gunn's Run property will be in my hands as of now. I have a feeling you will love it there as much as I."

"Maggie," Eliza said excitedly on the telephone, "Dunstan is coming home! He is alive! Can you believe it? Dunstan's alive! All of us are going to meet him at Kingston Wharf. Please come. I know you are married now, but he might like to see you, and your family. Everyone is so happy; we are just so bowled over."

Maggie gripped the phone tightly. Her palms went sweaty and she felt light-headed as she absently reached down and patted her warm stomach. Esau came up behind her at the counter and lovingly caressed her, then rested his hand on hers as he kissed the nape of her neck. "How's our new baby, my sweet?" he whispered, and he grinned, feeling his child kick beneath his fingers.

Maggie sighed deeply; Esau's passionate touch was more mesmerizing and more potent than anything anyone could ever offer her. And she leaned into him with a sigh as he held her from behind.

"Eliza," she said choosing her words, "I'm very happy for your family, Dunstan especially; but no, I'm sorry, we won't be coming to see him. Esau and I are having another baby. We want to spend as much time together loving each other and caring for our little William."

Esau gently wrestled the phone from her hand as he found her lips and covered her mouth with soft kisses. "Please give everyone our love" was all Maggie managed to say before she hung up the phone to return her husband's welcome caresses.

Everyone came to welcome them home, as Dunstan Gunn and Aynsford Collins, dressed in army uniforms, arrived by steamship at Kingston Wharf. Eliza and Lucas were the first to greet them, though there were dozens of strangers congregated there out of curiosity.

Wilemina, dressed in a broad hat, rushed forward, one hand clutching Ezekiel, the other, Ruth. Then there was Uncle Joseph in his wheelchair, forcing his way to the forefront, for wasn't it his nephew who was coming home?

Last of all was Roslyn Collins, her hair blowing in the breeze as she stood nervously to one side, her thoughts in turmoil. What if Dunstan didn't like what he saw, she thought to herself, and what if she didn't live up to his expectations of her?

But she need not have worried. When Dunstan came down the gangway, he anxiously searched the crowd. He waved to his waiting family, for there were Mother and Mr. Samuels, and there were Eliza and the tall, handsome black man she held on to so tightly, who must be her husband Lucas.

He patiently watched as a smiling Aynsford and his radiant wife Edith Collins proudly walked arm in arm out into the tropical sunshine. But Dunstan hesitated once more to search the crowd, unaware of the figure he cut standing there in uniform, waiting. His blonde hair gleamed in the sunlight, as gulls and scavenger birds wheeled across the blue Caribbean sky.

Then, at last, he saw her, and he knew at once that the young woman who stood apart from the others, with her long, dark hair streaming in the wind was Roslyn Collins. He raced down the gangway like a man driven, never once stopping until he at last reached her. He took her hands tenderly in his and wheeled her round to the delight of everyone present. There was a loud burst of spontaneous applause when he drew her to him and kissed her unabashedly.

Less than two months after his return from the war, my father, Dunstan Gunn, married my mother, Roslyn Collins Gunn, under the shade of the spreading banyan tree at Gunn's Run. The sound of distant waves crashing against the shoreline and the wind sighing and quarrelling in the banyan grove were no match for the soft, binding words solemnly spoken between my parents.

I, Charmaine Gunn, am the first of their three children. My sister, Marguerite Anne, and I are both as blonde and as blue-eyed as our father; it is only my brother, Thomas Edward, who, though blonde, is as hazel-eyed as our Uncle Aynsford.

It wasn't until I was in my mid-twenties that social upheavals involving senseless murders, drug wars, and various forms of violence began to erupt all over the island and the Jamaica my father remembered from his childhood lost its innocence.

Those Jamaicans who were financially able pulled up roots and left the island, feeling obliged to do so, though knowing full well that there would be repercussions. There would be economic hardships for those left behind, and the country would suffer the great loss of some of our most educated, influential and valuable citizens.

My father and mother were amongst those who reluctantly decided to emigrate. It was their vision to live in a society that ideally reflected their values, where culturally diverse citizens could live harmoniously. Toronto, Canada, despite its long, cold winters, was exactly that place.

I was the last of the family to finally leave Jamaica, and the last of us to close the doors on Gunn's Run. Perhaps it is because I am the one who finds it most difficult to let go of my loves, my love of the island, and even the love I was never destined to share with a wonderful Eurasian man who often visited Hedley, whose name was William Lazarus.